The VALLEY

First published 2018 by
FREMANTLE PRESS
25 Quarry Street, Fremantle WA 6160
(PO Box 158, North Fremantle WA 6159)
www.fremantlepress.com.au

Cover design by Nada Backovic.

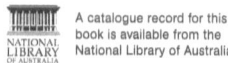

A catalogue record for this
book is available from the
National Library of Australia

The Valley. ISBN 9781925591187.

Fremantle Press is supported by the Western Australian State Government through the Department of Cultural Industries, Tourism and Sport.

Publication of this title was assisted by the Commonwealth Government through the Australia Council, its arts funding and advisory body.

The VALLEY

STEVE HAWKE

FREMANTLE PRESS

Steve Hawke grew up in Melbourne but found his way to the Northern Territory and then to the Kimberley as a nineteen-year-old in 1978. Captivated by the country, the history and the people, he stayed for almost fifteen years working for Aboriginal communities and organisations. He now lives in the hills outside Perth, but continues his strong association with the Kimberley, returning most years. His writings on the Kimberley include *Noonkanbah: Whose Land, Whose Law* (1989), the children's novel *Barefoot Kids* (2007), the play *Jandamarra* that premiered at the Perth International Arts Festival in 2008 and toured the Kimberley in 2011, and *A Town Is Born: The Fitzroy Crossing Story* (2013). *The Valley* is his first novel for adults.

For Sam and Tony,
for helping me to get out there in the wild country.

Author's Note

Some of the towns and geographical locations in this novel are real enough, but the imagined stations and communities and characters that lie at the heart of the story are entirely my creation, and bear no relationship to the real world.

Similarly, I do reference actual language groups of the Kimberley, in particular the Bunuba. I have worked for many decades with the Bunuba community. But that work has been a jumping-off point. In this novel I am not describing actual Bunuba country, or real Bunuba people. And nor should it be thought that this work is endorsed in any way by the community; it is my imagining, and my responsibility.

Three of the characters have appeared in my other work. Dancer and Andy first came to life in my children's novel *Barefoot Kids*, and Marralam is a fictional warrior in my stage play *Jandamarra*. It took the idiosyncrasies of my wandering mind to bring them together here.

Family tree

Bunuba skin names in italics

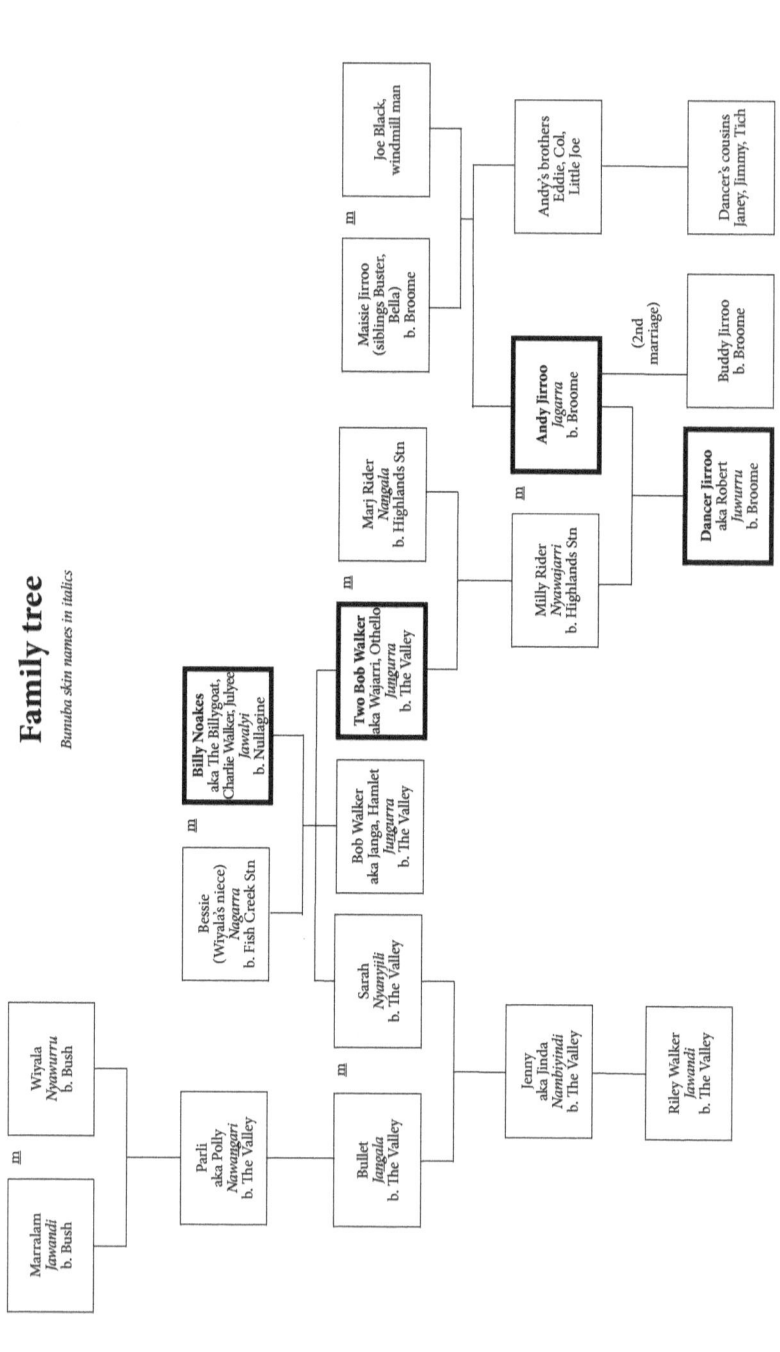

Prologue

The faint path veers right, but three steps to the left on the trackless granite, a different, hidden path beckons. Riley does not hesitate, despite the years.

The afternoon sun is warm as they make their way beneath the looming overhang, but the morning cold lingers in the shadowy depths. Dancer glimpses desiccated animal bones, but Riley's quick tread allows no close examination, and before he knows it the vista opens on a small glistening valley enclosed on all sides.

The cousins halt as one, hands touching featherishly. Riley, slight and dark. Dancer, heavy-set and gangling all at once, yellow more than brown, like an adder asleep in the sun. The skeleton of the hut is weathered grey beneath the reds and browns of the cliff. The rusted sheets of iron lie amongst the green vegetation like twisted flakes from the rockface. As their eyes sweep across the stark remains, they both see the bones. They hesitate only a moment.

The bones lie with arms folded, at peace. The flesh had withered before the hut's walls had crumbled, before dingoes or other predators could disturb the remains. Riley shows no fear, even when the skull falls apart at his touch. He merely steps back.

At the foot of the bed is an ancient tin trunk. With the lightest of nudges, Riley elbows Dancer forward. Dancer carefully removes the two smooth stones weighing down the lid. As he reaches out to touch it, the disintegrating skull fills his mind's eye. He eases the lid open, amazed at how readily it comes free.

A parcel wrapped in oilcloth sits at the top. Dancer gently unwraps it. He senses Riley step closer, feels his cousin's breath on his shoulder.

There are two pouches of worn leather. He can't help a small smile as he realises that each is made from the balls sac of an old-man kangaroo. Carefully he lifts them, and holds them up. Riley reaches over to take them.

Bending close, Dancer can just make out the pencilled scrawl on the top page of the fragile, yellowed papers: *The Last Will & Testament of William Noakes.*

Part One

1

Poison Hole, 1916

The ground birds are sheltering from the heat of the day. The only sounds breaking the silence of the bush are the occasional clinking of a buckle against a harness ring, the muffled steps of his horse and the two mules, and the odd snort as one of the animals tosses its head at a bothersome fly.

It's Billy's first solo trip, and he's enjoying having no chores and the freedom to daydream. He's trying to work out if he's turned sixteen yet. It was March when he stepped ashore in Derby. That must be six months ago now, but since he found his brother details like dates and calendars seem to have lost their meaning.

He dallies at Packhorse Creek, letting the horse and mules drink their fill, watching the play of light on the water and the fish fry darting about in schools. These are the times he likes best, being alone in the bush. It's only a few miles to the camp now, following the creek down, but there is no incentive to push on. He isn't expected until tomorrow. If he times his arrival right supper should be ready, and apart from unloading the stores and turning the mules out, he might be able to take it easy. Billy rarely gets a chance to take it easy.

As he tops the second-last crest he realises there is no smoke rising from the camp. Strange for this time of day. Kites are spiralling, dozens of them, their whistling cries filling the air as they swoop and wheel. Uneasy now, he flicks the reins to urge the horse into a brisker walk. As the camp comes into view he knows something is wrong. There's no-one in sight; not at the blacks' camp, not around the kitchen boughshed, nor at the bark hut.

The knot in his gut tightens as he stands the horse and scans the camp. An open flourbag in the dirt. Packs loose on the ground. Des's chair overturned. Jones keeps a clean camp. Every item is precious out here, two hundred miles from town; between scavenging dingoes and inquisitive munjons, it doesn't pay to leave gear lying around.

Then he sees the empty brew bucket. Fear takes hold.

꘎

The camp at Poison Hole is the furthest north in this part of the Kimberley, days of riding beyond the battling pastoral leases. Jock 'Twelve Inch' Jones has been here three years. A lanky Scotsman with deep set, burning eyes; tough as they come, making a living of sorts as a dogger getting a pound's bounty per scalp, and topping up his tuckerbags now and then with a contracting job for one of the station owners.

Twelve Inch had taken on Des eighteen months back for a fencing contract. For reasons that escape Billy, except perhaps that they are both of Scottish blood, they've stuck together since. He was not impressed when Billy turned up, tagging behind Des. 'Two white men in a camp's one too many in these parts,' he'd growled. 'Three's plain feckin' ridiculous. No passengers here, kid. Ye'll work like a blackfeller or ye'll roll your swag.'

Des had been only a touch more welcoming when the brothers were reunited at Mount House. He'd cleared out for the Kimberley when Billy was a babe, and hadn't expected to see any of his family again. He'd tried to talk Billy into heading back to Derby.

As they'd approached the Poison Creek camp the first time, Des said, 'He's not called Twelve Inch for his weddin' tackle, though that's a fearsome enough sight. It's for the barrel on that revolver of his. Special mail-order job from America, only one like it round here. Stay out of his way as much as you can.'

Twelve Inch scornfully dubbed him 'The Nullagine Billygoat', but mostly ignored Billy except to bark orders.

Until he went on a bender. He'd arrived back in camp one morning with a gleam in his eyes, and brought the brew bucket out from the hut. Twelve Inch was in a rare jovial mood as he presided over the brewing. First came 'the base'.

'Ye've got to get that right, or the metho'll kill ye,' he grinned at Billy. 'We don't mind a bit o' mayhem, but we don't want to be turnin' our toes up just yet, do we now. We Scotsmen know about these things. Read the Scottish play, laddie? *Macbeth*?'

Billy shook his head dumbly.

'The witches, laddie, the three witches. The middle one was in me family line, they say. Eye of newt,' he cackled, as he threw a handful of pepper into the simmering water in the iron bucket.

Boiled sugar and treacle and a dash of curry powder went into the murky broth. But the pièce de résistance, in his eyes, was the handfuls of white bark he stirred in. Billy recognised it as the same type the natives burned to ashes, and mixed with the tobacco they chewed.

'Gives it a kick, laddie, a kick like a mule,' Twelve Inch exulted.

The sun was getting low. After much tasting he decided the base was ready. Rubbing his hands together, he fetched two bottles of methylated spirits from his hut and emptied them into the bucket.

While Twelve Inch waited for the brew to reach perfection, Des took Billy aside and gave him some rare brotherly advice. 'Join in or clear out. He's inclined to take a set against anyone that's sober when he goes on the grog. That waterhole a couple of miles upstream's not a bad spot for a spell.'

Billy made the wrong call. The lovingly prepared base could not mask the raw, astringent bite of the meths. He couldn't stop the reflex that spat the foul mix out. Twelve Inch scooped him another measure. Glittering eyes fixed on Billy, he hissed through clenched teeth, 'Drink it.' The pannikin trembled in Billy's hands. He gagged and spat again, unable to control himself.

'Eatin' me tucker's one thing. Wastin' me grog's another, ye mangy billygoat,' Twelve Inch snarled, unbuttoning the flap of his holster. He took a big draught himself, then drew the revolver. 'Drink!'

This time Billy managed to swallow. But the fire in his throat was unbearable. He retched a spray that reached almost to Twelve Inch's boots.

The first shot was in the air. Billy looked despairingly at his brother, but Des's eyes were fixed firmly on the ground as he took a sip. Was that a smirk being suppressed?

The next shot buried itself in the dirt, a yard from Billy's right foot. He leapt and ran, with Twelve Inch's mad laugh ringing in his ears.

⚓

The memory overwhelms Billy as he surveys the camp. The terror. The mosquito-ridden desolation of the two nights cowering at the waterhole, no swag, no tucker, until he crept back. The sight of Des and Twelve Inch comatose in the dirt.

He leads the horse and mules back to cover, tethers them firmly, then edges towards the camp, rifle in hand. He steps anxiously into the open and makes his way to the hearth. The ashes are cold. He stands a long time. No thoughts. Just dread. And a vivid, momentary flash of his mother Mary, coughing her last.

A whimper from the hut.

Thinking Twelve Inch must be in there, dead to the world with one of the women, he approaches on tiptoe. But not quietly enough. The whimper becomes hysterical screaming. Bessie! A hand goes to the breast pocket where he's stashed the neatly folded neckerchief.

Bessie had come up with her parents from their country to the south. She was to become the second wife for old man Thursday, anointed by Twelve Inch as the boss of Poison Hole's native camp. Her cheeky smile and shining breasts have woven through his dreams every night since. He'd used his shilling to buy the neckerchief, thinking she might wear it, folded over her hairbelt to cover herself. That she might flash that smile at him.

'Bessie?' he whispers.

The screaming stops. 'Who dat?'

'Billy.'

'Billy? Where Twelbinch?'

'I don't know. What's going on? Where's Des?'

'Aaieeee!' The cry echoed. 'Where Twelbinch? Where him?'

'I don't know! What's happened?'

'Lemme out! Lemme out! Your brother he binish. Twelbinch been killim. Shootim. They been arguin'. Drunken one. Twelbinch been killim, him an' ol' man Thursday. Where my mummy? My daddy?'

'Nobody's here. Nobody.'

She wails again, 'Quick now. Quick. Before he come back.'

In the dim light he is confused for a moment. When his eyes adjust he realises she is pulling frantically against a chain. A leg-iron holds her shackled to the hut's centre pole.

Mind a frenzy, feet of lead. Des! Fear escalating. White-faced, wide eyes staring.

She is cringing now.

'No, no. It's all right.' Hands up, palms out. Frantic to reassure her. He grabs a blanket from Des's bed. She cowers as he drapes her. He steps back, hands raised again. She clutches the blanket, shrinking to a tight ball, averting her bruised face.

'Axe. Grabbem axe. Cuttim chain,' she pleads.

'The key?'

'Twelbinch gottim. Longa pocket.'

❧

Poised to strike at the chain, he suddenly pauses, realising the ring of axe on metal will carry through the bush for miles.

Twelve Inch must be disposing of the bodies. Des's and Thursday's at least. The others too? Thursday's first wife Nora, and Bessie's parents. Or have they fled? He has already thought of flight himself, when he went out for the axe. But on the big bay stallion Twelve Inch would outride him with ease.

Billy is a witness now. Twelve Inch cannot afford to let him live.

❧

Bessie is sleeping at last, though fitfully. Billy sits the rifle across his knees and steels himself to wait. He has never fired it, not even a kangaroo for the pot. Get through the night, he tells himself, face the morrow when it comes. Just don't let him find me here asleep.

The lock had resisted his every effort to prise it open. With night approaching, he'd eventually calmed Bessie somewhat by bringing her tucker. As she ate he pressed her for what she knew. From her tearful, garbled account it seemed that after a day on the grog Des had fallen asleep. Twelve Inch prowled the camp, still drinking his witch's brew, talking to himself. Suddenly he'd shouted to Nora, demanding Bessie be sent up to his camp.

When Thursday tried to protest, 'Dat Twelbinch just pullim out dat rebolber, and shootim ol' man straight out. No word. Nothin'. We just standin' there. Can't believe. Then he been growl, like a dingo, "She got no promise man now. Come here you bitch," he been say longa me. "Time you were broken in".'

She tried to flee. A shot whistled past her head. Des was woken from his drunken torpor. She'd seen him staggering to his feet as she was being dragged to the hut. After being chained, she'd seen nothing but heard plenty. Arguing. A cry of fear from Des. Another single shot from the revolver.

Her mob were crying out for her until Twelve Inch roared at them to shut up. 'He been tellem siddown la camp. Anyone move, anyone runaway, anyone makem noise, they the next one gettim bullet, he been tellem.' She heard horses being led in. He grabbed a few things from the hut, gave her a slap to shut her up, left her a small bowl of water, and told her he'd be back. She'd been here on her own, imagining the worst, since yesterday afternoon.

❧

All he wants to do is let go, shut down. His mind hasn't stopped racing, but he has been paralysed by fear. Terrified any sound might betray him. Too scared even to see to the horses. Lying in wait is all he can think to do.

Twelve Inch will come. The question is when. Travelling by night holds no fears for him. Billy figures if he's made camp, it won't be close by. He will come soon, or not until well after daylight.

This leaves the dawn hour. Perhaps. He doubts his chances, but can think of no other plan.

The mules are loaded with stores, and the camp is full of useful items. Before first light he will get everything loaded. The last job will be to take an axe to Bessie's chain, then mount and ride. Over the back country to Halls Creek if he can find his way, then east for the Territory, perhaps even Queensland. Leave this terrible country behind.

❧

He starts awake. Stifling a gasp, he grabs the rifle. Boots walking. Gear being dumped. The flare of a match, then the glow of a kerosene lamp. When Twelve Inch pushes open the door he will be facing his own bunk, and Bessie. Des's bunk where Billy sits is out of the immediate line of sight. He lifts the rifle, trying to keep a steady hand.

19

As the light and the boots approach the door, Bessie can't hold back a cry of fear. 'Quit yer neighin', filly,' Twelve Inch rasps. 'Breakin' time. She's been a rough few days, an' I'm ready fer a change o' pace.'

The door is kicked open and Twelve Inch towers, one hand holding the lamp. His flies are already unbuttoned, and the other hand is undoing his belt buckle.

'Stop there.' Billy can hear the quaver in his voice.

Twelve Inch whirls. 'Billygoat. Ye're back already, ye mangy excuse fer a man. Make yer useless brother look good ye do. What a surprise.'

'Where is he?'

'Who?'

'Des.'

Twelve Inch just grins and takes a step towards him.

'Stop there!' It sounds as panicked as it feels.

Twelve Inch lets go of his belt and flips open the cover on the revolver's holster.

'Stop!'

The shot booms in the confines of the hut. Twelve Inch springs back as the bullet whizzes above him. The shadows from the lamp whirl crazily as he gets his balance back. His trousers slip down around his knees and the revolver is no longer in snatching distance as its weight pulls his pants down further.

'Ye've not got the balls to kill a man, Billygoat,' Twelve Inch snarls. 'We both know how it's goin' to end.'

'The key. Where's the key?'

'Fer her?'

Billy nods.

'Ye're in the feckin' Kimberley, laddie, not merry old England. Think ye're a chivalry knight or summat? That's a gin. An' she's mine.'

'The key.'

Twelve Inch leans down and starts to pull up his trousers. 'It's in me trousers pocket, Billygoat. Wait now.'

Suddenly the lamp is flying through the air in his direction, and Twelve Inch is snatching for the revolver.

Just before the glass of the lamp explodes against him Billy gets a shot off. Twelve Inch is hit, but staggers forward, roaring with rage and disbelief more than pain as he claws for his gun. Billy shoots again, one-handed, and misses, as he bats at the flames of his burning shirt. Bessie leaps, with just enough slack in the chain to land on Twelve Inch's back. Her momentum knocks him forward onto Billy. His belly is pressed against the barrel of the rifle as it booms once more.

Twelve Inch's dead weight pins Billy to the ground, the rifle wedged between them, digging into his ribs. Smells of gunpowder, blood, kerosene, burning cloth and flesh almost overwhelm him. And Bessie screams without cease.

Somehow he jerks free of Twelve Inch. For a few moments he can do nothing but gasp for breath. But the flames are feeding on the kero. Grabbing blankets, he manages to douse them, burning his hands and forearms in the process, and adding the acrid odour of burning wool to the foul stench in the hut.

And Bessie screams.

He wants only to lie back and breathe, to be alive. But Bessie screams.

He crawls back to Twelve Inch. The only way he can turn him over is to put a shoulder to his guts, and push. Slowly he rolls, blood and intestines spilling. Billy fishes through the wetness for a pocket, for a key.

Hands slippery with blood he fumbles with the lock, screaming back at her to shut up. When he finally makes it turn and the hasp of the leg-iron springs open, Bessie tears herself loose and flees into the night, still screaming.

Billy drags himself into the open air, crawls to the hearth two dozen yards away, and collapses.

2

The Valley, 1943

Wajarri sits on a smooth granite boulder not yet warm from the sun, watching his twin brother Janga head back down the valley with their father Billy, towards the towering bluff marking the point where the main south fork starts.

He will wait here, as he has been told. The boulder sits beneath a narrow pass between two hills. Each year they come up here soon after the rains have finished to check the short fence of rusty barbed wire that blocks the pass – rusty to ensure that it does not glint in the sun – and carefully arrange spinifex and branches to hide its presence.

Short of climbing the precipitous ranges, the only other exit to the valley is down a difficult path that follows a narrow creek cutting through the range to the north. In some parts it is barely wide enough to push a mob of cattle single file. Each year they also block this path where it exits the range, creating a jumble of driftwood and bushes that looks for all the world like flood debris.

Wajarri and Billy camped nearby last night. Wajarri knew Janga was somewhere close. Billy caught his curious survey of the surrounds when they woke with the first grey of dawn, and the game was up. He merely called Janga's name in that quiet yet penetrating voice of his, and waited. It took longer than Wajarri expected for his brother to show. His defiance was short-lived though. No force was needed. Just, 'You. Wait here,' to Wajarri, and, 'You. Come with me,' to Janga, who glared at Wajarri with a desperate, jealous anger, but nevertheless turned and followed. It will be night before Billy rejoins Wajarri if he takes Janga all the way back to their camp in the south fork. But he will wait.

The boys have ventured outside the valley occasionally, but never further than the big river to fish, or to nearby hunting grounds; and never without Billy or their mother Bessie. It used to be that once a year they took a mob of their quiet cattle down through the path by the creek. The fearsome white man their father called Stumpy would take the cattle and hand over bags of flour, tea, sugar and salt, and whatever items Billy had ordered the year before. Vegetable seeds, rolls of fencing wire, tools that needed replacing – and always two new dresses for his mother and one for his sister Sarah.

But two years ago Stumpy had talked excitedly to his father, in high English that the twins couldn't follow properly, about a 'jabbanee war'. Last year he was not there to take the cattle, and there was no whitefeller tucker for them. Bessie was proper cranky.

Janga is the one who longs to come on this journey. Their parents' stories have made Wajarri fearful of the outside world. But whilst Billy needs one of the boys for the plan he has in mind, he refused to let Janga come, telling the boy, 'They steal the pale ones like you. Ye'd never come back.' His gaze moved across the twins; Wajarri near as dark as Bessie, Janga almost as pale as Billy. Yet their features so alike. Their mother had named Wajarri for the rich brown boab nut, and Janga for its creamy pith.

❧

An idle day is a rare treat, but with that look of his brother's still haunting him, Wajarri finds little pleasure. A small goanna easily caught makes for a better meal than the salt beef he carries. He walks to a small spring, drinks deeply, and watches a pair of rainbow bee-eaters on their never-ending forays above the rockpool. Mostly he follows the shifting shade amongst the boulders, watching for Billy.

Peering into the gathering gloom he begins to wonder if his father will return tonight. He thinks of retracing yesterday's journey. But the moon is thin. Already the bats are streaming overhead and the first dingo's howl has become a chorus. It is a night fit for spirits. He builds the fire, telling himself it will help guide his father. Yet he can hear the disapproval. How many times have he or Janga stoked a night fire, for Billy to pull the branch away with a curt, 'Ye want the whole world to know we're here? A fire's for cooking.'

He thinks of the nights he and Janga have camped out together. Janga building a blaze to shame this one, talking wildly of venturing on past this saddle, or beyond Stumpy's creek. And he would've, despite their tender years, if only Wajarri would've followed, would've been his companion. But Wajarri always stayed silent.

Janga can stand before a charging bullock and turn it with a look, or leap aside just as it seems he will be trampled. Wajarri can calm an uneasy mob with his song and his manner.

Already Janga can spear a roo from twenty paces. Wajarri has no such need – he can stalk to ten and be sure his spear will drive home.

Janga harbours no doubt. And if he happens to be wrong, why, he laughs and moves on, just as confident of triumph in whatever comes next. He fears only their father.

But for all his talk, he will not leave without Wajarri.

Wajarri draws his blanket tighter round his shoulders and watches the embers.

❧

It's still dark when Billy prods him awake. There is a tight set to Billy's mouth that discourages Wajarri from asking any questions. For eleven days they walk. Fast paced days that begin in the milky greyness before dawn, with the rising sun on their faces as they head eastwards.

At first they follow the big river upstream, with the lush waterholes becoming smaller and further apart each day. On the seventh day Billy bears north across a barren spinifex plain broken with gullies and hillocks of tumbled boulders. It is the roughest day's walking, but his father presses on, making no concessions for him. Eventually Billy leads down one of the gullies, and near the end of the day lets out a rare smile when they reach another river – this one bearing east by north, the opposite direction to his own big river. Always the ranges loom, reminiscent of the home valley and the country he knows, but forever changing in shape and feature.

On the last day they leave the river, following a tributary upstream. Billy is more cautious now; slowing the pace, staying well back from the water, keeping always below the ridge line of hills. They make camp early, well before nightfall.

'He's an Afghan, see, a Mohammedan,' Billy tells him that night. 'He's not tied up with those coppers and the station mob.' Wajarri can hear an uncertain edge in his father's voice. 'I reckon he'll do us right. He's a trader, like all those cameleers. He'll see the price is good.' Billy reaches across and lifts his chin with a finger. 'Ye right, lad?'

Wajarri nods. He has no words.

'I don't know who he's got there with him. It's only ever been a small turnout from what Stumpy said. We'll see what there is to be seen in the morning before ye go down. But ye're not to be talking with any of 'em, ye hear. Ye just ask for Mister Sohan, and do what I've told ye. Savvy?'

'Yuwai.'

'Then get some kip.'

But the emu travels well across the sky before Wajarri can sleep.

◦

'That's him now.' Billy can't keep the excitement from his voice. They've been perched on the ledge for an hour. Wajarri has watched the light slowly reveal the valley. It's the first camp he has seen other than their own, and there is much to take in, but his eyes are drawn to the camels. Huge, strange beasts looming in the dim light. Yet somehow familiar, milling as they wake just like a small mob of cattle.

His eyes shift to the man. The distance is too great to distinguish features as Sohan steps out into the small yard of his homestead, unrolls a blanket, and prostrates himself.

'What's he doin'?' Wajarri asks.

'That's how the Mohammedans pray.'

'Pray?'

'Talk to their god. Don't ye worry about that. We're set, lad.'

Billy pulls papers from the saddlebag that he normally wears slung over a shoulder. Then a small leather pouch made from the balls of an old-man kangaroo. Weighs it once more in his hand. He smiles to himself, then digs for a pencil and writes one more thing at the end of the list. He sees the boy's questioning look.

'Two pounds of boiled lollies.'

'What's that?'

'Something for Sarah. You boys might like 'em too. Are ye ready?' Wajarri nods. 'Just do what I've told ye. I'll be here, watching every minute. If anything goes wrong I'll be down in a flash.'

◦

Wajarri's heart hammers as he approaches the camel yard. Sohan is singing as he works, with an occasional word for the beasts as he clips a nosebag of feed to each bridle. None of the words are familiar. Without warning the man swings round, beaming at him. 'Greetings, young master.' He waits for an answer, but Wajarri is rooted to the spot. Sohan smiles even more widely. 'Never mind my wrinkly face, my eyes are sharpish, young fellow. I spotted you sure enough, sneaking across from the hills there. Old Sohan has eyes in the back of his head.'

The words wash over him. Wajarri is listening to the singsong lilt of the voice.

'Do you speak any English, boy? The King's English?' Wajarri manages a nod. 'Aha! The lad is not deaf. But is he dumb? Do you have a name?' He touches his own breast. 'I am Sohan.' Then reaches out with an open palm, almost touching Wajarri. 'You are ...?'

Instructions forgotten, all Wajarri can think to do is hold out the pouch and blurt out, 'Ottelo.' Without thinking he has given the name his father calls him.

'Ottelo?'

'The black prince,' Wajarri explains.

'The black prince? I do not follow, young man, but never mind. What have we here?'

Taking the pouch, Sohan eases the drawstring loose, and peers into it. He can't quite control the start of surprise. 'By jiminy, as my old sergeant major would say. By jiminy indeed! Sergeant Major Jones, British Indian Army, fifth regiment of Karachi. A Welshman he was, and very fond of that expression, and others not fit for young ears like yours.'

The torrent of words rolls on as Sohan inspects the gold and assesses the boy. Eventually he slips the pouch into a pocket of his breeches. He scans the hills with a keen eye. The lilt and the expansive manner have gone when he speaks next. 'Tell me, where is your ... let me guess, your father? Is he watching us now?'

This time Wajarri grasps enough of the words to understand. He cannot help but glance over his shoulder.

'Aha. It is as I thought.'

With an elaborate twirling of his hand Sohan salaams towards the hills, then with the exaggeration of a mime artist he places an arm round Wajarri's shoulders, and draws him close, so they stand side by side.

'Wave to him,' Sohan suggests, raising his own free hand.

Instead, Wajarri hands over the paper he has been gripping. 'There's more gold.'

The pantomime helps put Wajarri at ease. Even so, when Sohan invites him into the house – a pole and slab affair not unlike his own – he will not pass through the door, and hence out of Billy's sight. So they settle at a bench in the shade of a spreading bauhinia tree, by a huge outdoor table cut from a slab of cypress pine.

Sohan brings hot sweet tea and damper. He finds a level of speaking at which Wajarri can mostly follow, though he can't help an occasional flurry. More than once he looks at the list. And he talks; on and on.

His tale is one of woe. Disputes with 'a rogue of a white man' in Wyndham whose name is on the lease papers for this station he has built, despair over whether he will be able to hang on here, and worst of all, the loss of his wife and children, taken away to a place called Moore River, far to the south.

This pricks Wajarri's interest. 'Why they been take your kids? Because they half-caste?'

'Not only that, Ottelo. There are many who think it evil for a native and an Afghan to cohabit as they call it. But yes. That is enough for them.'

He must tell Janga about this, he thinks. It is true what their parents say.

'My Adam is just your size. Or was the last time I saw him. He is a good boy. Very handy with the horses and the cattle, though I cannot get him to love the camels as I do. By jiminy I miss him, Ottelo. But what can I do? The policemen and the protector have more say in his life than do I.'

He summons a smile. Looks at the paper once more. 'Can you read, Ottelo? Can you tell me what is on this list?'

Wajarri grins, and recites the list of stores and supplies, ending with, 'An' two pounds of boiled lollies.'

'That is remembering. Not quite the same as reading. Can you? Read?'

Wajarri shakes his head shyly.

'But you know what reading is?'

He nods.

⌁

Wajarri can feel his father's eyes upon him, almost sense the impatience and anxiety beaming across the valley. He summons the courage to interrupt Sohan's ceaseless flow of words. He points at the list. 'Will you?' he asks.

'Aha. It is time for business is it?' Sohan examines the paper again. '*The drovers' camp on Stoney Creek*. I know it. Though I've not been that far west for many a year.' Sohan reads from Billy's note, '*Then two days travel south by west to the river. Light a fire atop the round hill on the south bank. I shall meet you there the next day.* How very mysterious. And without a signature.' Sohan shakes his head. 'A most difficult delivery I must say. And how am I to know I will not be chasing shadows?'

'There's more gold!' Wajarri says fiercely.

Sohan laughs, 'You know what, Ottelo, I believe you. But I note these instructions say the third full moon from now. You must tell your father it is not so simple. I can get the stores, I can load my camels, and I can make the journey. These things I can do. But I am just a bloody Afghan after all, at the mercy of others as I fight my battles. I cannot promise to be there on the stated day.

'Tell him to look for my fire on the third full moon and then each new moon and full moon, for another three months. You follow?'

Wajarri nods. 'Full moon an' new moon, three months to six months.'

'You are a sharp lad, close-mouthed or not. Tell him that if I have not come by then, I may not at all, and he can keep his gold.'

'You will come!' Wajarri's exclamation is command as much as question.

Sohan puts a hand on his knee. 'I will do my very best.'

❧

Sohan tells him to wait, and disappears into the house. Wajarri bounces to his feet, thinking of how pleased his father will be, and of the tales he will tell Janga. He prowls, examining tools and paraphernalia, but is drawn down to the camel yard. Absorbed by the beasts, he is caught by surprise when Sohan pads up beside him. Sohan puts down a bulging flourbag and asks, 'Would you like a ride?'

'Yuwai!' Wajarri does not try to hide his excitement.

Sohan calls to the camels in a language that Wajarri cannot follow. Before he knows it Wajarri is nervously touching the hump of a kneeling camel. Following Sohan's instructions he takes a handful of hair and swings himself astride the backslope of the hump. On Sohan's command the beast unfolds itself. There is a rush of vertigo and a touch of fear as the camel rises to its full height. But as Sohan leads the camel on a lap of the yard he is soon laughing in delight, perched so high as he sways with the languid gait.

It is over all too quickly. Sohan too is laughing as he whooshes the camel back to its knees, and Wajarri springs off. 'That must do for now. But I promise you another ride when we meet up at the round hill. How about that?'

'Yes please.'

'Ah, I wish my Adam would take to them like you!' He sends the camel on its way with an affectionate slap. 'Perhaps you two lads will meet up one day. Would you like that, Ottelo?'

Wajarri grins his agreement.

Sohan squats down. He looks Wajarri in the eye, and speaks with a serious voice. 'Tell your father he has an agreement. Not a word shall pass my lips. I shall be at the round hill between the third and the sixth moon, Allah willing.' He straightens to his full height again, saying, 'Tell him too, that I look forward to meeting him. I am guessing that he has many tales to tell, even if they are for my ears alone.'

He picks up the flourbag. 'Some supplies for your journey home.' Then from one of his voluminous pockets he draws a comic book. 'You should tell your father you want to read. This is Adam's favourite story. It helps him learn his reading.' He opens the comic for Wajarri to see. 'Look, it has pictures too. It is about a man who lives hidden away. They call him The Ghost Who Walks.' He tucks the comic book into the flourbag. 'Tell me, Ottelo, does your father have a name? Is it ... Charlie Walker?'

Seized by panic, Wajarri clutches the bag to his chest, turns on his heel, and runs for the hills. He does not look back when he hears Sohan calling after him, 'Don't worry. I will say nothing.'

◈

The last morning of the return journey. Billy scrapes sand over the remains of their small fire and hefts his saddlebag. 'Just remember, lad, that what I've done was for his own good. His own. Yours. All of us.' With no further explanation and an air that brooks no discussion, he sets off at a faster pace than ever.

Until that moment the return journey has seemed so much quicker and easier than the going. Wajarri has spent the days rehearsing and refining the stories he will tell Janga, and practising under his breath his imitation of Sohan's lilting voice. The one afternoon they'd made camp before sunset, he cajoled Billy into reading the strange story in Adam's book. It made no sense to him, but was nevertheless wonderful; whenever there was a moment to spare he would pull the book out and pore over the pictures. But after his father's words this morning he trails behind, with a sense of foreboding.

He is still trailing as they near home, his dread rising when Janga fails to appear on the track, even as the camp comes into sight. Then the shouting from Billy. 'Bessie! Bessie! Where the hell are ye?' The anger in his voice. 'Did ye give him the axe?'

Bessie in the door of the hut. Gashes on her forehead still raw as she screams at him, 'Yuwai. I been givim axe. You fucken bastard.'

Wajarri sees the chain, still with its heavy padlock, looped around the corner post of the boughshed. The blunted axehead. The leg-iron at the end of the chain, smashed open. The dark stain of the dried blood in the dirt.

Mother is wailing, beating and clawing at her head, opening half-healed wounds afresh. Amidst the wailing she screams Bunuba words.

'What's she saying?' Billy demands. 'What the fucken hell's she saying?'

Wajarri sinks to his knees. Holds the leg-iron. Translates.

'He's gone ... He's gone, an' he's never comin' back.'

3

Heading back to Broome, 1989

The breeze is hardly a feather; just enough to cool the sweat on his forehead. The blades of the windmill stir, making a rod coupling beneath him creak softly. Andy tests the platform, high up on the mill tower, then sits and lets his feet dangle and his eyes find the horizon.

In every direction the thrusting granite ranges of the Kimberley plateau turn the skyline jagged. The hills are close to the east and the north. Banded, folded rockfaces dotted with precariously perched trees – boabs, bauhinias and an array of eucalypts. The range recedes to the west. From its foot a scrubby plain stretches south, patched with meadows of ribbon grass and curly spinifex, and etched with the meandering tree lines of the creeks. Beyond the plain the next range is distant enough to take on a blue-green tinge. That ridge line sits beneath the paler blue of the mighty King Leopolds, the ancient spine of this country.

It could hardly be more different to the landscape Andy has grown up with; the endless vistas of Roebuck Plain and the Indian Ocean on either side of Broome, stretching towards distant, ruler-straight meetings with the sky. But he has come to love it just as well.

Will this be a goodbye?

He discovered this country and its secret delights through Two Bob and Milly, but this perch on the mill is his private place. They would probably understand, though it seems a bit ghoulish, even to him sometimes. A dozen years ago Andy's father was greasing the mill head when the old platform collapsed underneath him. The manager came looking the next day, assuming a breakdown, but not ruling out the possibility that old Joe had smuggled a bottle and gone on a bender. He found Joe dead at the foot of the tower.

Two Bob had pointed out the track without comment during Andy's first year on Boxwood Downs. Andy had borrowed a station ute a few Sundays later and made his way out. That first time he came without any preconceptions. But as soon as he got out of the ute he found himself drawn. Hands and feet carried him up the steel ladder as if of their own mind. It was only when he reached the platform that he stopped to think. He tested the replacement timbers carefully before stepping off the ladder. And then he looked around.

He can still remember the shock of that moment. The still, silent, abiding power of the country he surveyed sucked the breath out of him. Jiir the sea eagle, his dreaming bird, gliding in a downward spiral and disappearing behind the northern range. For a moment he felt his father, as a benevolent, welcoming presence.

This place seems always to greet him with the familiarity of an old friend. Sitting up here with legs dangling, back leant against the tower, he can dream, remember, or just float, as the mood takes him.

But not today. His spirit is unable to connect, to reach past the turmoil and the fug of despair that envelops him.

❧

Seven hours driving will get him back to Broome and baby Robert. But the other half of his heart has been left back at Highlands. Milly wouldn't even come out of her room to say goodbye. He could feel the eyes of everyone in the small community follow him to the car, but only Two Bob was in view, sitting in the shade of the boab tree, hand gently tapping his thigh with the beat of an ancient song.

Two Bob waited until Andy started the car before unfolding his lanky frame. He approached, and then just stood watching the road. It was Andy who broke the silence. 'I'm sorry, lambara. I just don't know what to do, an' she doesn't want me here.'

Two Bob flicked a hand – the 'nothing' gesture. Andy wasn't sure if it meant shut up, or perhaps agreement that there was nothing he could do. Or both. 'Might be she'll come good by'n'by ... Might be.' After another short silence he bent down to look in through the window. 'You tell ol' Buster to keep an eye on that little Robert. Tell him I asked.'

'I will.'

Two Bob rested a hand on Andy's shoulder for a moment before stepping back. Andy eased into gear and left Highlands behind, holding the memory of that hand.

Now, after climbing the mill, there is nothing to look forward to but the road. The only thing he really knows is that he is too young, too green to deal with this. He blinks back a tear, grips the wheel tighter, and tells himself to remember the good times.

❖

The Boxwood turnoff. Only a couple of miles in to the station, behind that spur. New boots and hat, his guitar and a half-full suitcase were all he had in the world when he arrived there three years ago, still shy of his seventeenth birthday.

Andy didn't think of himself as a troublemaker, but whenever his mum chuckled and reckoned he was the one out of the four boys who took after his father – 'lovable to be sure, but oh what a handful' – he would swell with pride.

He and his mate Georgie just knew they were the coolest kids in town, and acted like they owned it. They were planning to enter the bull riding at the looming rodeo, and decided they needed some practice. Down behind the meatworks, backing onto Simpson Beach, were the holding yards for the cattle awaiting slaughter. It seemed obvious. The half-moon provided plenty of light. With Georgie working the gate, Andy managed to manoeuver a couple of steers into the race leading to the empty yard and get his makeshift bull rope on one of them. He offered Georgie first ride, but knew he'd decline.

It was less glorious than he'd expected. He sure as hell didn't make the eight seconds for time, and he hit the dirt hard, shoulder first. Dead arm and no wind, he lay where he'd fallen. The second steer charged out of the race as Georgie ran to Andy's help, leaving the gate swinging. Somehow the panicked beasts managed to bust the rails and head for the beach, followed by the hundred head from the next yard. The night fishermen on Simpson Beach lived on the story for weeks.

How Sergeant Griffiths managed to link him to the great escape, Andy didn't know. But a few days later the gruff, burly copper pulled him aside and told him that his card was marked. 'I can't pin that stunt down at the yards on you, but don't go thinkin' you've got me fooled, or got me beat boyo. I'll be comin' down on you like a ton of bricks first chance I get. Take that as a warnin' – and a promise.'

Despite his bravado, it put the wind up him. There was no planning, no forethought, but when he bumped into Big Al Steer a week or so later at the bakery he found himself asking if there were any ringing jobs going on his stations; preferably up the Gibb River side, he added, remembering a run he'd done as a young tacker with Joe one school holidays. Serendipity: they'd just lost a man at Boxwood Downs. 'Can you start Monday? Me manager Goldy's headin' back up then.'

⁓

Goldy dropped him at the single men's quarters saying supper was at 5 pm. The first man he met was the head stockman, Two Bob Walker. 'Some of me mates call me Wajarri though,' he said with a wink. By the time supper was finished Two Bob had him pegged.

'Andy Jirroo eh. What relation for that ol' man Buster?'

'He's my uncle.'

'I know him little bit. Strong feller that one. My Marj knows him more better, from all them Land Council meetings. That old Joe Black was mixed up with all them Jirroo mob wasn't he? Poor feller.'

'He was my dad.'

'Ooh, sorry young feller.'

It turned out that years ago Joe had contracted to repair a couple of mills on Highlands. Two Bob had offsided for him, and remembered him as a good gudia to work for, and a generous man. With this connection established Andy was taken under the head stockman's wing.

Two Bob was a veteran of the time of packhorses, mules and jerry-built bronco yards, and proud of it. Despite being well into his fifties he could work a mob of cattle and sit a horse at day's end better than any of the younger men under him. Of a night-time round the fire he was the best yarn spinner in the camp.

His yarns were all of Highlands, the next-door station, where the road ended. 'You reckon this place is old style,' he told Andy. 'Only thing changed at Highlands since I been start there in the forties is the new coat of paint the ol' boss been put on the homestead twenty years back.' But the Highlands mob had a falling out with the boss there, and had all moved to Snake Springs, a new community set up on the Gibb River Road on a small block of land excised from one of the big stations. Two Bob couldn't stand having nothing to do, and had taken the job on Boxwood.

Andy might've been green, but he took to the life as if born to it. Long weeks in the stock camp living out of a swag, eating beef and damper, with tinned fruit for a treat. Pre-dawn starts, night shifts tailing the mob of cattle, evenings around a campfire listening to the tales of Two Bob and the other old ringers. The occasional day off at a waterhole to have a bogey and wash the jeans and shirt turned stiff with dirt. He embraced it all.

◆

Lost in his memories, Andy realises he is about to hit the Gibb River Road. He pulls up at the tee junction as a convoy of tourist four-wheel drives flies past, throwing up roiling clouds of dust. He waits to let it settle, bemused by the silly buggers who think they are in the wilds. Coming from Highlands, it feels like hitting a superhighway on the outskirts of town.

A left turn, two bends, and there is Snake Springs. Behind the store that fronts the road, beyond the dozen or so houses, he can glimpse the bare posts and beams that were once the frames of the Jimbala Wali humpies.

Where he first met Milly.

He doesn't stop.

◆

The first proper weekend off that season at Boxwood he spent alone in the quarters doodling with his guitar; Broome was too far for a weekend, and besides, he had no vehicle. Second time round Two Bob took pity and told him to jump in when he went to Snake Springs to see his family.

Milly Rider took her surname from her mother Marj's side. The Riders were the biggest family at Highlands. A shy slip of a girl, she'd endured the minimum three years at the hostel in Derby for high school like a prison sentence. Apart from that she'd hardly ever left the tiny community there on Highlands until they moved to Snake Springs.

When Two Bob saw the two of them making eyes at each other, he just smiled that crooked smile of his. And he kept letting Andy tag along on the odd weekends off. By the end of the year the two youngsters had really fallen for each other. Hard.

❧

There's the backtrack to Bullfrog Hole. He can feel his dreams unravelling with each landmark of their lives that he passes.

Andy saved up enough that year to buy a beaten-up old Hilux during the wet season break, proudly anticipating Milly's delight. They would have their own wheels! But in the meantime Highlands had gone on the market and the government had bought it for the mob. Two Bob pulled out from Boxwood and returned home as the manager. So instead of driving west to Snake Spring on his days off Andy would head east into the hills, to Highlands.

His romance with Milly was conducted as she guided him to her favourite camping spots amongst the hidden valleys and waterholes of that remote country. Andy had always fancied himself as a bushman, but he was a novice next to her. She could track anything, rustle up a feed of bush tucker any time of year, build a neat little fire and have a billy boiled quicker than he could gather the firewood. And it never seemed to take her more than ten minutes to catch a feed of bream. She wielded a handline like a maestro, casting with unerring accuracy amongst the snags.

Her very favourite place was a billabong called Bullfrog Hole. They only went there a handful of times. It was a hell of a trek from the Highlands side, right down at the southern limits of the station. The old women of the community frowned on it; they reckoned it was too close to the debbil debbil country the other side of the big river.

Milly held no such fears. Each time she would check the ground, confirm that no-one else had disturbed their place since the last trip. The idyllic waterhole was so rarely visited that giant bream virtually jumped onto the hooks. The lovers revelled in their solitude, the proprietorial feeling that this place was theirs alone. When Milly fell pregnant she had no doubt that their child had been dreamed at Bullfrog Hole; that was their baby's Unggurr, its spirit place.

❧

Inglis Gap, with the bay for the tourists to take in the endless view of the lowlands they have just traversed, before they head into the 'wilderness' of the plateau. He is going the other way. Last time he did the run to Broome, Milly was sitting beside him. 'All downhill from here,' he murmurs.

Two Bob and the Rider mob at Highlands were almost as happy as Milly and Andy when the pregnancy was confirmed. But Milly was young and small, and the child she was carrying was a big one. The Community Health nurse wanted her to move into Derby, but she refused point blank. Then in the sixth month there was a scare, some spotting and bleeding. The nurse insisted she couldn't stay out there at Highlands, hours from medical assistance. Andy pulled out of Boxwood, and the two of them packed their meagre belongings into the old Hilux and headed to Broome. As they left the hill country, Andy knew that beneath Milly's smiles and silences she was scared.

❧

Forty clicks to go, the Port Hedland turnoff. It is almost tempting, the thought of flight, escape. He was nervous last time with Milly on board, but never before has he dreaded arriving at Jirroo Corner, the only home he has known.

Joe Black hit the jackpot like never before one night in one of the old Broome gambling houses. In the only prudent move of his life he bought the big corner block with the winnings, and set up his woman Maisie Jirroo and their brood of young boys there. He couldn't keep up the discipline, and slipped back into his drinking ways, but thankfully for their sake he never gambled the house away, and luckily, he left a will. He and Maisie had never got properly hitched, and without that bit of paper anything might've happened after the windmill accident.

Maisie had to work herself to the bone to keep them all in tucker. There were times they wouldn't have got by without a hand from her brother Buster. The boys grew, and the house seemed to become smaller. They all played guitars from a young age and Joe Black's joint became Jirroo Corner, a house of music.

But when Andy arrived back there with Milly it seemed to have gone out of tune. The yard was a building site as his oldest brother and his wife worked on their new cottage. No back yard jams. The women were gentle with Milly, but could not get close. Through three months she said hardly a word except to answer questions in a soft whisper. Even alone with Andy she was silent and withdrawn. He promised that as soon as the babe was ready to travel they would head back to the bush; Snake Springs, Highlands, she could choose.

One morning Andy's mother Maisie didn't get up, she who always beat the rooster's crow. They found her dead in her bed, taken by a heart attack. Two weeks later, Milly left a house in mourning to go into hospital.

Baby Robert was born strong and healthy. And large, a ten-pounder. Milly lost litres of blood, and had to stay in hospital for weeks after the birth. She never seemed to recover properly. She pined for her family and the hills of Highlands, and would turn silently to the wall when the doctors insisted she was not strong enough to return, not with a new baby.

When she made it back to Jirroo Corner she stared at the bedroom wall for hours on end. It was never clear to the Jirroos what was wrong; some combination of postnatal depression and 'women's troubles' was the best they could establish. Andy was too young and too overwhelmed to know how to reach out to her.

In the months that followed, Milly was in and out of hospital. Andy's Auntie Bella often had to care for Robert. She watched with deepening concern; she reckoned that Milly never really bonded with little Robert. Andy told Bella and himself that was bullshit. But if any of them tried to talk to her, Milly just retreated further into her shell.

And then she simply vanished.

❧

Frantic searches by the Jirroos and everyone Andy could rope in proved fruitless. The police turned up no leads. The Kimberley grapevine was silent. A week and a half later, a road train driver heading into Boxwood found her at the station turnoff from the Gibb River Road. Two Bob took her home to Highlands, but she wouldn't tell her father, nor anyone else, what had happened in the intervening days.

Auntie Bella offered to come with Andy as nurse for baby Robert, but in agonised phone calls Two Bob and Marj counselled Andy against bringing the babe. Andy left him in Bella's care, and headed inland full of fear and apprehension.

He begged and pleaded with Milly. Raged at her. Tried every way he could think of to break through the wall of silence that surrounded her. To no avail. He offered to go back and fetch Robert and move to Highlands. But he could get no more response than a noncommittal murmur.

Mostly she wouldn't move from her room. Some mornings she would take a handline, and walk to a nearby waterhole. With a shake of her head she would command Andy not to follow. She'd be gone all day, and not once did she bring any fish back.

Her family were convinced a bad spirit had entered her. 'Remember,' they told Andy, 'we been tell her not to take you fishin' down near that debbil debbil country.' Whether it was an ancient spirit or a modern psychosis that had Milly in its grip, it seemed nothing could draw her back to the world.

Andy felt almost as lost as Milly seemed to be. Gutted by failure. Shamed in the eyes of the Rider clan. Unable to meet

Two Bob's eye, he muttered that he had to get back. To work, and to baby Robert. Two Bob had just nodded, and watched from the shade of the boab tree as he packed his gear into the ute for the horror trip home.

⟡

Andy doesn't return to his casual job down at the port. But he's of little use to Bella in caring for Robert. A nineteen-year-old Broome boy learns little of parenting skills, and he is battling to keep his own head above water. He feels more lost, more alone here, amongst family, than he did the morning he left Highlands. Bereft. He spends hour upon hour pacing the yard, contemplating the ways in which his life has turned to shit.

One afternoon Bella loses patience and shouts at him to bugger off, to get out from under her feet for a while. He goes looking for his old mate Georgie, but finds his younger sister, not long past her eighteenth birthday. She is heading for the pub.

A week later, he is still drunk when he takes the call.

He can't understand Marj over the crackly line from Highlands, and they finish up shouting at each other. Two Bob comes on the line.

Milly has failed to return from one of her 'fishing' expeditions. Her tracks just vanished in some stony country. They've been scouring the country for the last three days, but nothing. 'She's gone, Andy,' Two Bob says gently, then hangs up.

4

Broome, 2005

Dancer's eyes are closed, tight. His hands clench the edge of the hard pew. He has been mouthing the half familiar words of the hymn. As it draws to a close there are shuffling sounds of people shifting in seats, and the odd cough. He feels the nudge of his father's knee against his own. Opening his eyes with a start, he realises that Andy and the others are already on their feet, waiting for him.

Dancer rises from his seat. Andy puts an arm around his shoulders briefly, whispering, 'Be strong, son.' They follow the others up, and Dancer takes his place at the rear. Andy is in front of him, taking the middle handle. In front of Andy is Nyami Micky. On the other side of the coffin are Dancer's uncles, Eddie, Col and Little Joe. It was Little Joe who'd asked him to be a pallbearer, to represent the young generation of the clan. Dancer knew it was right as soon as it was spoken. He was the oldest of the five. The one who'd been closest to Buster. He steeled himself for the day, distraught, yet proud.

The high-roofed church, full of light, is overflowing. It seems like all of Broome is there. On Eddie's signal they lift the coffin to their shoulders. It feels so light. He glances sideways, and reality hits home as he realises that Nyami Buster's gnarled old foot is inches away on the other side of the polished wood. The others feel the coffin shake a little at his shudder. Opposite him, Little Joe looks across sternly. Dancer braces. Tells Little Joe with a look that he will be ok. They set off at a slow march down the aisle.

Out of the corner of his eye he can see heads turn, aisle by aisle, following their slow progress. He realises it is not just Broome that has turned out. They are here from communities up and down the coast. Dancer has not seen some of them since his initiation ceremony up at Garnet Bay two summers ago. And dozens of old men whom he doesn't know, but recognises as the lawmen of the Kimberley come to farewell one of their own.

He can feel eyes on him. Not the coffin. Not the six of them bearing it. Him. He shifts his head slightly to look at the mourners on his right. His eyes are drawn to an old man sitting next to the aisle a few rows ahead. Tall and lean, with angular features and a bald spot, he is wearing jeans, cowboy boots and a bright checked shirt, all new from the shop.

As they draw level, Dancer notices Andy incline his head ever so slightly. But the old man is watching Dancer, not his father. The man nods gravely to him.

❧

It has rained that morning, an unseasonal early storm. The earth is steaming. At the cemetery many of the mourners have no choice but to stand in puddles of pindan-coloured water. Dancer does his best to shut out the voice of the priest, desperate to avoid the final reality of burial. Instead he tries to summon memories from the countless hours he has spent with his Nyami; the man who one night gave him the name all know him by now, when he was little Robert stomping in time with the men as they danced in the firelight for Jiir the sea eagle.

Once again, on Eddie's signal, he joins the others. They stand braced, holding the ropes, sweat running down their faces and saturating their white shirts. The supporting planks are pulled away, and the six of them take the weight of the coffin, two to a rope. It seemed so light at the church, but as they lower it into the freshly dug earth the burden seems more than he can bear, tearing at his shoulders as if it would pull him down into the grave. The gentle thud as it hits the bottom sounds louder than thunder to Dancer.

❧

When they get back to the house he heads straight for the bedroom he shares with his half-brother Buddy, tears off his tie, pushes the door shut, and throws himself on the bottom bunk that he has grown too big for.

He tries to ignore the murmur of voices and greetings as the wake gets underway. But lying there on his back, fingers clasped behind his head and forearms clenched to his ears to block out the noise, he can't shut out that thunderclap of coffin meeting earth at the cemetery. Suddenly Dancer is bawling; great, racking, body-shaking sobs. He doesn't try to stop when the bedroom door creaks. Through his tears he can see Buddy standing in the doorway, biting at his lip.

'Fuck off bro,' he manages to get out, before turning to the wall and curling up in a ball.

Gradually the sobbing subsides, and he is able to straighten his body out. But when cousin Jimmy calls from the other side of the door, he doesn't answer. Jimmy says hesitantly, 'They want us to play. We said we'd do a couple of numbers.'

'I didn't.'

'Come on cuz. You know he'd want us to.'

'He's not here though, is he. Music isn't always the bloody answer you know.'

'Dancer,' Jimmy pleads.

'Fuck off Jimmy. You guys play if you want to, but leave me out of it today.'

Dancer doesn't want to hear them playing. Doesn't want Andy or the aunties coming in to see if he's ok. Sneaking out the front to avoid the wake in the back yard, he heads to the vacant block next door and climbs up into the cab of Andy's truck. His safe place. But then he hears the band starting up. He climbs down, and stalks off into the gathering dark.

~❖~

His brain catches up with his feet when he turns a corner and realises Kim's place is only two doors down. He wonders whether this is a good idea. Things haven't been going too well between them lately.

Kim's mum is surprised. Doesn't Dancer know she's at Jess's place for the weekend? He declines the offer to come in and give Kim a call, makes his excuses and heads back out into the streets before the interrogation can start.

The wake will be in full swing now, and it's still the last thing he feels like. He's never quite sure what reaction he's going to get from Kim these days, but the thought of curling up on a sofa with her and watching a movie at Jess's feels right at the moment. Jess will be cool with it. She's half an hour in the opposite direction, but that's the way he heads.

Jess answers the door in her Saturday night finery; micro skirt and heavy makeup. She hustles him out into the yard, whispering that Kim's not there. They reach a safe distance from possible parental ears, but before Jess can start on her story she registers Dancer's bedraggled formal clothes, and dark mood. 'Oh shit, you've been at the funeral haven't you. Are you ok?'

'Not really.'

'You poor thing. Listen, I'm getting picked up any minute for the party. Kim's done a runner. I said I'd cover for her, but if her olds call here, we're both in the shit, big-time. Do you want to come? There'll be room in Greg's car.'

'Where's she gone?'

'Oh god. Do you really want to know?'

'Maybe.'

'She's in one of her moods. You don't want to see her tonight.'

'Where's she gone?'

'Dancer, come to the party. I'll share my bottle with you.'

'I don't drink, remember.'

Jess puts a hand on his shoulder. 'You're a really nice guy, Dancer. Believe me, I'm always telling Kim that. But you've got to lighten up. That's her biggest bitch with you, you're so fucken serious.'

A car pulls into the verge.

'That's Greg. Come on, Dancer, come with me. I haven't got a date tonight. You can keep all those gross bogans away from me.'

He shakes his head. 'There's only three bogans in Broome. Where's she gone, Jess?'

Jess fixes him with a look. 'I didn't tell you this. Ok?'

'Ok.'

'I think she's gone to Paddy F's.'

Jess pulls a half bottle of vodka from her shoulder bag and takes a slug, runs back to her front steps calling a promise to her dad that she'll be back by eleven, then down the driveway and into the car.

❧

Dancer has never been into Paddy F's. The closest he ever got was sitting in the back seat with a mate, while the mate's big brother went in to score. He's sick of walking now, but his stubborn streak has kicked in.

It's a duplex in a short backstreet of state houses. A few have been auctioned off and tarted up by their new owners, but most have that dilapidated air of public housing; scruffy yards and old bombs in the driveways. The back yard is fenced off to hold a bull terrier that throws itself against the palings in a frenzy the moment he sets foot in the front drive. He hesitates, but he isn't going to turn tail now.

It takes an age for his knock to be answered. Paddy F appears, but the flyscreen door with its heavy security mesh remains locked. 'Don't you know the rules, kid. Someone's got to vouch for you first time.'

'I don't want to score. I'm looking for Kim.'

'Wha'd'you want with her?'

'I just want to see her.'

He hears movement. As Kim appears she stumbles, and catches herself with one hand against the wall, and one in Paddy F's back. 'I told you to stay inside, girl,' Paddy F growls.

'Sorry, thought I heard my name.' Her words are slow and slurred. Dancer can tell she is stoned, completely ripped in fact. She peers out, and realises with a shock it is him.

'Dancer!' She is happy stoned. 'It's Dancer, Paddy. He's cool. He's my boyfriend.' There is the slightest pause as she exchanges a look with Paddy F. 'Sort of.' She giggles. A shiver runs down Dancer's spine. Then she remembers, and is all concern in a gush of words. 'Oh Dancer, I'm sorry, I forgot. You've been at Buster's funeral. You said you were going to be at the wake tonight. What's wrong? Are you all right? Was it awful? Paddy, let him in. It was his grandfather's funeral today. Oh you poor thing.'

'I felt like chilling out. With you. Will you come for a walk with me?'

'I'm too freakin' stoned to walk anywhere, Dancer. You said you were going to be at the wake.' She turns to Paddy, who has been watching impassively. 'Please, Paddy, please. Let him chill out here for a bit.'

'He's not stoppin' for long.' He unlocks the screen door. As soon as they are in the living room Paddy settles into his easy chair and unpauses the DVD. *Pulp Fiction* resumes mid scene, and consumes his attention. Kim collapses back onto the sofa. Dancer is relieved to see they have been sitting separately.

'Can I get myself a drink of water?'

'Help yourself,' Paddy murmurs.

Whilst Dancer is in the kitchen he can half hear a whispered conversation. When he rejoins them, Kim is grinning as she packs a bong. 'This'll chill you out big-time, Dancer. It's Paddy's stash. Hydro. Only for special guests.'

Paddy looks up from the movie. The look he gives Dancer is conspiratorial, amused and menacing all at once. Dancer was going to decline the offer, but something in that look changes his mind. He takes the bong, and leans over for Kim to light it.

⌖

Most of Dancer's friends are seasoned drinkers and smokers, or at least think of themselves as such. He simply refuses to touch grog. Mainly out of solidarity with Andy, who is a reformed alcoholic. But he's also heard enough stories and seen enough confronting evidence on the streets of the town to be turned off its attractions.

He's tried ganja a few times, usually to go along with Kim. But the truth is, it doesn't do much for him, and he doesn't like what it does to her. Sure, she gets happy, but there is a looseness around her edges, he senses, that contrasts with the feeling he gets of drawing in tighter on himself. A couple of times when they've been stoned she has come on strong to him, offering herself. Both times, something has held him back. The first time they laughed it off awkwardly. But second time round she got angry, and accused him of not really loving her. Never the argumentative type, he refused to explain himself and bit his tongue to refrain from pointing out that she'd never been this hot to trot when straight.

None of those dynamics come into play tonight. Before he has even finished exhaling the lungful of cool white bong smoke Dancer is pinned back in his armchair by an overwhelming force, as the room is sucked away from him. Kim is right, this is nothing like the dope they have shared before. He can dimly hear her laugh, and then her voice, but although he is aware she is talking to him, the detail of her words is lost in a fog.

He has no idea how long it is that he rides the tiger, glued to the chair in a state of immobility, with his mind and senses taking him to unexplored places. It's not all bad by any means. John Travolta is definitely the best actor he has ever seen; how could he not have realised this before? The tracery of lines on his palms and the delicate movements he can make with his fingers are intricately fascinating. The piercing clarity with which he remembers a walk through the dunes at the back of Eagle Beach with Nyami Buster is blissfully real, then gone in a flash and completely impossible to recapture.

But amidst the insights that seem so profound are waves of panic that come with the awareness that he has lost control. That he dare not speak, for he has no idea what he might say. That if he fought his way out of the grip of the chair he would likely collapse. That Kim and Paddy F are laughing at him. Are they?

Is this tripping? Fuck, it must be. Is this tripping? Am I tripping? Fuck. Fuck. Fuck.

The panic recedes, without disappearing. The room is swirling less. He takes a deep breath. Another. He can sense sanity within reach. If he can just ... just, keep breathing.

The phone rings. Paddy F returns in a few moments, suddenly businesslike. 'Time for you to get goin', kid.'

Dancer can manage no more than a grunt in response. Fighting the nausea that it induces, he manages to sit up straight in his chair. 'Ok ... Ok, I'm going.' At least that's what he means to say, but he can tell the words aren't coming out right, with his thick, dry tongue refusing to follow directions.

'Get him a fucken drink, Kim, quick,' Paddy snaps. 'And then get him out of here. You said he'd be able to handle it, you silly bitch.'

The room starts to spin again as Dancer forces himself out of the chair. He just saves himself from falling, then staggers after Kim into the kitchen. 'Whass going on?' he whispers. 'Who's he think he is, calling you bitch? Whass going on?'

She shooshes him frantically. He realises that maybe he wasn't whispering like he thought. 'Don't you dare embarrass me, Dancer. Here, drink this, and pull yourself together. You've got to go.'

'Come with me.'

'No way! Look at you.'

'Come with me. Whass he up to?' He tries to hold her, but she shrugs him away. 'You shoont be hanging here, Kim.'

'Dancer, I'm warning you.'

A knock at the front door shuts them up. They hear the curse from Paddy, then his low, angry, 'Stay in there,' as he shuts the kitchen door on them. The voices are muffled through the door, but they can hear a gruff question, and Paddy saying, 'It's cool, come out the back.'

'Whha the fuck's going on, Kim?'

She scurries to the kitchen window. 'It's bikies, two of them. Full patches and all.' There is excitement in her voice. 'Must be where Paddy gets his supplies. I'm gunna tell him he's got to give me some of the good shit to keep me quiet.'

Dancer downs the glass of water and pours himself another as Kim rabbits on. 'He'll give me some anyway I reckon. He wasn't even going to boot me out when they rang. It was only you he wanted to get rid of. He must think I'm cool.'

'Kim! Whha you talking 'bout? We gotta get out of here.'

'No way. Just sit tight like Paddy said. You're such a bloody kid sometimes.'

The glass slips as he goes to put it down, and shatters on the floor. Kim screams as she jumps backwards. Outside, the bull terrier launches into a frenzy of barking. Dancer feels like his head is about to explode. The door is pulled open, and there is Paddy exclaiming, 'What the fuck!' with the pair of bikies looming behind him.

'The chick's bleedin',' one of the bikies observes.

Dancer looks down and sees that there is a cut on Kim's calf. It isn't deep, but there is plenty of blood, seeping out amongst the shards of glass.

'Is that black prick givin' you a hard time, girlie?' his bald mate asks.

'No. It was an accident,' she answers quickly. 'He just can't handle the ganja.'

Paddy steps in, boots crunching the glass shards, grabs a dirty tea towel and flings it at Kim. He leans in close to Dancer and hisses, 'Get the fuck out of here. Right now.'

Dancer edges past him. Tries to signal Kim to come with him, but is ignored. He makes it out of the kitchen, but the bald bikie steps forward to block his path to the door.

'Hey toerag.'

Dancer keeps his eyes down.

'I'm talkin' to you.'

Dancer can't help shaking as he looks up.

'Keep your fucken mouth shut, if you know what's good for you.'

The bikie steps aside. As Dancer lets himself out, he hears the man snarl at Paddy, 'It's like bloody amateur hour mate, you better lift your friggin' game.'

The dog is still barking wildly as Dancer fumbles his way off the porch in the dark. He sees the gleam of metal too late, and trips over the stand of one of the bikes. Still half out of his senses, the rage and humiliation burst forth as he gets to his feet. He plants a foot against the fuel tank of the Harley, and pushes with all his might. It topples, coming down against the other bike, and both go to ground with a crashing of metal and splintering of headlights and mirrors.

For a moment he is shocked into stillness. But only for a moment. As the door bangs, and the porch light comes on, he is off. Across the road, down into the drainage ditch on the other side, crouching as he runs.

'You're dead meat, you little cunt. You hear me! Dead meat!'

The angry shout echoes as he gains the cover of the bush. He crashes on, heedless of the scratching branches and grabbing roots. All he can think of is the Eagle Beach track a hundred yards away.

Part Two

5

Two Bob's pew is about halfway back, but he can pick out Andy sitting in the front row.

Next to Andy, that's gotta be ... Yeah, that's him!

When Dancer joins his father and uncles as a pallbearer, Two Bob cannot take his eyes off his grandson as they make the slow procession down the aisle, bearing Buster's coffin.

He didn't recognise me. But why would he.

The rest of the mourners depart. The sight of Dancer has unnerved him. He doesn't feel up to going to the burial. He rubs at his bald spot before he puts his akubra back on and gets stiffly to his feet in the empty church.

❦

He'd wanted to hide when he saw Rosa coming. Thought she was still chasing him to get involved with all the station humbug again. It's not that he doesn't care. He would be heartbroken if the station is lost. It's just that ... That looking after Riley is enough to cope with? Too much painful history involved? He's just an old pensioner now, with weary bones? All these excuses flitted through his mind as he put on a smile.

But she hadn't come about station business. A funeral notice had come in on the fax. 'Buster Jirroo. He was family for Milly's boy wasn't he? Thought you might want to know.'

'Yuw. Andy's uncle, on his mother's side.'

It wasn't until that evening that the realisation hit him. Robert would be there! Dancer! A compulsion seized him to lay eyes upon his grandson. For the first time, he left Riley to look after himself, laying in a supply of tins and frozen bread, and promising to be back after two nights.

◦

He tells himself he should hit the road now. Plenty of time to make it to Derby before dark tonight. Maybe even a bit further. Camp on the road. That way he can be home with plenty of daylight still tomorrow.

Blachan.

The thought is suddenly there unbidden. It must be from seeing Andy. He'd love some to spice up his stews. He finds himself walking the two blocks from the church to the courthouse gardens. In the unfamiliar bustle of the markets he spots a likely looking stall. 'You're in luck,' the young woman smiles in answer to his query.

He walks away with three jars, plus one of mango chutney on the house, feeling ridiculously pleased. *Should hit the road,* he tells himself again as he stows the booty in the ute. But instead, he drives to the cemetery. It is deserted now, but the freshly filled grave is easy to find. *I'm older than you were Buster,* he thinks, as he pays his respects.

A glance at the angle of the sun as he starts up the ute. Plenty of daylight still.

Longest time since I been in Broome. I'll just have a little bit of a look round.

Driving the streets of the old town he recognises a gaggle of cars from the church service parked outside a corner block. He pulls over down the street a little bit and watches the comings and goings; men in white shirts and dark pants, women mostly in black. He can't kid himself any longer.

Even as he walks up the driveway he shies away from contemplating his actions, falls back on the familiar ground of wondering how Riley is doing. He mounts the verandah steps and stands there at the front door, at a complete loss when a woman appears.

'Come on in. I'm sorry, old man, please forgive me for not recognising you, but all are welcome on this day.' As she steps aside to usher him in, he takes off his hat and introduces himself.

'Two Bob Walker.' He hesitates. 'Dancer's grandpa.'

The woman's jaw drops. Her eyes dart to a photograph in the hallway. Following her gaze, he sees a photo of Milly and Andy and baby Dancer. She recovers herself, puts a hand on his arm and says, 'Wait here, I'll go and get Andy.'

He can hear singing from the back yard. Kids' voices. He wants to flee back to his car. He does turn to go, is about to step off the verandah when Andy appears. The two men look at each other across a gulf of sixteen years. Two Bob drops his eyes. 'I'm sorry, Andy. It's a bad time.'

'Mmm.'

'I was ... I was wonderin' if you could ... if I could ... see Dancer.'

'He's taken off somewhere. He's pretty upset. Him an' the old feller were real close.'

Two Bob feels his heart tearing. 'Could you tell him I came?'

'Sure.'

'Could you ...' He has no idea how to finish the sentence. 'Maybe I'd better go.'

He can't look up at Andy. He puts his hat on as he turns away.

'Come back in the mornin', old man. He'll be here then. We'll have a cuppa tea eh.'

⚬

But Dancer isn't.

There.

Andy is about to go out looking for him and tells Two Bob to come back later.

'But I can't. Riley. I've got to get back.' Panic rising. Of all the scenarios he had imagined last night this was not one of them.

Grasping for something, anything, to keep this tenuous thread from breaking, he latches on to the first thing that comes to mind. 'Andy, you gotta ring me. You gotta come up. The station. It's in trouble, we might lose it. Rosa's asked me to help.'

But Andy is not listening. 'I've got to find Dancer, Two Bob. He never showed up last night. Come back later on. Ok?'

He leaves Two Bob standing there in the front yard, twisting his hat in his hands.

6

'Jee-sus Dad!'

Dancer's head whirls, catching a glimpse of the bullock as it is thrown in an ungainly arc to the road's verge, dead before it lands.

'You're awake! Sorry mate. But I'm not gunna roll the truck for some bullamon that decides to walk in front of me.' Andy grinds down through the gears as he approaches the single-lane bridge. 'You do what you gotta do, boyo.'

The truck crawls across Willare Bridge with a rhythmic clunking. Dancer looks down, taking in the murky green of the late dry season waterhole of the Fitzroy River. He can feel the momentum of the road, of change, of saltwater country receding and river country rising. And with it he feels the weight of the last few weeks starting to ease. He turns to his father.

'And that's what you've been doing, hey Dad?'

'That's what I've been doin'.'

'Wanna tell me?'

'Willare comin' up. Time for breakfast. What you reckon?'

'I reckon. I'd kill for a bacon and egg burger.'

'Two for me.'

❧

Dancer has no memory of making his way from Paddy F's to the shack at Eagle Beach. He can dimly recall plunging into the ocean when he woke the next morning, but feeling no better for it. He was afraid. A dull dread, blunted by sheer inertia in the aftermath of that fateful bong, as if he'd been wrung out and tossed aside; by emotional overload from the weeks of sitting with Nyami Buster through his final illness; from holding himself together for the funeral; from the shame of fucking up the night before. He felt overwhelmingly weary.

The fear became razor-sharp that afternoon. He and Andy were in the yard, sitting in the cab of the truck, as he tried to explain what had happened. Two Harleys rumbled slowly past, then turned and crawled by again, with the bikies giving them the evil eye each time.

Dancer still doesn't know how Andy sorted it out, and still doesn't feel reassured. He made it through the next day at school in a fog, hardly acknowledging the condolences for Buster. Jess cornered him, tried every way she knew to prise out some sort of account of what had happened. Kim was freaked out, she reckoned, and told her to tell Dancer that she never wanted to see him again.

Walking home with Jimmy and Buddy, his gut churned at the sound of the two Harleys turning the corner. When the bikes U-turned, and idled slowly along beside them, it was all he could do to stop from breaking into a run. He kept his eyes firmly on the ground as the one with the ginger beard snarled at him, 'Your old man's saved ya skin kid, I'll leave you be. But ya card's marked. You better not cross me again.'

He spent the next two weeks in a funk. Refusing to go to school, to even leave Jirroo Corner. Andy could hardly get a word out of him; frantic with worry, he remembered his Sunday morning encounter with Two Bob.

◦

Andy concentrates on the tucker until he's demolished his first burger. He takes a gulp from his mug of tea. 'It's a strange world.'

'Meaning what?'

'B&E burger at Willare. I was just thinkin' I had the same thing way back, when I was headin' up the Gibb River Road to escape from Broome.'

'What were you running away from?'

'You've heard that ol' story about the great Simpson Beach stampede eh?'

'Just once or twice. How true is it?'

'Depends who's tellin'. Thing is, though, we couldn't claim the glory. Not till ol' Sarge Griffiths left town. Somehow he knew it was me an' Georgie. Couldn't prove it, but he knew. He cornered me one day an' told me my card was marked. He was gunnin' for me.'

'Your card was marked?'

'That's what he said.'

'That's what the bikie said to me. The red-haired one.'

Andy shivers. 'Same mentality. He was a bad bastard, Griffiths. Maybe not as bad as these fucken bikies, but I was spooked. I pulled out of the band an' lined up the job at Boxwood. Had a bacon an' egg burger here on the way up. I was only a year older than you are now mate. An' I didn't have an ol' man to help me sort my shit out!'

'How did you sort it out, Dad?'

Andy watches Dancer and chews a bite from his second burger. 'They're thugs. Thugs an' scumbags. An' they want your guts for garters. That's the truth of it. The way they see the world no-one gets away with disrespectin' 'em. But they're not completely fucken dumb. They've come to town to do business with Paddy F an' his type. That was me angle.'

'You went and fronted them?'

Andy nods through another mouthful.

'In their clubhouse?'

'It's just a shed in the light industrial area.'

'Still.'

'I didn't go on me own. I've got a few scungy mates from when I did time for the car smash. They set up the meet, an' came to cover me arse.'

'So what'd you say?'

'I told 'em if they want to do business in Broome they need to show it some respect. I said if any harm comes to you, every blackfeller in town'll be on their case. Theirs an' every dealer they supply. I told 'em it wasn't worth it.'

'Weren't you shitting yourself?'

'Deeply. But I offered 'em a deal as well.'

'Yeah?'

'Yeah. We'd stay quiet – no losin' face for anyone. You got that clear?'

'Got it.'

'An' compensation.'

'How much?'

'Ten K.'

'Ten K?! It was only some scratches.'

'What? You stopped to inspect the damage did you?'

'Where'd you get the money from?'

'I've got three months to pay.'

'Shit Dad ... I'm so sorry.'

Andy balls the burger wrappers into a tight wad as he pushes to his feet. He hurls them into the bin.

'I'm sorry,' Dancer repeats. 'I just ...'

Andy is on his way back to the truck, speaking over his shoulder. 'Your uncles'll bail me out if it comes to that, but I'd rather they didn't have to. I've got that hay cartin' contract when we get back from Highlands, but that's not goin' to be enough on its own.'

7

Two Bob tries to tell himself it doesn't matter if they make it tonight or in the morning, but he's not sure he can stand another night of anticipation. Either way, he's going to have the stew ready, just the way Andy likes it. Or used to. He slides the rough-cut potato chunks into the camp oven and gives it a stir.

He hasn't been this edgy since ... since he can't remember when. He is by habit a man of caution and deliberation, but from the moment he watched Dancer gather himself and lift the coffin to his shoulder he's been running on raw instinct. He's not sure what he has unleashed, or whether he'll be able to ride this bronc.

The thud as the boab nut hits the hard-packed earth not two feet away startles him. The nut bounces, rolls, and comes to a stop at his feet. It has cracked open. The janga, the yellow-white pith, is exposed.

He reaches down and picks it up. A segment of the chalky fruit has broken loose. Breaking the habit of a lifetime, he plucks the piece of pith from the nut and places it on his tongue. The tart, lemony taste floods his mouth. His first instinct is to spit it out. But he holds it in, then swallows, and lets the flavour and its memories overwhelm him.

~◈~

Bessie sent the boys out, telling them they better not come back without some sugarbag. They made a day of it, tracking wida the bee, and found two nests. Bessie mixed the honey with the janga she'd gathered and pounded, to make up a sweet paste. Janga thought it was a great joke, eating himself. But Bessie railed against it. Wajarri and Sarah shared her unease.

They couldn't always find sugarbag. Without it Wajarri could hardly bear to swallow the bitter pith. Mother would prepare it for them, but refuse to eat it herself. On these days her haranguing of Billy would become merciless.

'You fucken whitefeller you, makin' us all live here like a bunch of munjons. I can't eatem my son. I want damper. I want tea an' sugar. An' nicki nicki. All my family still there Fitzroy side. I'll take 'em this lot kids and fucken leave you here on your own you bastard.'

The twins and their big sister Sarah had learned to take these outbursts with a grain of salt. For all the fire she displayed when this mood took her, they knew she feared the world beyond, and especially feared for the fate of her children in that world. Nevertheless, she could keep it up for hours at a time. Billy could lay down the law ruthlessly to the children, but he had a different manner with his Bessie. His silence served only to goad her on.

At the turn of the year, as the days started once again to lengthen, Billy disappeared for a few days, as he sometimes did. He returned in good humour, with his precious pouch of gold heavier than it had been, and informed them all that he was taking Wajarri with him to Moonlight Valley to find Sohan the cameleer.

'I'll get ye a camel load o' flour, and a whole saddlebag full o' chewing tobacco, me darling,' he promised Bessie.

Janga was outraged. But Bessie was just as adamant as Billy. Many a time she'd told them the tale of her young brother. Back at Fish Creek he'd been snatched away one day by the police patrol, never to be seen or heard of again. Every time she told the story she cried anew. And until he grew old enough to be able to shrug her off, every time she would hold Janga close, whispering, 'An' he was darker'n you, Janga. Darker'n you.'

٭

He's gone ... He's gone, an' he's never comin' back.

Two Bob winces. He can still hear himself translating his mother's grievous wailing when they returned home that awful day. Can still remember his father's anger disappearing in the instant. The way he stood there, frozen, as she snatched up the leg-iron and began to beat him with it, screaming in English now, 'You're allasame Twelbinch, alla fucken same.'

Only when Bessie swiped herself with the iron, reopening her mourning wounds afresh, did Billy move. He grabbed it, threw it aside, and held her tight. She wailed, and beat her hands against him as their blood mingled.

This time his mother really did want to leave. But Sarah would not. She'd spent her life absorbing her parents' fear of the world beyond the valley, believing as a matter of faith that she'd be stolen away like Bessie's young brother if she left.

Bessie's grief hung over the camp. The only relief came on the days when Sarah would take her out looking for bush tucker. When Sohan's smoke signal came, Wajarri helped his father cart the stores back into the valley. But by the time the rains came, he could endure no longer without his other half.

With dread in his heart, one morning he followed the creek north, and found his way to Highlands. To Janga, who had become Bob. Wajarri became Two Bob. He had never eaten janga again.

٭

The boab nut can only be a sign from Bob. But telling him what? He stirs the coals under the camp oven. The *Oprah Winfrey* theme tune wafts on the air.

Riley must be up.

He breaks off another piece of pith, and sucks on its sourness as he ponders, and remembers.

The only other sign Bob ever gave him was unmistakable, the night before he left the valley. He'd followed the dream's instructions, and after two days had spied Highlands; the gnarled monster boab he sits beneath now, the homestead and outbuildings, the humpies of the camp, and down beyond them the post and rail yards.

He hovered for hours on the ridge, watching, waiting. Sure of his dream one moment, full of doubt the next, wondering if he should turn tail back to the valley. Then as evening approached he saw Bob make his way to a snappy gum on a low rise, where he stood and watched. With his heart singing, Two Bob whistled the call of the kite hawk, and moved out from his cover. Bob came running.

He stretches as he looks around. The yards are hardly recognisable now, though a couple of the original posts remain. The humpies have been replaced by a scattering of houses. The office and clinic appeared a few years ago. Then the telecom tower like a skinny, overheight windmill that has delivered a phone, a fax and the TV signal that has changed Riley's life. But the boab tree is still here, and Highlands is still the end of the earth, eighty miles in from the Gibb River Road with nothing but the rough station tracks beyond.

8

Highlands.

The word, the name, the unknown place has been a mystery in Dancer's psyche all his life. Yet in his funk he has gone along with this plan with little thought, and hardly more than grunted okays.

Andy eases off the pedal as the car in front decelerates to take the turn for Fitzroy Crossing. Once it is gone, he floors it again and straightens in his seat. ''Nother forty kays an' we'll be on the Gibb River Road. Headin' for the good country.'

'What are we going to be doing up there, Dad?'

'Remains to be seen, to tell you the truth. Your grandpa's not really one for phone chats. I finished up just sayin' we'd come up an' play it by ear.'

'He was the one in the cowboy shirt hey? Going a bit bald?'

'That's him.'

'He was staring at me.'

'Yeah.'

Dancer moves in his seat, looks across at his father. 'He's my own grandfather, and I've never met him.'

Andy keeps his eyes on the road as he shifts down a gear to ease into a dip, then back up again. 'It's complicated … He's a good man, Two Bob. One of the best I know. But it got complicated.'

❧

Dancer waits.

And waits.

Of course it's bloody complicated. As if I haven't worked that out by now.

The silence rolls on. Half an hour later Andy leans the truck into the turn for the Gibb River Road, at which point he plucks a Pigram Brothers CD from the array he has in a sleeve on his sun visor. Mowanjum on the right. The bitumen narrows from double to single lane width. Still nothing from Andy except his soft accompaniment to the music.

Andy has only ever sung harmonies and choruses in the band, but Dancer is always struck by how pure his father's voice is when he hears him sing alone. His rendition as he breaks into the Kimberley trucker's song is note-perfect.

> *Unfolding like a flower, dewdrop in the dawn*
> *Rising like a mountain, through the foggy morn*
> *Riding this live dream, catch me if I fall*
> *Starting to rise now, my shadow's up the wall*
>
> *And I'm rollin like a road train, four dogs and thirty ton*
> *Gliding like a mountain, towards the blazing sun*
> *Gliding through the valley, the wedgetail is my friend*
> *Winding like a river, to the bitter end.*

It's been like this for as long as Dancer can remember. The mother he never knew. If anything touches on her, even faintly, Andy snaps shut like a hermit crab in its shell.

It's about to change, one way or another. He can feel it in his guts. He hasn't really taken in the how or the why through the madness and despair of the last two weeks, but they are heading towards her.

There had been that one moment, three years ago now. 'This is your Unggurr, your spirit place,' Dad had said on the bank at Bullfrog Hole. It had opened a window in Dancer's heart. A window that flickered alternately with an alluring light and a murky shadow that scared him deeply. But Andy had offered nothing more in all the time since.

Dancer has no choice but to wait. He knows from long

experience that pushing, asking, questing will only serve to set him back.

There's something about the sensation of rolling like a road train down this thin strip of bitumen that helps him deal with the unease that he feels.

The bush is changing. There are more boabs on either side of the road. Then they float down a gentle descent and plough along the road's furrow through what seems a limitless, almost treeless plain dotted with a city of dun-brown anthills. There is a faint shimmer of the ranges ahead. It's a landscape too old and wondrous to concern itself with his problems.

He eases back in his seat and watches the anthills.

9

When Bob limped into Highlands he told the mob he'd come up from Fitzroy side; that he'd had a fight with the boss at Fish Creek Station. The boss had chained him up and gone for the police, but he'd escaped before they got back. And he told them that he had a twin brother who would follow him as soon as he could.

The high country was still a wild world in the 1940s. The ranges to the north-east, where the headwaters of the big East Kimberley rivers rose, were known as the Outlaw Country; home to gangs of horse thieves until not too long past. There were still a few fellers who hadn't taken to the station life, roaming the ranges living by the spear. There'd never been many whitefellers, and at that time there were even fewer than usual, with Stumpy and others having taken off to the war. Amongst black and white it was a country of closed mouths, minding your own business, and taking people at face value. When the pale-skinned youngster turned up, the Highlands mob took Bob at his word, or at least chose not to ask too many questions.

He joined the stock camp as the junior man; horsetailer, woodchopper and cook's offsider. It was the cook who gave him his new name. When Wajarri arrived, and the same man saw the two of them side by side, he said with a laugh, 'Well if he's Bob, you must be Two Bob.'

The twins cobbled together a camp of bush timber and scraps of iron; a bachelors' camp at a slight remove from the rest of the humpies of the Highlands families. It was understood between them that the lost valley they'd come from would remain just that; it was not their place to betray the secret. This reserve, the obvious hole in their life stories, was not questioned, but it hung as a mystery that marked them as different and apart. They were accepted, even put through the law, but not embraced to the mob's bosom.

Year in, year out, like all of the men and a good number of the women, they worked the cattle. When the great cycle of the annual muster swept down to the southern reaches of the Highlands run, the stock camp would set up at Bullfrog Hole, the waterhole closest to the valley. And each time, Bob's demeanour would harden. To the day he died, his heart remained unforgiving towards their father.

Two Bob excelled in the stockman's arts, year by year moving up the hierarchy; his steady, methodical manner getting the job done whatever it might be, his quiet humour making him well liked. Bob equalled him in skill, but didn't share his passion for the craft. He was a young man of dreams and daring and a quick temper, who did the job because that was his lot, not his love.

Bob came to life during the wet season layoff, when for a couple of months the mob were not at the beck and call of the manager. They were free to immerse themselves in the joys of swapping visits with relations on neighbouring stations, walking the country, hunting and socialising; and to turn their attention to the business of ceremony. Bob distinguished himself as a singer and dancer in the wanggas and junbas that filled these nights.

When Wiligula the Jalgangurru became aware of Janga's ability to send dreams and messages, he was taken under the old man's wing, and began to progress in the ranks of the lawmen, to learn the arts of the healer and wise man. The twins came to understand that though they would remain ever joined in spirit, their temperaments and talents would see them take differing paths.

✤

Two Bob had been at Highlands three years when the Boxwood boss turned up one day and told them that he was the new owner. Stumpy had been killed in the big war, he said, and he'd taken up the lease.

The new boss didn't last long, nor his successor. They came and went every few years. Some were new owners with grand plans, believing they could defy Highlands' reputation as a battler's graveyard. Others were managers who just wanted to get the muster out of the way – it wasn't a place that attracted ambitious employees. Some bosses were rougher than others, some years the weekly tucker ration was better, but the comings and goings of the whitefellers made little real difference to the lives of the mob.

Two Bob was the constant through it all. Even before he became the head stockman, he was the trusted one who stayed behind when the rest of the mob went walking, saw to the essentials and made the emergency repairs after storm damage, until the road dried up enough for the year's business to get underway. Sometimes there would be a whitefeller camped in the homestead with the title of caretaker, but more than one of them fled to town, unable to cope with the isolation. A good few spent the wet in a rum-soaked stupor. Other years the boss just locked the homestead and took off for a couple of months.

When the law business was at Highlands, Two Bob played his minor part, taking brotherly pride in Bob's prominence. But when the mob took off he was happy to stay behind. He had another kind of business.

The year after they got the news of Stumpy's death there was great excitement amongst the Highlands mob as the working year wound down. They were heading east to Turkey Creek. It was a two-week walk to get there, but plenty of country to see and hunting to be had on the way, and a new ceremony from the

Territory side to take part in.

Two Bob saw his chance, and made his excuses. Highlands had become his home, and stockman his vocation, but the valley and those he had left behind were never far from his thoughts. The tiny community who still called the valley home. He felt that he had to let them know of Stumpy's passing. There would be no resumption of the annual supplies. And he'd heard that Sohan had turned loose his camels, and disappeared from Wyndham and the Kimberley. How would they all get by?

He spun a yarn to the caretaker about checking a couple of mills whilst fitting in a bit of hunting. He took off with a packhorse loaded with bags of flour and other supplies, as well as his riding horse. He even managed to palm a few sticks of nicki nicki from the store for Bessie.

When he got to the round hill he wondered whether he should light a signal fire.

With that thought he realised that he no longer belonged to the valley. He would be a visitor, not entirely certain of his welcome in a place that turned its back on outsiders. But there was no reason to think they would be on the lookout for a fire. He rode on to where the creek emerged from the cliffs. There was a thrill of familiarity, and a tightness in his chest as he began disentangling the jumble of driftwood that concealed the path into the ravine.

10

It is but five days ago that I buried my only daughter Sarah.

Yesterday I bade farewell to her grandson Riley. He was perched upon Othello's shoulders, and happily did he wave back at me as they turned the corner of the track. They will be through the gorge by now, that portal to the world beyond, and on the road to Highlands. 'Hold the lad close,' I asked.

For many a year now Othello has been the lifeline for me and mine, but our peculiar arrangement has run its race. I told him not to bother with disguising the entrance any more. There's naught to hide. He begged of me to go with them, but he and I both knew the walk to be beyond me. The pneumonia is in my lungs, and I know not how long I will last. Even if I could have gone, I do not think I would have. I am a sinful man who has shunned the world.

Last night I wrote my Will & Testament, and double-wrapped it in an oilcloth, along with the stones it promises. They are secure in my trunk, laid atop the red dress of Bessie's. It was a night of turbulent reflections and recollections. In the witching hour the fancy struck me that a way to calm the storms besetting my thoughts might be to give them shape as words on a page. A sinner's confession, if you like. But to whom? As of this day, I am truly Robinson Crusoe.

How I delighted in that tome as a young'un. Defoe and Dickens were my favourites from Mother's library. On her deathbed Ma had urged me to head for Perth, and to find gainful employment as a clerk. She had schooled me well, for an outback boy. But I took my own counsel and, after burying her in

Nullagine, did make my way to the port of Cossack, and thence by steamer to Derby. I was seeking to find the only flesh and blood left to me, my older brother Desmond, known as Des, whose last known address was 'via Mount House Station'. And thus my course was set.

Where to begin? Perhaps as I began my Will & Testament:

My name, my true name, is William Noakes. I was born in the Nullagine goldfield in the year of 1900. Mother Mary Noakes, boarding house proprietress. Father Rudolph Noakes, mining engineer and prospector, lost on Gallipoli's shores.

But there is more to tell than the brief accounting in my Will. I have had many other names. The Billygoat. Julyee, as Bessie and her people called me, once they decided to spare me. Many years ago, when I needed a name to give a stranger, I made Julyee into Charlie, and for a surname I chose Walker, for that is what I had become in this horseman's land, the man who walked.

It is a strange affair in this country, the business of names. My Othello is now known as Two Bob. His mother called him Wajarri, that being the name in her language for the nut of the boab tree. His twin brother she dubbed Janga, for the creamy white pith of that same nut, whilst I called him Hamlet.

We are all of us less clever than we think ourselves, but both Bessie and the station fellow at Highlands who renamed Othello were closer to the mark than I. The man saw them for what they were, two of a kind; Bob and Two Bob. Bessie knew that they were two parts of a single whole; Janga and Wajarri, pith and shell, pale and dark, indivisible. I chose to bestow them with the names of the white prince of Denmark and the dark prince of Venice; a fancy that none but I embraced.

I call myself a sinful man. I confess to two great ones. Many smaller, but two of consequence. A murder, and a grave injustice on my own flesh and blood. The latter scarred me more. Hamlet held a deep resentment towards me until the day that he died.

The murder first. Yes, call it that, for all the truthful reasons I might advance by way of justification.

In the late dry season of the year of 1916, some weeks before the first storms, I did shoot Jock Jones, more commonly known as Twelve Inch, at Poison Hole on the Packhorse Creek, some three days ride north by west of Mount House Station. The next day I did burn down his hut, with his corpse still inside, and then did abscond, taking with me many of his goods and possessions.

There. It is said.

It is true that he would have killed me without a thought, had I not got in first. It is true that he had earlier shot my own brother, and almost certainly Bessie's parents, amongst others. Yet it is also true that I lay in wait for him, gun in hand, knowing what would come.

I would like to explain myself, to justify my actions, but that bald confession must suffice. The Reaper stalks this valley as I write, and I shall be his prey. If that sounds overly morbid, there is a more practical matter too. My supply of salvaged pages and pencil stubs is scant. I shall spend what time and stock I have to write of those I've loved, and wronged.

11

Two Bob tests the stew, breathes in the aroma, pleased with his efforts. It's ready if they get here tonight, but it'll be even better by tomorrow. Even so, he adds another dollop of blachan. He can't help peering down the road yet again. The waiting is getting to him. There's a deep-seated tension in his body, a restlessness that provokes an uncomfortable memory of his first return to the valley.

He was edgy as well as expectant as he walked his horse up the valley towards his old home. Would his father make him welcome, or scorn him as a deserter? Would they all still be there, still be well? Had Bullet come back to Sarah like he promised? And Bullet's mum, Parli, the last of the old families, living there in the old camp across the creek?

Sarah and Parli were the only ones around when Two Bob rode in. And Sarah's baby Jinda. He'd become an uncle! His parents arrived back from their hunting trip to find him dandling the child with a silly smile on his face. Bullet strode into camp as the sun was setting.

Two Bob's worry about how they would all survive in Stumpy's absence turned out to be misplaced. Billy, ever practical, had come up with a solution, as he explained while they butchered a bullock and hung the carcass ready for salting.

He'd taken a string of mules along the old backtrack through the Leopolds and come out to the north of Halls Creek. 'Not as far as Sohan's, but the mules slowed me down something terrible.' Billy grinned as he wiped the blade clean. 'At least it meant a month on me own without having to put up with

Bullet's bad moods and unfriendly tongue.' Presenting himself at the trading post as Charlie Walker, prospector, he had more than enough nuggets to obtain the goods on his list and load up the mules for his return journey.

For those few days Two Bob once again became Wajarri. Little brother, young son, the junior member of the small community. It made him realise that in a strange way Bob had always been so much older than him. Billy didn't speak of Bob. Or remark on Two Bob's departure or long absence. It seemed that as far as he was concerned life went on as normal.

Mostly that was how Bessie and Sarah acted too. Sometimes of an evening as they all ate together, Bullet would catch his eye, with a look that was knowing, questioning, almost laughing, as if challenging him; but he said nothing.

◦

Two Bob swirls the dregs at the bottom of his oversized pannikin, then flicks them into the smouldering ashes of his small fire. He eases himself to his feet, and uses a stick to lift the lid of the camp oven. Aah, that smell!

Ol' Bullet. I wonder what happened to you at the end, wadu, my brother-in-law.

He'd always been a bit fearful of Bullet. The big boy scaring the twins witless just for the fun of it when Bessie left them in his care. Bob had got his measure early on. Sarah had been devoted to him. But he'd always somehow held the edge over Two Bob. He'd liked to boast that his family were fighting men, and that he would be too.

Bullet's dad had died not long before the twins were born, leaving Parli to raise her son alone. His uncle's family was one of the trusted handful that came and went from the valley at times, especially in the wet season when it was common enough for blackfellers to be walking the country. But after Bob's escape from the leg-iron they'd never come back.

Bullet had gone with them, leaving Sarah to look after Parli with her crippled leg. He returned, as promised, but never to stay. He came and went at his own fancy, with no explanations. When he was there, he and Billy barely tolerated each other.

◆

The day before Two Bob left the valley he sat with his mother up by the spring, helping her strip the bark she would shred and weave, just like when he was a kid. Three times he tried to find words, and could not. Bessie placed a hand on his knee. 'We know he's all right. He talks to Parli in his dreams. He can dance that emu wangga eh?' Two Bob laughed with relief. He talked to his mother for the next three hours of the life he and Bob were now leading.

Most years he was able to find a way and a week to return. He would take small gifts from Bob for mother and Sarah; a bright neckerchief, or a mirror. One year he took a tightly wrapped pouch and handed it to Parli without ever knowing the contents.

He'd sit with Parli sometimes, marvelling at the nimble way she manoeuvred around her camp, ignoring his every attempt to assist. Billy had fashioned her a very serviceable crutch, on which she roamed far and wide. But close to home she found it easier to fold her bad leg beneath her, use the callused heel of her hand as the crutch and move in an awkward but remarkably effective scuttling sort of way. She had a laugh that made him laugh. Her tales of childhood made it seem that the valley had once had a cast of thousands.

She loved to tell the story of his parents' arrival in the valley, and remind him that he was lucky to be alive. 'My daddy the one been savem your daddy eh! My Bullet, his daddy the one was gunna put a spear longa your daddy's guts! Too many daddies eh!' She would cackle with laughter at her own joke. As the years passed she took to teasing him about whether he had a sweetheart at Highlands who might help him become a daddy too.

He would help his father with one task or another that was more manageable with two sets of hands. It became a ritual that the two of them would slaughter and salt a bullock each time he visited.

With Stumpy no longer taking an annual quota, the cattle numbers in the valley had got out of control. His stockman's eye was quick to note the poor condition of both stock and pasture. On his third trip back in, Billy agreed to a suggestion, and they spent three days on a two-man muster; him on his Highlands horse, and Billy ungainly as always on his old mule. The stock were nowhere near as quiet as the old days when he and Bob had worked them year round; 'Best coachers in the Kimberley,' Stumpy used to say, as he took delivery of the near-tame beasts. But they managed to cut out all but a handful of the bullocks and half the cows, and push them out through the top entrance to the valley, before remaking the fence.

Billy was always curious for information about Highlands and the world at large. Every now and then he would say something that showed Bessie had passed on to him the stories Two Bob told her of his brother. But only once did he broach the subject directly. They were replacing one of the main upright poles in the kitchen boughshed that the white ants had got to. 'Have ye asked your brother if he might come with ye one time?'

Two Bob nodded.

'And?'

When Two Bob shook his head, Billy closed his eyes whilst he took a deep breath, then turned to the newly cut replacement pole lying beside them. 'Here, give me a hand with this bastard.'

And always Two Bob would while away some time at the spring where the creek emerged from the cliffs that ranged behind the camp; the perfect little waterhole where he and his brother had spent so many hours splashing and playing. He'd sing the song for the spring that Parli had taught them. He'd clear any debris that might have accumulated, wade in to the dark, shady spot where the water seeped from the rockface, and press his forehead against the rock's cold, damp surface before cupping some water in his hands to drink.

Then he would sit with his mother and sister and tell them stories of his and Bob's life at Highlands, while Jinda played alone in the pool.

12

A new morn.

I'd write of those I've loved, I said last night. Foremost of the few is Bessie.

After shooting Twelve Inch that fateful night my last action was to free her from the chain on which the beast had held her. When Bessie shook me awake next day my clothes were red with Jones' blood, and sticky with his gore. The flies were feasting.

Whilst I had lain asleep she had crept out from her place of hiding to investigate. She could find no foot tracks leading from the natives' camp, but hoof prints and drag marks convinced her that bodies had been removed. She believed her parents had met the same grisly fate as my Des, and her intended husband. Yet for all that, she was far more sensible to the needs of the moment than was I.

She urged me to the waterhole to cleanse myself, and pressed me as to my intentions. It became clear that she meant to not let me from her sight. She was a stranger to that country, and feared her fate whomever she might encounter, black or white. She seemed to think she might gain protection from my company.

The days that followed remain somewhat unclear in my mind. They have the texture of a dream in which vivid moments are interwoven with confusions and absences, but now I have set myself to this task, long-forgotten details are coming back to mind.

I was enveloped by dread. Two white men could not go missing without an investigation. Barely three years earlier a pair of detectives from Perth had scoured the countryside for months interviewing all and sundry as they sought to prove a case in a suspected murder by one white man of another.

I had neither the skills to conceal what had just taken place, nor the nerve to withstand an interrogation. My only course would be to plead the deed was self-defence. Yet I did not feel innocent. My fevered imagination was filled with visions of incarceration, or even the spectre of the gallows.

Such were my thoughts as I scrubbed and scrubbed in that waterhole, like Lady Macbeth in the Scottish play, as Twelve Inch called it, seeking to cleanse myself of all trace of the man I had killed. I had heard talk of a route winding through the Leopold Range that came out to the north of Halls Creek. I thought to seek that track. When I emerged from the water I told Bessie that I had resolved to ride for the Territory and beyond. To vanish, was my intention.

I cannot properly explain the reasoning in my mind at the time. Indeed, reason was perhaps not uppermost. For the purpose I had in mind, the sensible course would have been to travel less encumbered. I think it must have been the presence of Bessie. There was no stated agreement or purpose between us, merely an understanding that for the time, at least, she would travel with me.

We departed Poison Hole with all the horses and mules at our disposal, laden with everything we could pack upon them. But first, we burned the hut. I forced myself in, a cloth bound over my nose, averting my eyes from the cloud of flies that swarmed around the corpse as I plundered what I could. I thought perhaps the fire might mask the manner of his death if discovery was postponed long enough. With a stench in the air, and smoke billowing, we mounted and rode with our plant, headed east.

To state it plain, we became hopelessly lost. I became increasingly panicked as we blundered into dead-end valleys and country that was dreadful harsh on the horses. But I could not countenance return, sure that my initial flight would be taken as a sign of guilt.

One night, with a dry storm rumbling in the distance, and lightning flickering around the hilltops, Bessie rose from her blankets on the other side of the fire, and came to mine. Little was said, but with that act, she seemed to take charge. The next morn, with her at the lead now, we turned south by west, instead of blundering haphazardly eastward. She may not have known the country but, unlike me, she knew where she was headed.

A peculiar light headedness took hold of me, a contrast to the weariness of body engendered by endless hours in the saddle, and the heavy tedium of packing the gear on and off. It was in part, no doubt, the pleasures of the nights contributing to this feeling in me. I was a young man, newly admitted to a realm of delight previously but imagined. But it was also a lifting, if not of fear, for that remained strong in me, then of responsibility. I had sensed disaster crowding in on me, and felt wholly incapable of finding a solution. It was a great relief to follow, though I knew not where, after such failure as a leader.

After some days like this, Bessie propped herself up on an elbow one night as she lay next to me. 'Mount House that way,' she said, in her pidgin English, gesturing to the west. 'Two days ride.' Sensing my alarm, she quieted me. 'I know this country now, little bit,' she said, explaining that she'd walked through this part of the country coming to Poison Hole, and that if we kept going we would cut across the wagon road from Fitzroy Crossing to Mount House.

It was that night my future was sealed.

With Bessie's guidance, I could have found and followed the wagon road to Fitzroy, and then to Halls Creek and on, as per my original plan. However, it became apparent that if such was my choice she was not of a mind to accompany me. She was close to her lands and her people now, and had another scheme in mind. I assumed that her intent was to return to Fish Creek, the station from which she had so recently come. But she shook her head and fell into a silence, then commenced a quiet sobbing.

Whilst we held each other close she made it plain. Why would she, an orphan now, return there? She had kin there to be sure, but none who might protect her from the manager, a man she seemed to regard in only slightly better light than Twelve Inch. It seemed that her proposed marriage to Thursday, and the long trek with her parents to Poison Hole, had been arranged to remove her far from this man's clutches. From the frying pan unto the fire, thought I.

There was more she had to say, but each time she began, the words stuck in her throat. My caresses were meant to help her find the words, to calm her. But before I knew it, we were consumed in the most passionate and abandoned embraces. I have experienced none quite like it in all the days since.

It was in the quiet aftermath that she told me of her scheme.

13

Wandering back down to the hearth beneath the boab tree after checking on Riley, Two Bob is musing about Sarah. His big sister. The only one to know nothing at all of life outside the valley.

An' this mob reckon I'm a munjon. He flicks his cigarette butt with a chuckle. *Sarah an' Bullet, what a pair.*

He almost steps on the snake. Jumps back despite himself as it slithers frantically away towards the long grass. Cranky for being so unobservant.

Ol' Bob'd read somethin' into that prob'ly. Just a snake though by my book.

⚬

Two Bob breathed a little easier if Bullet was absent when he arrived in the valley. The drawback was that it meant Sarah would be fretting. Sarah, always scared and nervous. She seemed amazed that he survived from year to year in that awful world outside. Even the gentlest of stories Two Bob told her, thinking they might amuse, seemed to make her flinch. When two years passed with no visit from her man she implored her brother to find out where he was, whether he was coming back.

Mostly he gave the annual races in Derby a miss. Too much humbug, and too many mosquitoes in that saltwater country. That year he did go in, and found Bullet's cousin Ganada. There was a silent understanding amongst the few of them who had once lived in the valley, but left. A quiet nod of acknowledgement, but no more. The fierce code of secrecy on which the valley community had been founded sat somewhere in the guts of them all. This time Two Bob edged Ganada to a quiet corner of the roiling paddock behind the racecourse where the mobs from every station in the district were camped, and dared to ask what had become of Bullet.

'Fucken wild man that one,' Ganada muttered. 'We thought he must've gone back there to die.' According to him Bullet had been nothing but trouble. Every station he worked on, he got bushed by the boss. He did time in Derby jail more than once. He had two kids by a woman over on Fossil Downs. Ganada's family worked out that he must be returning to the valley at times to see his mother Parli. 'But we never heard nothin' about Sarah, or any baby.'

Bullet had found his way somehow to the mission down at La Grange, with all that desert mob. Word came back that he had got into an argument with one of the desert men. A spearing left him bleeding badly. He had walked away from La Grange swearing vengeance, and not been heard of again.

Two Bob always regretted that he did not think to find a lie, or at least a gentler way of breaking the news to Sarah.

Poor thing, first her feller, then her little girl.

Jinda followed the course of her uncles; defiant departure. She needed no chaining nor dream to cause her flight. Just an almighty blue with her mother. She had gleaned enough information from Two Bob on his visits, and had enough bush sense to find her way. Unlike him she had not skulked on the hill looking down. She had marched into the station camp one night calling his name.

Thank god Bob had been there, and grasped the situation in a flash. A gesture silenced the girl, and sent her to his camp. With the haughty authority of the medicine man he had become, he informed the gawkers that this was his niece, his sister's daughter from Fish Creek. Go back to bed, he told them.

❧

Two Bob was in Broome at the time, feeling like he'd won the lottery. He'd just become the first Highlander to get his own motor car, thanks to Joe Black the windmill man.

Since he first started getting wages a couple of years earlier Two Bob had been squirrelling away whatever shillings he could from his one pound a week. But until Joe rocked into the camp at Blundstone Bore two days late and rather the worse for wear, he'd thought he was still years away from his dream.

Joe had contracted to re-equip a couple of mills. As was the custom, the station provided a man to assist, and Two Bob had been assigned to the task. Joe reckoned Two Bob was the best offsider he'd ever had. They shared the work of the camp, yarning away. Joe was happy to wash the dishes of a night, and didn't seem to care a bugger about all the little ways whitefellers usually had of showing they were the boss. He had to do a run back into Broome mid contract, and had a big win on the cudja cudja at one of the gambling houses while he was there.

'How much you got?' he asked Two Bob the night he got back.

'What?'

'Saved up. For that motor car dream you were tellin' me.'

Sixteen pounds and eight shillings was all. But that was enough for Joe. He'd already ordered a new car with his winnings. He even filled the ute's tank for Two Bob's trip home before they shook hands and waved goodbye.

Back at Highlands, Bob hadn't been able to keep Jinda silent for long. He had no idea how to deal with the angry and confused young woman. By the time Two Bob got back she had jumped in the back of a stores truck returning to Derby. Two Bob thought about turning around and trying to chase her, but he didn't have enough money left for the fuel.

❧

Two Bob raises himself from the flour drum seat with an old man's groan, feeling at his stiff back and wondering how he will go in the coming days, bumping over the station's backtracks with Andy. He prowls the wide circle of speckled midday shade around the boab, flicking aside a stick here, stooping to pick up a fallen nut there, and trying to hold his spine straight and loose like the gun rider he had once been. Loose limbs are a thing of the past though, as he well knows.

All this remembering. He supposes it is inevitable, given what he has set in motion. And it is easier than thinking about how he is going to manage what is still to come. That scares him.

You're the one always knew what to do, Marj.

He turns towards the small cemetery where her headstone dwarfs all the others.

He used to tease her that it was the Landrover she wanted, not him. She did love sitting up there in the front beside him as they poked along, with a bunch of countrymen crowded on the back. Marj had picked him out, even if it was from a small pool. She didn't want to marry up with some feller from outside and have to leave home, she told him, and there was no other bugger straight for her round here.

The confirmed bachelor, the head stockman who never so much as looked sideways at a girl, was snared. He'd been terrified at first, but despite what everyone else thought, by some mysterious quirk of chemistry Two Bob and Marj suited each other almost perfectly. Oh, she would give him the sharp end of her tongue when others were around. In the stock camp the other men would make sly jokes about who wore the trousers in Two Bob's camp. He would smile wryly at the jokers, and change the subject with another story; he knew how things stood.

14

The folly of love. That is the only way I can explain it.

Many years ago, before the termites had devoured the Collected Works of William Shakespeare that I stole from Twelve Inch, I read the tale of Romeo and Juliet. It is a story from centuries past in another world, but is all I know of love as it may be conceived of in the world beyond this valley. Yet I dare to declare that Bessie's and mine was such a youthful love, conceived too against all odds in an atmosphere of madness. Why else would she take such a chance?

As we lay together that night Bessie told me of her uncle Marralam, a man she knew only by the tales of her mother. He was a survivor of the time when the country was inflamed in conflict as the police hunted the outlaw Pigeon, whom she called Jandamarra. Not just a survivor, but a comrade in arms, and a man of fearsome repute.

In Pigeon's time a secret pocket deep within an unknown valley was their safest refuge when they retreated from the battle. One never breached by the troopers who scoured the country seeking their sign. Even in nomadic times of old it was but little known and used. A sort of no-man's-land where the Boonooba territories abut and overlap those of other bands, out of the way of the usual routes the people followed in their daily business.

Marralam had sworn a vow, to himself and to Pigeon, to 'never live like a whitefellow's dog' in the station camps. Imprisoned after Pigeon's death, upon release he made his way by foot the hundreds of miles from Roebourne back to his lands, and made haste for the valley, where he forged a refuge for the last of the munjons unable or unwilling to wear the yoke of the white man.

The redoubt had only ever been mentioned to Bessie in fearful, reverent whispers, and always with dire warnings of the perils to any who might reveal its whereabouts, or even its very existence.

Bessie meant to find her uncle, and to join his band.

Her tale of Marralam's lair was meant as explanation, not invitation. That night, though, I was not of a mind to bid her farewell. What's more, I'd been growing ever more afraid that the events at Poison Hole may have come to light whilst we blundered around the countryside. If they had, I gravely doubted my chances of making it across the border to the Northern Territory. To disappear with her into the valley of the munjons seemed to me a sensible course of action.

'I'll come with you!'

The look on her face when I said it!

'He'll put a spear longa you,' she cried.

'I'll take my chances,' I begged.

'Might be longa me too, for bringing you.'

Yet even as she spoke she held me close. With all that had happened we felt ourselves alone against the world. She could not lead me to this valley, she said. But if we travelled to the place she knew, and waited, we would be found. She undertook to plead my case, if given the chance, but that was all she could promise.

'Lead the way,' I answered, drawing her to me again.

The spot was a hillock of modest size on a plain south of a goodly river. I was happy to stop our wanderings, let the animals out on long hobbles, and put my feet up. At Bessie's insistence, I left all the weapons in clear view by our campsite. Each day she climbed the hillock, and lit a clump of old-man spinifex, sending a cloud of oily smoke roiling into the sky.

We had been at the camp a little over a week. I was by then well rested after our travels, and had begun to let down my guard somewhat. Indeed, with the pleasant idleness of the days, it had rather the feel of a holiday. I strolled from the river to our camp, well pleased with the brace of bream I had caught for our dinner. I hung the fish in a branch and set about stoking the fire for a billy of tea. Squatted down in this manner, I sensed a movement, and looked up to see two men facing me, spears poised.

The vivid memory of that day is of Bessie's scream. It was all a blur of fear and chaos as she screeched and begged and cried, and the two men snarled and glowered. Somehow she stopped them. The elder of the pair lowered his spear. I had no doubt from what she'd told me that this must be her uncle Marralam. He held out his arm to still the younger man. My life was spared. Though for how long I knew not.

With Marralam barking orders, Bessie led me blindfolded up a steepling path. The next thing I saw, when the cloth was torn from my eyes, was this valley I have called home ever since.

15

It's funny the way he feels better now when he finds himself remembering Marj. Talking to her. For so long it was so hard, so painful. He doesn't know why, doesn't want to know, but lately it seems like she's become his mate again. The memories have gradually become nurturing, not an agony.

Marj felt liberated by the hundred-yard move from the scramble of ramshackle huts where all the Riders lived, across to the Walker camp. She supervised the rough-and-ready extensions to Two Bob's hut, and generally took charge. He said yes to everything, not trying to hide his delight at the change in his circumstances. They worked out early on how to make each other laugh, and to give each other the space they needed.

Her favourite week of the year was the Derby races. She loved the hubbub of it, the furious exchange of gossip, the news and speculation of new times coming: the Gurindji mob going on strike in the Territory; a referendum in Canberra. It still wasn't to his taste, but he could hardly refuse Marj, with as many of the Rider clan as could squeeze aboard coming along for the ride.

He often encountered Jinda in there. She would either ignore him, or scream at him to fuck off. Jinda had become Jenny, and fallen in with a ragtag group dependent on the down-at-heel whitefellers who floated around the backblocks of the town in makeshift, impermanent camps. And dependent on the grog they supplied.

The first time Marj witnessed Jinda's screaming, she challenged Two Bob. He held her eye but gave no answer. 'You and your secret family humbug,' she said with a glare. 'One day I'll get to the bottom of it.' But she backed off. An unofficial policy of 'don't ask, don't tell' was mutually accepted.

∽

Two Bob's annual valley pilgrimage always started with a visit to Bertie Ahmad's camp in Derby. Bertie had closed down his trading post that catered to the drovers and prospectors and other battlers of an era that had all but disappeared. But the shopfront had only ever been a part of his business. He was a go-to man for the bushmen of the Kimberley hinterland with goods of dubious provenance – a station manager doing a little business on the side, or a countryman who had mysteriously come into possession of some item of value.

Billy was no longer up to the trek through the Leopolds to Halls Creek, but still managed to coax a little gold from his secret reef. Bertie, in retirement on his block behind the meatworks, was happy to receive a visitor like Two Bob, and exchange a stack of grubby old notes for some gold flakes. Money in hand, Two Bob would head to Elders at a quiet time the next day, load up with stores then head back up the Gibb River Road.

Many miles before the Highlands turnoff, he would turn in on the back road to Bullfrog Hole, and begin the slow crawl over the old track that no-one graded any more. It was the only time in the annual cycle of his life, dictated by the slow rhythms of the muster and the familiar patterns of Highlands, that he felt the pressure of the ticking clock. The slow track. The walk in. Back with his father and the mules for the stores. The work waiting at the station. Marj's silent disapproval. And the undercurrents of the handful of stolen days in the valley.

∽

Bessie and Sarah seemed to shrink ever inwards. There were fewer stories each time of their own year past, and fewer questions about his own stories; except for Sarah's avid attention to his tales of her daughter Jinda. And tales they were. His renowned stock camp yarns were recollections with the odd embellishment, but for Sarah he concocted a whole new life for Jinda in which she had settled into a job as a cleaner at the hospital, and lived in a little house with her feller who was a gardener there. Each year as he made his slow way along the backtrack he rehearsed the latest instalment he'd created. This imaginary Jinda became almost more real to him than the Jenny he encountered at the races. When he drove away from Bullfrog Hole the deception sat like a heavy stone in his guts.

Year on year Billy seemed less energetic, less attentive to his routine of gardening, repairs and improvements. Each time Two Bob tried another way of raising the subject of them leaving the valley, his father's response was curter than the last. How might they emerge from the valley and explain themselves to the world? Two Bob could never offer a plausible answer. Sarah simply remained terrified of the world beyond.

Each year the trip depressed him more.

Until the time he took Milly.

How did I get away with that? That's right! It was when Marj had to go into hospital first time, for that diabetes business.

The look of delight on Bessie's face when he walked into the camp with Milly perched on his shoulders is something he has never forgotten.

Little girls. I reckon they're different to boys, the way they make everybody go soft.

The clock wasn't ticking the same way that year, with yet another change of managers back at the station, and Marj in hospital. But it was Milly that changed the feel of things. Even Billy couldn't stop smiling.

She was a solemn little girl, who tended to react more to the twittering arrival of a gaggle of zebra finches at Billy's birdbath than to the cooings of her aunt and grandmother. But nor did she object to their constant attentions.

For the first time since he had begun his returns to the valley, the night-time silences did not hang heavy. They would all watch the sleeping girl dreamily instead of each wondering what the other was thinking. When Two Bob took Milly up to the spring to splash about in its cool, shaded waters, and exclaim with delight at the flash of a skimming rainbow bee-eater, he was able to drift back in his mind to his own childhood when all had seemed simple.

He never said anything to Milly, but somehow the girl divined that their trip to the valley was something private between them. She said nothing to her mother when Marj returned. The silent mutual conspiracy of 'don't ask, don't tell' between him and Marj seeped down to embrace their daughter.

16

I am granted another day, though my rheumy lungs and ebbing strength suggest a need to press ahead.

Just why did Marralam spare me? I would not have been the first to die at the end of his spear, and if that had been my fate, it would have troubled him not at all. I think it did me some credit that I had disposed of Twelve Inch. And as I would discover, a natural curiosity was one of his qualities. He glimpsed an opportunity in those frantic moments to observe at close quarters one of the hated whitefellows. It was intended to be a temporary reprieve at first, I suspect. But he soon surmised that I posed little threat; a blundering, fearful youth likely to perish if he tried to flee, easily tracked down if needed. He chose to give me a chance.

Now I am the inheritor of his domain. What irony.

At our first encounter I would have guessed him between fifty years and sixty. He was not an overly tall man, but well built and heavily muscled, with a proud and fierce demeanour that could, when he so chose, be overwhelming and intimidating. He was, by experience as well as by natural inclination, a warrior.

He had reclaimed his wife Weela from Fish Creek and arrived back here some ten years or thereabouts before Bessie and I. Their daughter Polly was five or six as I recall. He maintained a secretive contact with a few of his trusted comrades from the fighting days. He allowed in a handful of others seeking refuge. Most particularly, I believe, women who had been misused, or who had lost their husbands, or both. And so this wee community of souls was born.

Not all of them welcomed my arrival, let it be said, but Marralam's word was law. Bessie and I made our camp on this side of the creek, somewhat apart from the rest. At first an ill-trusted novice, by my diligence and reliability, and gradually by my ingenuity and resourcefulness, I grew to be accepted. By most. As the years passed I stopped fretting so much about our circumstance and my fears of pursuit, and settled into the life I was leading as something ... what? Natural to me, I suppose.

In our fifth year here there came the moment that made any notion of departure unthinkable. Bessie suffered two miscarryings before the happy event, but, our Sarah arrived.

It was Bessie who made the point one night as we lay here, watching Sarah sleep. 'You know we can't ever leave here now.' She made clear, after her own manner, that anywhere beyond this little world, our circumstance would be seen as far from natural. Our precious daughter would be branded a half-caste and taken from us, and we would be torn asunder. For though every white man assumed his right to empty his loins upon a black woman, none out there would accept his right to live with that woman as his mate.

'It seems we are stuck here,' I said.

'Julyee.' She drew me close, for the first time since our daughter had been born.

Of all my names, Julyee is the one to which I cleave. My skin name. Other names might change with time and events, but a skin name is immutable. Bessie was Nagarra. As her man, I was therefore Julyee.

It was not really until the birth of Sarah that my probation was completed in Marralam's eyes. After that, though I was a much younger man than he, we started to become friends. Despite the limitations of our pidgin versions of English and Boonooba, we spent many an hour in spirited conversation. He was something of a philosopher, in his thirst for knowledge and comprehension of a society he scorned. He spoke with a great pride of being the last still holding fast to the old and true ways. He conveyed a condescension bordering upon contempt for his fellow Boonooba who had surrendered their independence, voluntarily or otherwise, for a life as the 'gudia's dogs'.

However, he would at times, by word or more commonly by a revealing pause or reflective silence, convey that the matter was not entirely straightforward. He sometimes questioned the wisdom of the course he had chosen. These are not his own words, but he admitted to a selfishness of motivation. This lay not just in the stubborn adherence to his old vow; but also in the ever-burning hatred he felt, and the knowledge that succumbing to the other world would be a constant humiliation and affront that he feared he could not bear. And because he could not contemplate such a fate, he forced the others to endure the harsh and lonely life of the valley.

In the consequences of his selfishness for his kin, I find echoes of my own story.

Ah! I muse and I ramble, my confession deferred. What is my defence for such indulgence? The account of my first great sin burst forth on the page almost the moment I started. Perhaps because I have confidence that for that sin I shall be, or should be, forgiven. It troubles me, but not deeply in my soul.

The second is another matter. I have no such confidence, for it involved the betrayal of those I have loved.

17

Everythin' was startin' to change by the time you came along, eh Milly girl.

Two Bob had done well out of the equal wages decision, with his wages suddenly shooting up to thirty-five dollars a week from the five it had been. He felt like a rich man. But he was in a small minority. All over the Kimberley the different mobs had walked off or been kicked off the stations as the old order broke down. A few of the young fellers who were laid off and a couple of families drifted into Derby, but most of the Highlands mob stayed put.

When he camped at the Derby reserve while Marj was in hospital for the birth, the number of people living there had more than doubled from a year before. Most nights it was a madness of drunken noise and intermittent fights. He was thankful that they were able to take Milly home to the peace of Highlands.

Marj was just about the only one who didn't go soft around the edges in the presence of Milly. She loved her daughter deeply, but maintained her businesslike attitude to life, whereas even gruff Uncle Bob fell under Milly's spell. When Two Bob was in camp, if the babe wasn't on Marj's breast, she was in his arms. And once she was weaned, she hardly ever left his side. It became another subject for jokes amongst his fellow stockmen.

Two Bob felt his life was charmed. The only shadow came from the valley. When Parli passed, and then his mother, they were down to two, Billy and Sarah. It had become a forlorn place to visit, but he had no choice.

He always timed the supply run for off-week, as it was called, when the fortnightly cycle of binge drinking fuelled by the pension and dole payments was at its low point. This time he'd loaded up at Elders, then spent the evening yarning with Bertie before rolling his swag on Bertie's verandah. In the pre-dawn glimmer he started the engine before he realised; she was sitting there in the passenger seat. Jinda!

It was only when the light improved that he realised what a mess she was in. Eyes blackened, one swollen shut. Dress torn and bloodstained.

'Got any gear with you?' he asked.

A brief shake of her head.

'Want to go back to the hospital, see if they can patch you up?'

Another head shake.

He pulled in at a bore, where she cleaned herself up as best she could. Then he delivered her home to the valley, along with another year's worth of supplies.

Milly was with him when he went the next year. At Marj's suggestion!

He chuckles at the weird irony of it all as he gives the stew a stir.

Marj and Bob had always been civil, without ever really having much time for each other. But they were the two who started to get mixed up in all the politics stuff, going off to Land Council meetings and what have you. He was proud of them. Especially Marj, who wasn't going to let the diabetes and all its complications slow her down; there weren't many women up front in those early days.

Somewhere in there they stopped being the Highlands mob, and became the Jimbala Wali Community, with Marj as the chairman. The name never took root in his mind. He knew all that politics business was not for him. He went to one of the meetings early on, and it was all too hard and angry for his liking. After that, if the Land Council couldn't pick them up, he handed the car over to Marj and stayed home looking after Milly.

On one of those long drives Marj put the screws on Bob, challenging the twins' Fish Creek story. Neither of them ever told Two Bob exactly what transpired, but the dynamic between him and Marj shifted. She let the 'don't ask, don't tell' arrangement stand, knowing that a confrontation would make him at best deeply uncomfortable. But with the odd comment she let it be known that Bob had spilled the beans – or some of them at least – and she stopped being so resentful about this silence between them.

That year when he gave her his usual mumble about having to take off for a week, she gave him a look, and said, 'Why don't you take Milly with you. I'm goin' to be flat out here.'

He and Milly arrived at the hut to discover that three had become four. Jinda had been pregnant. Milly couldn't have been more delighted. It was like having a real live doll. For the three days they were in there she hardly let go of her little nephew Riley.

&

Jinda's dissolute years in Derby had taken their toll. One morning she didn't wake up. Two Bob arrived in the valley to find toddler Riley in the care of his sixty-year-old grandma and eighty-year-old great-grandpa.

Billy and Sarah's lives had narrowed down to the most basic of tasks. They survived, and they doted on the boy. They both knew it had become ridiculous. But both of them had also gone beyond the point of being able to change it, to take the momentous step of leaving, even for Riley's sake. Two Bob had the only blazing row of his life with his father, but there was no persuading him.

Instead he started to go in two or three times a year, taking powdered milk and tinned fruit for Riley. And he built three huge piles of firewood. Big enough to create a smoke smudge on a far horizon. He told them he would watch every morning that he could. If Riley needed help, light the first pile. If he had not come within the week, light the second, and then after another week the third.

They all knew it was less than adequate, but could think of no other scheme.

18

In the year of 1929 a miracle unfolded in this room where I sit and write. I can think of it no other way. It was a most bewildering experience when I was ushered in by Polly, that first time I beheld the mewling pair each grasping for a teat; so like in feature as two peas in a pod, yet such a contrast in hue. I was overcome with manly pride and love. Yet there was at the same time something almost disturbing in the sight; one near as dark as his mother, the other near as pale as I, creamy and stark beside his mother and his twin.

Othello and Hamlet. Wajarri and Janga. Two Bob and Bob. My flesh and my blood. My heart and my soul. My agony.

As young'uns they were an unbridled joy to Bessie and I, and the rest of us here in the valley. But as they grew I came to realise that they were a mystery as much as a miracle. It was an intrigue to us all to watch them. So unalike in temperament, yet always, it seemed, in harmony with each other. Othello was a steady young soul. Hamlet, though, confounded me; there was indeed a fire in him.

Marralam breathed his last a few years after the twins arrived. My brood aside, his daughter Polly with her gammy leg was the only permanent resident left. Her son Bullet and her two cousins and their families still came and went back then, but the responsibility of leadership fell by default upon me. I speak now with hindsight, but with his passing something changed profoundly here. This place had been founded as a defiant warrior's retreat and fastness, bound to the stories and deeds of a time of war. With him gone, it became instead a mere hiding place.

At the time, I had no such thoughts. Indeed, they were my golden years, that decade when the lads were young. I knew full well how odd our situation was, but fancied that I would not change it for the world. I was the head of a family I adored, and given our peculiar circumstances I provided for them well.

After Sarah's birth, having abandoned any thought of departing the valley, I gradually transformed our boughshed into the dwelling it is now. I instigated a scheme of irrigation for the kitchen garden that I cultivated. And most importantly, I came to an arrangement with Stumpy Maclean.

Maclean had taken up his run to our north, which he called Highlands. He was clearly a hard-working and assiduous man, determined to make the most of the lease he now occupied. Two years running he had mustered his southern flank, making camp at the selfsame waterhole near the hillock where Bessie and I had waited. Such activity was much too close for comfort as far as Marralam was concerned. Bessie told me that there had been talk between he and a couple of the younger men about an ambush. But they well knew that the disappearance of a white man would inevitably lead to inquiries and searches that would imperil our fastness.

Well, I knew something of the man. He was the one the police had investigated so thoroughly but unsuccessfully for a murder without a body! I had encountered him during my days at Mount House before I reached Poison Hole. The men there admired the coolness and nerve he displayed in the face of the investigation. He was a man who looked to his own business, caring little for proprieties or the sentiment of others.

Marralam agreed to the plan I suggested. It entailed a very great chance at the outset, should my estimation of the man be mistaken, but Marralam recognised he no longer had the power to ensure our survival by his will alone. The beauty of it was the obvious benefit it provided to all the parties.

Stumpy was a man to rapidly assess a situation. He showed no surprise when I walked into his camp. Indeed he laughed. 'The Billygoat! You're looking a bit raggedy arsed there lad. I thought you'd be in the Territory. And where's your brother?' They never found poor Des, I thought. But quickly enough we got down to business. His closing words were, 'You hand over the cattle before I hand over the goods.'

Thus was sealed a bargain that served us all well for nigh on twenty years. The arrangement was simple enough. By enclosing the valley at its two entrances Marralam had already created a supply of beef more than adequate to our needs. I offered the surplus to Stumpy in return for a supply of goods. The first year it was twenty head. But as we started to manage our stock, we were able to provide him with fifty, sometimes sixty head of quiet bullocks each year, walked down the ravine to its outlet only a short ride from the billabong that he had christened as Bullfrog Hole.

Each year, as we handed over the bullocks, I would also deliver a list of goods and supplies for him to bring to Bullfrog Hole the next. I have no doubt that he profited handsomely from the transaction. But from our perspective, so did we. The necessities and the small luxuries were both provided for. And each year I was able to obtain tools, equipments and various items that made our life here more amenable. This scheme was in place before our boys were born, but from a very early age they became adept young stockmen, and soon exceeded me in proficiency.

I became confident enough in Stumpy — or should I say in his desire to keep our arrangement intact — that I broached the matter of our tenure. For two years I asked for nothing but basic supplies on my yearly list. In return, Stumpy took out a new pastoral lease, which, at my request, he registered as Maryvale. Most of it was steepling rock on which no beast would ever graze, but it included this valley of ours. That year, before the exchange of stock and goods, he signed the deed I had drawn up, assigning the lease to me.

My Maryvale. Named for my mother. A valley of no horizons, where the steep walls delay the sun's appearance and hasten its departure; but I have never found it gloomy. The lease papers and the deed with mine and Stumpy's signatures are secured in the trunk with my Will.

I also took to embarking on occasional ramblings further afield. I steered clear of Stumpy's domain to our north, but explored the other three quarters, gradually extending my range. As I learned to read the country more closely I became fascinated with the nature of the rocks and ranges that were so dominant. This in turn led to my discovery of a thin and somewhat fickle seam of gold in a belt of quartzite some two days walk from home.

I liked to think of myself as a prudent man. Though I had no plans at all to change our situation, between the lease and the gold that I secreted, I felt I had some insurance, should mischance befall us. As sure enough it did!

Stumpy Maclean, the foolish man, decided it was his duty to take the fight to the Emperor of Nippon. Now, that was an action that seemed out of character with the man I knew. Perhaps he had at last tired of his life as Lord of Highlands, and wanted a new adventure.

The bell was tolling for this fool's paradise.

19

Two Bob hums the song of the spring. The song that Parli taught them both in the time before he can remember. He pulls a small chunk of the boab pith from his pocket, and sucks on it, smiling at the sourness.

You never really forgave me, did you, for goin' with the old man. For leavin' you behind, locked up. I didn't know. I told you that, but still you didn't forgive me.

Two Bob looks up at the new moon, a thin silver sliver amongst the branches, halfway towards the western horizon. The edge is coming off the midday heat. There are a good couple of hours of light left, but the day is on the decline.

◦

Marj and Bob were at a Land Council meeting. Down at Billiluna in the desert country, which was as foreign to Two Bob as France. There were none of those premonitions that twins are supposed to get, and which he would have expected.

His theory is that it happened too quick for Bob to call out to him – Marj said he had a big heart attack right there in the meeting, and lay down dead on the spot.

He didn't know what to feel. He just had to live with the hole that was left.

◦

Eh brother, I might be readin' you wrong, but I don't think so. You're givin' me the go-ahead. It's time to sort things out.

He is feeling old. And strangely nervous. Of all his blood relations and family, only Riley and Dancer are left.

Let's just hope I don't fuck it up; I'm not as clever as you were.

20

My hand is shaky this morn.

Was it prudence or fear? A mixture perhaps? I had the means – my stash of gold. And if I'd acted that same year whilst the lads were younger and Hamlet more amenable, all may have turned out differently. But I dithered, eking out Stumpy's last consignment as the rains failed us two years running. But worse than the hard rations was what I can only describe as a loss of harmony amongst us.

Bessie's general mood and occasional fits of temper were certainly not improved when the supply of chewing tobacco ran dry. She would grumble about this shortage or that, or watch with disapproval as I began to struggle with exercising my fatherly duties.

Our Sarah had been besotted with Bullet for many a year, had always pined when he departed the valley. Whereas Bullet and I had never got on. We had words during one of his visits, and he departed angrily to seek his kin. He swore to Polly and Sarah that he would return, but cursed me as he left. Sarah, unfairly I believed, held me responsible, and withdrew her affections from me.

Hamlet took her side. He had become increasingly defiant, and I knew not how to deal with him other than to become ever firmer in directing and disciplining him. He would bow to my authority when he had to, but only because he had to. My love for him did not diminish, but his for me did lessen.

I would watch him. With his brother, his mother, his sister, he was as high-spirited and as charming as ever. He and Othello went about their tasks with the cattle like a pair of old hands, working in perfect harmony. It was only when he and I had dealings that the air would become thick with tensions. It came to seem that in the daylight hours only Othello could find a smile for me. Yet of course, I knew him to be entirely sympathetic with his twin, and would not have expected it to be otherwise.

It came to its boiling point when we had consumed the last of the flour. There was meat aplenty still, but nary a vegetable. The tea and sugar and tobacco were long finished. The johnnycakes the ladies made from the seeds they winnowed and ground had once been a treat for us all, but they too were exhausted.

The time had well and truly come to make use of the gold I had been hoarding. It was Stumpy who had told me of Sohan the cameleer, and his block at Moonlight Valley. There was a chance he was no longer there, or that he might be away with his camels when I visited. But I could think of no better scheme. I conveyed none of my doubts to Bessie and the children when I laid out my plan.

Ah. I think back now on our foolishness. As if Hamlet was ever going to live a life here in this valley, with all that curiosity and energy and charm he had. But Bessie was just as adamant as me that Hamlet should not accompany Othello and I. Should things go awry, I might pass myself off as an eccentric prospector, and Othello as a native in my employ. But a fourteen-year-old as pale as his father, and identical to his brother in all but hue of skin? It was beyond explanation.

It is also true, though I would not say it, that I was reluctant to embark on this chancy adventure with him. I could rely upon my Othello to play his part. When it came to Hamlet, I had no such confidence. I had guessed a two week walk. The two of us would not last that long in each other's company!

And so, with stern admonitions on my part to Hamlet to care for his mother and sister, Othello and I departed. We left later than I had planned, and made it only as far as our valley's eastern exit that first night.

In truth, I was not surprised at what unfolded the next morn. Othello's demeanour gave the game away. He may perhaps have laid an eye upon his brother, but more likely it was that sixth sense they shared.

It took a great effort on my part to maintain an outward appearance of calm. I called out, and when Hamlet finally appeared his manner was defiant. The look exchanged between us remains burnt in my memory. Yet he bowed to me. Not a word crossed our lips in the hours it took us to return to camp. He walked as slowly as he dared, knowing that my fury and frustration were mounting.

When we reached the final turning that leads into this hidden pocket, he simply sat. He deliberately forced me to take him in hand. Yet the moment I did, he resisted not. Oh how many times have I replayed that day in my mind? Each time I released my hold on him, he stopped and regarded me, almost mildly, until I was forced to take a hold again and lead him on. And so we entered the camp, me grasping his wrist, Bessie and Sarah fearfully watching. I let go of him there in the kitchen boughshed. He let his arm drop and stood motionless as the women edged closer.

It took every ounce of self-control in me to keep my voice calm. 'Will you stay?' I asked. It came out as a whisper, almost, the first time.

He looked not at me, and answered not.

'Will you stay?' I asked again, louder. The same response.

'Will you stay?' I shouted.

This time he met my eye, but still he said nothing.

'By God you shall!'

I find it hard to believe, still. That I remembered it. That it was there at all. But in that moment I did not hesitate. I marched to the hut where I kept my tools, and there, buried in a dark corner amongst other unused, long-forgotten items we had brought to the valley all those years ago, I found it. And back I marched.

Bessie realised what I was about but was unable to stop me. In a blind fury, I secured the chain around the boughshed's post, and before he knew what I was doing, I sat Hamlet on the ground, and snapped the iron around his leg above his ankle.

The poor boy was too shocked to protest.

With my blood still boiling, I glared at the three of them and departed.

There! I have confessed at last.

I did chain my own flesh and blood. And I used the same chain and the same leg-iron that had been used to chain his own mother.

But there is something worse than that.

I took the key with me.

Oh I feel wretched.

It was so long ago, that fateful day. There is more I would like to say, of my dear Bessie, of my Sarah, so recently buried, of her Jinda, and especially of, or even for, Riley, but the chance is past.

I know not what else I should have done that day. But what I did was wrong and was foul. It tainted all. This place, and those of us who remained.

I am sorry to all of you.

My greatest trait was stubbornness. I fear it did not serve us well.

It is done. I am going to sit by the spring.

21

Two Bob was on the track to Bullfrog Hole within fifteen minutes of seeing the smoke on the south-west horizon.

'Did Bob tell you about Riley?' he asked Marj.

'He told me.'

'I dunno what's goin' on, but he might be comin' back with me.'

Marj held his eyes. He couldn't read her face, which disturbed him.

She reached in through the car window, laid a hand on his forearm, squeezed briefly.

Two Bob stretches his arm out, remembering that touch. It is an old man's limb now, the skin is looser, the muscle weaker. He remembers her words too, and the surge of love he felt.

'Get goin' then,' she said.

❦

He came back to chaos at Highlands.

It was one of those stories that never made any sense, but everyone who'd been there, and a lot who weren't, enjoyed telling it. He's heard many versions over the years. The manager had come down to the camp looking for him and somehow it had finished up in a spectacular shouting match between Marj and the boss that had gone back and forth around the camp, up to the homestead and back.

Marj had cited every slight and injustice of every owner and manager back to the time of Stumpy Maclean. The manager had denounced her and Two Bob and 'every other black cunt in the

Kimberley' as 'useless, unreliable bludgers not worth feeding', and threatened to run them off the place.

'You can't run us off, you fucken white cunt,' Marj had raged. 'We're fucken leavin'. See how you go on your own runnin' this fucken cock-rag turnout, you mangy white prick.'

When Two Bob drove into camp with Riley, Marj was already on her way to Snake Springs spearheading the exodus. The two working vehicles in the camp had been precariously loaded with people and possessions, and headed off. Thankfully Milly had been left behind with orders to fill him in, make sure the pot plants were watered, and complete the packing up of their camp. She was fifteen by then, not long back from the hostel in Derby that she hated so much – scarily beautiful in Two Bob's eyes, with that quiet manner and faraway eyes – and delighted to reunite with her nephew and take him in hand.

The next days were a madness of packing, driving back and forth and unpacking as the exodus was completed. At one point the manager cornered him. Two Bob rather enjoyed the moment; the gammon, half-hearted apology, the barely masked fury, the offer of a big pay increase for him and two of the other boys. He nodded what might have been a thank you, or a dismissal, and got on with the packing.

For a while there it was fine. There was so much to do for a hands-on feller like himself, building boughsheds and makeshift camps for the new Jimbala Wali camp on the eastern side of Snake Springs, the Highlands side. But the only good thing he could say for the camp was that it was better than being in Derby.

As far as he could tell Riley seemed fine, happy in Milly's care. To his amazement, no-one was asking questions. Was it just the turmoil of the times? Was it the old Highlands way of minding your own business, leaving those Walkers to their own devices? People who didn't know them seemed to assume that he was Milly's child. He wasn't going to rock any boats by offering up explanations that no-one was asking for.

He thought many a time about heading back to the valley, but something about the look in his father's eye as he handed Riley over and waved him away made him know it was pointless. What would he find? There was no-one left to bury the last man standing.

Once the new camp was set up, Two Bob found himself at a loose end for the first time in his life. It didn't sit well. Marj had plenty on her plate, but she recognised the signs. It was she who urged him to ask about a job at Boxwood Downs. He argued half-heartedly against it; what if she got crook again and had to go to hospital? Marj retorted that Milly was old enough to look after herself now, for a while at least. Herself and Riley.

He started the new season in the Boxwood stock camp, living in the single men's quarters. It was the first time he'd ever worked anywhere other than Highlands. He missed Milly and Marj something terrible, and fretted about Riley, but found himself loving it. Boxwood had a proper vehicle plant! Equipment that didn't break down all the time! And a better class of horse for the stockmen.

You were right about that, Marjie, it was a cock-rag turnout they were runnin' here.

When the new head stockman they'd recruited from the Territory didn't work out, Big Al's manager Goldy promoted Two Bob into the role, 'for now'. Then the new lad they hired in for the camp to fill the hole turned out to be old Joe Black's son Andy. The two of them took an immediate shine to each other. 'For now' just seemed to roll on, with no further mention of finding a replacement for the Territory feller.

22

He heard the news from Goldy, who'd driven out to the stock camp with supplies. 'Your old joint's on the market again, Two Bob. I asked Big Al if he was goin' to have a crack at it.'

'What'd he reckon?'

'Said he'd love to, but he's a bit stretched just now. If it's still there next year he might. Reckon it probably will be too. No offence, but it's a bit of a basket case in the good times. No way it makes sense the way the market is now except as an add-on to this place.' He was watching Two Bob keenly as he said this, but got no response. 'S'pose you mob might have a go eh? Government's buyin' every other joint in the Kimberley for youse.'

'Might be. It's not up to me, boss.'

But he knew there was no 'might be' about it. Marj trumpeted the news as vindication, and immediately embarked on a campaign for Highlands to be acquired for Jimbala Wali. She'd had another bad turn, and this time was down in Perth for a month for tests when the news broke. But that just made it easier for her to get access to the government mob to lobby and plead and plot.

Two Bob was surprised at how ambivalent he felt about the prospect. There was nothing he desired more than to put an end to their exile at Snake Springs, and the eternal cycle of changing owners claiming lordship over their country. It belonged to them. Marj deserved it. But ...

Goldy knew what he was talking about. Two Bob was on a hiding to nothing if Marj's campaign was successful. It was assumed that he would become the manager. And he would. But it was one thing having been the reliable old head stockman on Highlands forever. It was another having the headache of actually running the place.

Two Bob had seen it on so many other stations across the Kimberley. The joy of returning to country as owners. Then the hard reality of trying to keep a run-down property with a rubbish herd afloat with no money. The blackfellers only got the busted-arse places. He knew what he was in for, but kept his ambivalence to himself.

The deal was completed during the wet season. He rang Goldy from Snake Springs to give his notice. 'Good luck, mate!' Goldy laughed. It was not malicious. 'Sing out anytime. I'll give you a hand where I can, but Big Al keeps me on a pretty tight rein.'

It is years now since he's set foot inside the old homestead building. He couldn't get used to living in it back then. Marj and Milly did a huge spring clean. Decades worth of detritus disappeared to the tip. They put a swing set in the yard for Riley which he never used, got the lawn looking green for the first time in thirty years, and brought the bougainvilleas back to life. He had to admit, the place looked better than it ever had. But it didn't feel like home. The minute he stepped inside the house, he felt out of place.

And he knew from day one that he wasn't really a manager. He had trouble making sense of the words that poured out from the government feller they sent to help him, let alone the numbers in his budgets; but he knew in his bones that those figures didn't add up in the real world.

Right from the start he could feel it slipping away. Since he'd pulled out, half the plant, shoddy as it was, had been sold off. He just didn't have the gear to do the job. The feller he had pencilled in as head stockman got on the grog and didn't show up. The muster never got into full stride. The truck broke down on the south run out Bullfrog Hole way. That meant they never even started the sweep through Blundstone's on the east side. The government feller muttered over his papers with a big frown. Elders kept ringing up asking when the freight account was going to be paid.

He bottled it all up. He didn't want to worry Marj, who was in her element. There was something wonderful about being their own bosses in this small world at the end of the road where they all lived in each other's laps. About not having to second-guess everything around how the manager might react, or what he might think or say. About letting it all hang out, for good and bad.

The meetings on the verandah planning a future. There'd be a proper office. A school – only primary, she acknowledged, but at least then the littlies wouldn't have to be sent away to the hostel. A clinic – her niece Rosa could run it when she'd finished her nursing course down in Perth. Marj could see it all. There was an energy and an excitement at Highlands that had never existed before. He felt like a wet blanket every time he gave his report on station business to the Jimbala Wali council.

◈

His joy through that year was watching Milly. The smile. The bounce in her step. The way she glowed with anticipation when she knew Andy was on his way out. What could be better than seeing the child you love happier than she has ever been in her life!

The spark that had been lit on the weekends off from Boxwood became a raging fire that first year back at Highlands. Marj didn't approve, but that was to be expected. Two Bob wondered how Andy managed to keep his job at Boxwood, with the amount of time he was spending at Highlands with Milly.

When she knew he was coming, she would wait on the verandah, with her bag of fishing gear and a change of clothes, singing away to Riley until she heard the engine. Then she would be on her feet, looking for the dust, and would run to the gate to hold it open. Two Bob was lucky if he got two minutes of station gossip in before they were gone.

Mostly she took Riley with them. But sometimes she talked Two Bob into looking after him for a weekend. Then there was hell to pay. For Milly as she extracted herself from Riley's clinging embrace. For Two Bob, trying to calm the desolate boy. Riley hated Andy.

How did something that seemed so pure go so wrong?

The question has tormented him ever since, and he has never come close to finding an answer.

23

Kerthunk. Dancer startles back to consciousness as the truck goes over a grid. The sensation in the truck's cabin changes from the floaty smoothness of the bitumen ride to the gentle shudder of the gravel. It feels good.

'He's awake again!' says Andy. He lip-points. Dancer spots the two pairs of brolgas in a graceful glide, low in the eastern sky.

They watch the brolgas out of sight before Andy speaks again. 'Do you think about your mum?'

Dancer is immediately tense. For all of his impatience of an hour ago, this is too direct. His answer is hesitant. 'Yeah ... Not so much think, as wonder. There's no picture there in my head to hang a thought on.'

'I do. Every day. Or every day since I've been sober. That's the excuse I used to give for me drinkin' – so I wouldn't have to think about her.'

It is a change of subject, but Dancer has to ask. 'What about Buddy's mum?'

'It's different, Dancer. You know it's different. I don't want to diss her. She gave us Buddy. In some ways I loved her too; but it was ways that were part of the mad drunk years. And most of the memories are sad, an' angry. An' guilty.'

He runs a hand through his hair. Scratches the crown of his head violently. 'I killed her! I got behind that fucken wheel with her sittin' beside me when I had no fucken right. I deserved every fucken day of the sentence I got.' A noisy, lip-flapping, tension-releasing exhalation before he continues. 'It's different, Dancer. Your mum, she ...' He takes his eyes off the road to hold

Dancer's eye. 'She's deep inside of me, tangled up with whatever part of me is any good.'

They roll on another couple of kilometres with Dancer blinking back tears before Andy asks, 'What do you wonder?'

'I wonder everything. Every fucking thing. All those little short words, Dad: How? What? Where? No-one's ever told me! And don't forget the main one. Why? ... Why? Why? Why fucking why?'

'Do you want to pull up for a spell?'

'Nup. Keep driving. Just don't go all quiet on me again.'

Dancer keeps his gaze out the passenger window. He knows this will be easier without eye contact, without the assessing sidelong glances. But he can sense the shudder as his father holds in a deep, deep breath.

'I've only got half answers to those little words. I'm tryin' to think, how much do you actually know?'

'Fuck all, Dad. You took us to Bullfrog Hole, and you told me it was my Unggurr. The rest of it I've heard more from the rest of the family than from you. She left me in Broome when I wasn't even one year old, she went back to Highlands, and she disappeared. That's about all I bloody know.'

Andy looks across at Dancer, who is still staring fixedly out of his window. Eventually he starts to talk. 'The doctors called it postnatal depression. The Highlands mob called it spirit sickness. That's about as much of a why as I ever got.'

But he's hardly got started when he yanks on the air horn. Up ahead a small mob of cattle startle. He holds the cord down, not slowing. The blare continues as the gap closes. The last weaner scurries clear in the nick of time, lost in the roil of dust the truck throws up. Still he holds the cord. Still it blares, with the cattle left well behind. At last he lets it rest, and continues speaking as if there's been no interruption. But Dancer can feel the effort it takes for Andy to keep on talking.

'Maybe they're the same thing, or two sides of the same coin.

Or maybe they're two completely different things, and she got a giant dose of both at once. But even then, they don't add up to a proper why. They're just words, labels.'

Dancer can't tell whether the sound that escapes his father is a rueful laugh or a choked-off cry. He glances across, but Andy's eyes are firmly on the road ahead. He gets the sense that his father has been rehearsing this conversation forever, but one wrong word, one wrong move on his part, and the thread might break.

'She had this serious, sort of sad look about her. Everyone used to say that. I'm talkin' about before it all went wrong. But no way was she a sad person inside. We were happy as a pair of mudlarks in a rainstorm. Then this veil came down. Not all at once. But it kept fallin' heavier and heavier on her.

'She was so gentle with you, Dancer. Right through. When you were asleep, she'd just lie there hour after hour, starin' at you. And every now and then she'd reach out a finger and stroke you, ever so lightly. She never stopped lovin' you, boy. Never. I'd swear to that. Swear to the end of me days. But she just ... She stopped ... connectin' properly. Even to you.'

Without looking at him, Andy reaches a hand across, and gives Dancer's leg a brief, light squeeze.

'As for me. That veil became so fucken thick, it was like she couldn't see me at all.

'Jesus, Dancer, I was only, what, three years older than you are now. I was completely outta my depth. I just didn't know what to do.'

Dancer keeps staring out his window, seeing the passing bush through a blur of tears, trying to disguise his intermittent sobs as sniffs.

'I'm sorry, boyo. You told me not to go quiet.'

'That's right.'

'You've got a right.'

'That's right.'

'I honestly don't know much about the rest, except that it was the worst time of my life. I don't think her mind was workin' proper any more. But I think she figured that the only chance she had to get her shit back together was to get back to Highlands. So she went.'

'Without me.'

'I think she reckoned that's what was best for you.'

'And you?'

'An' me what?'

'What did you do?'

'I followed her up there, mate. Left you with Bella and drove this same fucken road we're drivin' now. But it was no good. That bloody thick black veil was still hangin' there. It was like I was invisible. There was no point. An' I had to come back. To you.

'All I could do was wait. Wait an' hope. I even tried prayin', Dancer, but that never felt right.'

For some reason this gets a strangled sort of laugh out of Dancer.

'What? Me prayin'?' Andy tries to sound indignant.

'Yeah.' Dancer points at a big, gnarled boab tree, resplendent in bright green foliage. 'Look at that one.'

'It's nothin' to some of the ones up at Highlands.'

'So what happened next?' Dancer holds onto the thread.

'Then I fucked up. I mean, you know, I tell you this story, an' I could throw myself on your mercy an' say that I had some pretty damn good excuses to lose it. But I let you down, an' I let her down, and that's the hard fucken truth of it.

'I can't even remember – an' it shames me to say this – I can't even remember the phone call from Two Bob to tell me she'd gone missin'. Basically I stayed drunk from the day I started, until they threw me in the cells after the car crash. You've got more to thank your aunties and uncles for than your father.'

'Shut up!' Dancer turns to his dad fiercely.

'Hey! That's not what you said just now.'

'No jokes,' Dancer says, and turns back to face the window.

'Dancer, I've spent your whole life runnin' away from this conversation. Sometimes I hoped we might never have to do it, that you might be able to just cruise on through. But you're not the cruisin' type are you.'

Dancer shrugs but does not reply.

'Mate,' Andy says, gentler now, 'I'm just a dumb bass player and truck driver. I've got no idea whether this is helpin' you or hurtin' you. Maybe it's both eh. That two sides of the coin thing. But here we are on the Gibb River Road headin' for Highlands, so I suppose it was about time.'

24

Marj and Two Bob tried to carry on in the aftermath of losing Milly, but their lives were blighted. How quickly it unravelled. He didn't have his mind on the job. The muster was a disaster. Late in the year Marj had to go down to Perth for her first spell of dialysis; her kidneys were starting to collapse from the years of diabetes.

When she had to go down again six months later, the rest of the Jimbala Wali council held a meeting. They praised Marj to the skies whilst avoiding Two Bob's eyes, but said they needed a chairman who was fit to do the job. A different family took over. Two Bob resigned as manager. It was a relief to move out of the homestead, back to his old camp.

He can't recall how, but he and Riley finished up in an aeroplane. He shies away from the memory of Perth. The hostel, the hospital, the taxi rides, the absent horizon, the never-ending noise are all an ugly blur.

Vivid still is the flight back, as he cradled a sleeping Riley close, pulled his akubra down over his eyes, and wept for three hours.

The Land Council organised her funeral, to his great relief. He stood tall and proud with a hand on Riley's shoulder, unable to resist the temptation to gaze upon the know-nothing young chairman who had replaced her, as the bosses of the Kimberley praised Marj, and offered him their condolences.

⚬

'Bugger.'

There is not enough tea left in the pannikin to even moisten his palate. He leans forward to stir up the coals, and slides the billy across to rewarm.

Wha'd'you say, Marj, am I doin' the right thing?

She was a woman of firm opinions and decisive actions. A driver. He has always been a watcher with second, third and fourth thoughts. A reactor, not an initiator.

We had somethin' good, didn't we girl.

He turns towards the cemetery.

I don't just mean the lovin'. Not many fellers I know would've given you the rein I did. An' I was the only bugger on earth you'd bite your tongue for, lettin' me keep me secrets all those years. Or pretend to.

An' for what?

For so long now he has buried it all. Billy, Bessie, Sarah, Jinda; he has honoured their secrets. The unbearable, unresolved pain of Milly. The ache for all those he has lost. But he feels like he has failed each and every one of them.

To devote himself to Riley. That is what he has told himself.

Until Rosa gave him that fax.

Until that moment of panic in Andy's driveway saw him abandon the cautious habits of a lifetime.

❧

The sunwarmed headstone gives ever so slightly as he leans back against it.

You tryin' to tell me somethin'?

He twists to rest a cheek against the smooth grey granite. Whispers.

'I don't care any more what it was Andy said to you that time. Robert's our grandson. Our only one.'

He places the cracked boab nut that fell at his feet this morning at the foot of the headstone.

'Bob's given me his blessin'. Least that's the way I'm takin' it.'

25

The bush rolls past as an unfocused blur. Five minutes or fifty, Dancer doesn't know.

He feels the feather-light stroke of a finger on his cheek.

He whirls, but Andy has both hands on the wheel, and eyes straight ahead.

'You missed it.'

'Missed what?'

'The Bullfrog Hole turnoff. Just then. Didn't want to disturb you – seemed like you were a million miles away.'

'I was.'

'Four hours in, that way. Another three from there to the Highlands homestead. It's got to be the most out of the way spot in the Kimberley.'

'I used to try to talk Milly out of goin' there at first, it was such a bloody trek. But she wouldn't take no for an answer. An' I could never say no to her anyway.' He chuckles to himself. 'It grew on me, though. There was magic in the air when we set up camp at Bullfrog Hole. Good magic for me an' Milly. Ol' Marj, though, she always got proper cranky when she found out we'd been down there. There was some weird vibe going on between her and Two Bob and Milly about it all that they never let me in on.'

'She was Milly's mum? This Marj.'

'Yeah.'

'What was she like? My mimi.'

'Fierce. But in a good way, mostly. Took me a while to win her over. Or I should say, for Bob and Milly to win her over for me.

Proper old style out here, you don't talk to your mother-in-law …
Then of course, when things went wrong, it was all my fault.'

Dancer almost wishes he hadn't asked. Being lost in dreams
of his mother seems like easier territory than this, but it is
something that has always gnawed at him. 'She never tried to
make it up with you? To … to see me?'

'She passed away within a year of your mother disappearin'.
Down in Perth. Kidney failure. They were hard fucken years, for
everyone.'

There are still a host of questions on the tip of Dancer's
tongue, but instead he finds himself saying, 'How about some
music for a bit?'

'Sure. Pigrams again?'

'Nah. Something fast and loud.'

'I don't do much in the way of fast and loud,' says Andy. 'See
what you can find in the glovebox.'

All Dancer can come up with is Bruce Springsteen. 'Thunder
Road' begins to swell as the guitar joins the insistent piano. He
realises it's a road song, urging him to wind down the window
and feel the wind in his hair. He does, and Andy follows suit.
Dancer turns it to full so he can listen over the rush of road
noise.

They eat up the miles, with Andy banging out drum lines
on the steering wheel and every now and then belting out the
lyrics. There is something weirdly perfect about the way the
wailing, growling saxophone winds down as Andy works down
through the gears, then Springsteen's incoherent groans of pain
that bring 'Jungleland' to a close just as the truck comes to a halt
at the Highlands turnoff.

'The Boss! It's a while since I've listened to that. Good eh?'
says Andy.

'Not bad.'

'That Clarence Clemons.'

'Who's he?' asks Dancer.

'The sax player. Big black dude about six feet ten. I used to dream about playin' sax. Didn't really fit the bill for a Kimberley cowboy, though. I got stuck with the bass.'

'Ever try playing it?'

'Couldn't lay me hands on one. They cost a mint.'

The truck's engine idles down, and comes to a halt. After the rush of truck noise, wind noise, music noise, they are enveloped by an almost silence; just the rustle of the wind rattling the stand of cotton trees, and the single cry of a curlew. Without a word to each other, they simultaneously open their doors and climb down.

'Boxwood, then Highlands,' says Andy. 'The road to the end of the world. If we keep goin' we'll get there just about dark, or we can make camp here and head in first thing. Your call, mate.'

'What's going to happen when we get there?' Dancer asks.

'Two Bob'll be waitin' for us. After that, I'm buggered if I know.'

Dancer stretches the truck stiffness out of his limbs. He turns a full circle. The junction sits in the middle of a plain that seems vast, but on every side the ranges loom in the mid distance. The new moon is halfway toward the western horizon.

'Let's keep going.'

⌀

Dancer can sense Andy's unease; can see it in the set of his face, and the occasional short, sharp drumming of his fingers.

'This is the first time you've been back in hey?' Dancer asks.

'Yep.'

'And my first time ever.'

'The Boxwood turnoff's not far now. Other side of that hill up ahead.'

'That's where you first met him hey, Two Bob?'

'Yeah. That first year at Boxwood ... I dunno, it's hard to explain. I mean, we got on well together. But it was more than that, much more. He never made any fuss about it, never said anythin', but he saw that I was a young feller out of his depth, an' he just made it his business to look out for me an' ease me path. An' he turned me into a good stockman, if I say so meself. He was like a father to me, even before he became my lambara.' He sees Dancer's puzzled look. 'That's Bunuba for father-in-law.'

Andy slows to peer up the Boxwood track. 'It's only a couple of miles in. Just behind that spur.' He smiles at a memory. 'Should've seen the dust I used to make on this corner. On me weekends off I used to come harin' down that track an' hang a leftie, headin' for Highlands fast as I could go without rattlin' me old ute to bits.'

Dancer smiles too, seeing his dad light up.

'Oh Dancer, what might've been. They'd just got the place back. Two Bob pulled out of Boxwood an' went home as the manager. Ol' Marj was just buzzin' – she was too busy an' too happy to keep givin' me a hard time! When Milly got pregnant, you know what the dream was? Our dream.'

'Tell me.'

'To bring you back here, to Highlands. Milly wasn't interested in livin' anywhere else. We figured that when Two Bob was ready to retire I might have enough experience, an' enough cred with the mob here, to be able to take over as manager. Ol' Two Bob used to say "one step at a time, Andy, one step at a time." But I thought we were goin' to spend our lives out here. Imagine that, saltwater boy!'

'Whoo ... That might take a bit of processing.'

They start to wind through a series of creek crossings offering glimpses of water, pandanus palms and paperbarks, and low hills of pale yellow-green spinifex with seed stalks dancing amongst the red-brown rocks. Dancer drinks it all in, suddenly feeling like he is seeing the country through new eyes.

◦

The road levels out again. Andy points down a sidetrack. 'There's a mill down there's got the best view. I'll take you in an' show you sometime.'

But Dancer has his mind on other things. 'So tell me again, what happened when Two Bob came to see you that morning, after the funeral.'

'He didn't come to see me; he was lookin' for you. But you weren't there, remember.'

'Dad!'

'It was completely fucken weird, to tell you the truth. I wasn't really listenin'. I wanted to get out and track you down. He started rabbitin' on about how the station was fucked an' he needed me to come out and take a look an' give him a hand.

'You've got to understand, Dancer. I haven't spoken to him since the day I left Highlands – when you were just a babe in arms. Everyone's had a big night at the wake. You've gone missin'. An' he's tryin' to talk cattle to me!'

Dancer nods slowly. He hadn't really thought about it like this before. This whole trip is just as weird for his father.

'I didn't exactly push him out of the way,' Andy continues. 'But I told him I had things to do. Truth is, if you hadn't got yourself in the shit, it probably would have ended there.'

Andy tugs the cord to give a couple of short, sharp blasts of the air horn into the emptiness. Dancer spots a couple of old mickey bulls in the long grass turn their heads in alarm. They snort, wheel, and gallop off.

They both sit in silence for a few moments.

'This day was always comin', Dancer. We're goin' back to your mother's country. It might be hard, but it should be good. That's the feelin' I've got in my guts. And neither of us wants to be in ol' Broome town just at the moment.'

'True.'

'Mind you, my gut has led me astray before. Once or twice.'

'Very reassuring, Dad.'

'Should see the Highlands lights soon. If they're turned on.'

26

Fifteen years now that he buried Marj. Fifteen years it's been him and Riley.

Riley is forever talking or singing to himself in quiet monotone while he draws; intricate pencil designs and sketches on whatever paper he can lay hands on. The TV is on from the minute he wakes until Two Bob turns it off after he has fallen asleep.

In the life the two of them lead there is no reason that Saturdays and Sundays should be different; there is no logic to it beyond habit, but every weekend they go bush, and Riley comes to life. Two Bob husbands his pension money carefully, using everything he puts aside to keep his old Hilux registered and running and fuelled up for these excursions. He might shoot a bush turkey, Riley might catch a few fish. But mostly Two Bob sits by a small fire, sipping his tea and worrying about the state of the cattle, whilst Riley walks the country. A couple of times a year they take a longer trip and set up camp at Bullfrog Hole for a few days. The routine is the same. He sits. Riley walks all day. But they never go into the valley.

Years ago they fell into the pattern of talking Bunuba when they are out on country. It is not the lingua franca at Highlands. Two Bob has hardly used the language since he left the valley, except for his brief trips back in. Riley has not heard it spoken other than by Sarah in his first few years, but it seems rooted in his psyche.

And at night, by the fire, they sing. Songs for the Highlands country that Two Bob has picked up over the years. Story songs.

Wangga songs. Bunuba songs learnt from Parli and Bessie, dredged up from his memories.

He has thought this will be the pattern of his life for the time he has left, or until the Hilux dies, for he doubts he will be able to afford another.

❧

He wishes Bob could have heard his nephew sing.

Whenever there is singing to be done, Riley is summoned. He always happily obliges. It's his only real connection with the rest of the community.

Two Bob has to admit he's not much more connected himself any more. He got involved when the housing plan was done, digging his heels in to get his new house in the right place; on the Riders' side, but separated out a bit, with an outlook to the boab tree and the country to the south.

That's us two. A pair of rogue bullocks, cut out from the mob.

It was a shock when Rosa came to see him wanting to talk station business. In his mind she is still the young girl who was the closest thing Milly had to a best friend. As far as he can tell she seems to be doing a good job of breathing some new life into the place since she got in as chair of the council. Marj would be proud of her.

Shocked, and he had to admit, flattered, but he'd offered her no encouragement. 'I'm an old pensioner, Rosa.' He can't blame her for that funny look she gave him when he did a backflip and told her that he and Andy were going to see what they can do.

❧

The sliver of moon is brighter now, as it dips towards the horizon. The sun is not much higher. A few more minutes and the light will start to fade.

They'll prob'ly make camp back on the road somewhere an' show up in the mornin'.

He puts his hands on his knees and pushes, levering himself stiffly to his feet, and for a moment is overwhelmed. It is not vertigo. There are too many loose ends in this scheme he has concocted on the run. In fact, he is not really sure what the plan is. Too late now.

He pulls the camp oven off the coals, makes sure the fire is safe, and turns towards home.

Bloody hell, is that a truck comin'?

Part Three

27

Lying on an old foam mattress in the back of the ute, Dancer has slipped into a semi trance of blue sky and wispy cloud jolting in erratic patterns. The hand gently shaking his arm comes as a shock.

He works himself up into a sitting position. Back braced against the rolled-up swags tied to the front frame of the tray as padding, he grips the side panel to keep a semblance of balance as the ute bounce-glides along the track.

Riley points. A steep bluff has appeared to their left. In profile it rises sharply to its peak, then slopes gently backward to merge into the low range that has been sitting to their north for some time. The skyline of the undulating range is stubbled with small white gums and the odd boab tree, distant yet clear.

Riley extends the rest of his fingers. The pointing finger becomes a gentle hand with which he seems to caress the line of the hills. He draws his hand back in a fluid motion until it hovers over the bluff. He begins to sing.

After a few bars he lets his hand drop and uses it to silently tap the song's rhythm. The view is lost as the ute dips into a small gully, but Riley's eyes stay fixed on the point where he knows the bluff to be. His song does not waver. Its pure clarity subsumes the engine noise of the ute, which seems to fade to a distant thrum.

Dancer takes care not to stare, but directs his gaze towards the range in such a way that Riley's profile is in his peripheral vision. Sitting cross-legged, Riley rides the movement of the ute like a surfer his board. His face is both calm and intense.

Only his lips seem to move. The song finishes on a long, guttural note that sounds strangely jarring in Riley's high voice. A broad smile breaks over his face, but he reins it in to a tight, shy grin as he turns to Dancer.

'Marnunbarrigu.'

Once again, he strokes the profile of the range, from Marnunbarrigu Bluff, westwards to the point where it dips to the horizon.

28

Riley says no more. He settles into his cross-legged slouch, riding the ute's undulations.

Dancer cranes his neck to peer between a gap in the rolled swags. Two Bob and Andy are deep in conversation, with Two Bob pointing something out with one hand, as the other gently guides the juddering steering wheel.

On the first day Dancer sat in the cab between the two of them. His big frame got in the way whenever Two Bob had to shift down to second gear. All three of them implicitly recognised that he was also in the way of the flow of conversation between the two cattlemen. That night when they got home Two Bob lined the back of the ute with the foam mattresses. In the morning he put the old esky in the middle of the front bench seat, and without a word, the configuration changed. No insult intended, none taken.

He settles back and braces against the swags, heels dug into the foam mattress, but he still has to reach out a hand to steady himself. He looks out again to Marnunbarrigu, overwhelmed by its grandeur. Straightening his gaze, he watches the station track unfold behind them as he recalls flashes of the last three days.

⚭

'Blachan killer stew!'

'Your recipe, Andy.'

'That's not a recipe, lambara. I just shook a dollop of Bella's mix into your stew one time.'

'Good though.'

'Yeah, it's good. You an' me always thought so anyway. Everyone else was a bit doubtful.'

'I picked some up when I was in Broome.'

Dancer breathes rapidly in and out as inconspicuously as he can, trying to cool his palate. He doesn't mind hot, but this is ridiculous.

It is the night of their arrival. They are perched on plastic chairs on Two Bob's verandah. A reality show is spouting loud nonsense from the TV inside. He can sense Riley staring fixedly at him from a dark corner as he wolfs down his stew. But he is watching his father and his grandfather. Trying to make sense of it.

There is an ease and a familiarity between them. An obvious joy in reconnecting. But both are as tense as roos in a hunter's spotlight.

❧

He sits up in his swag the next morning, momentarily uncertain where he is. Andy's snoring a few feet away is comfortingly familiar. The looming shape of the truck behind him in the pre-dawn greyness reminds him: Highlands.

He shrugs out of the tangle of blankets, steps free of the swag, and takes in what he can in the dim morning light. Off to his right an improbably huge boab tree. He can just make out the girth of gnarled, irregular trunk, and against the lightening sky an intricate network of branches. In front of him a gently sloping plain, grasses waving in the early morning breeze. The road they came in on last night cuts across the plain, disappearing into the murk.

Two Bob's house sits like an outlier, slightly separate from the others, and facing away from them. Beyond his place there is a scattering of boxy houses, then a transportable that looks like it could be an office, more clearly visible than the other buildings thanks to the light on the verandah with its swarm of moths. Next to it is the store. Beyond them another scatter of houses.

STEVE HAWKE

Across the way a bougainvillea hedge half hides a saggy-roofed sprawl that must be the old homestead and its outbuildings.

He wants to walk and explore. But he is a stranger here, and doesn't know who may be watching from the verandahs or windows of the houses. He nervously prowls the apron of grass in front of the truck, then heads down to the boab. Under its branches there is an old flour drum, and a fireplace in a ring of smooth stones. He holds a hand over the fine ashes, and can sense a faint warmth still from yesterday's fire. The ground around the fireplace is raked clean in a wide circle. The rake leans against a pile of firewood.

He places a palm against a bole of the enormous, knobbled trunk, as if in salutation. It is cool against his hand. Calming. He cranes his neck to peer up through the branches, with random leaves and pendant nuts, to a sky beginning to blue.

❧

Turning to find Two Bob approaching with a billy and the makings for tea.

'Up before me! Not many young fellers do that.'

'I always get up before dawn. Always have.'

'You musta got that from me. I always had to shake your ol' man awake.'

'Nyami was the same, might be it came from him.'

Two Bob chuckles. 'Might be too. Most of us old-timers can beat the rooster. He was a good man, your grandpa. One of the best. What you call him?'

'Nyami.'

'Broome lingo?'

'Yawuru.'

'You know the Bunuba word?'

Dancer shakes his head.

'Jaminyi.'

Dancer nods, but does not try to say the word.

❧

Waiting in vain for Two Bob to talk after the initial chitchat about how he takes his tea, and the size of the boab tree.

Until the sudden blare of the television.

'Riley's up.'

❧

The blaze of anger in Riley's eyes when Andy suggests the TV is a bit loud.

❧

Riley's refusal to acknowledge Andy.

❧

Riley always staring at him. The way his eyes slide away whenever Dancer returns his look. He half remembers something he saw on TV about body language and lying.

❧

Riley bent over his drawing, concentrating intensely, refusing with a shake of the head to join them in an inspection of the station plant. The moment they step off the verandah he springs up and turns the TV volume to high.

❧

In their swags last night. They hear the TV being turned off. Night sounds emerge. A mopoke. Before Andy can fall asleep Dancer asks, 'What'd'you know about Riley?'

'Mystery boy! It's sort of a long story that I don't know the beginnin' for.'

'Huh?'

Andy lets out a sigh. 'When I started courtin' your mother, he was in the way, you might say. First glance, you would've sworn they were mother and son. Only that didn't make sense. He was about four I reckon. An' she was fifteen.

'I had to ask her, actually, once we got to know each other proper. Just to be sure. She just shook her head in that way of hers, an' smiled at me. "His mother's passed on has she?" I asked her. She nods. I wait for her to say somethin'. She can see I'm waitin'. We were lookin' in each other's eyes. After a bit she says, "He belongs to me and Dad." That's all.'

'That's pretty weird.'

'Yep. Pretty weird.' He expels a breath forcefully. Suddenly he moves in his swag, and is propped on an elbow, looking at Dancer. 'Hey, you're not thinkin' ...?'

Dancer suddenly understands the unfinished question. 'No no! No ... I just meant it's weird.'

'No ... Yes. It was pretty weird. But she never offered up anythin' more.'

They lie back in their swags, elbows out, fingers linked, heads resting in the palms of their hands. Still the mopoke calls.

'See that shootin' star?' Andy asks.

'Yeah.'

'Make a wish?'

'Yeah. You?'

'Yeah. You can't blame him for not likin' me, Dancer. Far as he was concerned, poor little bugger, she was his mum. An' then I come between 'em. It's as simple as that I think. Looks like he still carries the grudge.'

'It's a long time.'

'Yeah. It's a long time. But none of us has been given the chance to get over anythin' ... I wish that mopoke'd shut up. G'night Dancer.'

Dancer watches the night sky for a long time, wondering if there might be another shooting star, but not sure what his second wish might be.

Other than that his mother's name has not been mentioned once. At least not in his hearing. And he is sure those two have not spoken about her in the cab of the ute.

29

Two Bob is cooking dinner. The TV is blaring. Andy is tinkering with the truck's engine; his preferred way of escaping everyone.

Dancer is down at the boab, trying to get Riley's song back in his head. He's been loving the days of driving; standing in the tray gripping the top rail, bracing his knees against the vagaries of the track; feeling the wind in his hair. Loving the grasses, the birds, the creeks, the ranges. But he has been feeling like a rather useless appendage.

Until the moment Riley started singing. Through the song he felt for the first time the pulse of his mother's land.

Marnunbarrigu.

He can hum a phrase here or there, but only fragments; the melody line escapes him.

He hears the Landcruiser with the bad exhaust start up from somewhere behind Two Bob's. Three days now and he has yet to meet anyone other than Two Bob and Riley. He knows that lots of the mob here at Jimbala Wali are relations of one sort or another. He has been bracing himself. But Two Bob has had them out on the road early each morning, and back late. He's not once mentioned any of the people in the houses behind his. And no-one has made themselves known.

Is Two Bob an outcast? Are he and Andy being shunned? He has no idea what's going on, but it doesn't feel right.

Nothing I can do, but.

He hums a phrase and can feel the next one on the tip of his tongue, when the lights of the Landcruiser sweep across him as it turns. It idles a few moments, as if uncertain, then swings towards him, creeping along so as not to raise dust. It pulls up by the pile of firewood.

Dancer stands up nervously as the driver and her companion approach.

'Robert?'

Her question throws him off balance. He stutters, 'No ... Yeah ... I mean ... Sorry. That's my name, but everybody calls me Dancer.'

'So I hear. I'm Rosa. This is my brother, Tim. We're cousins for your mother. Your granny was our Auntie Marj.'

Suddenly Dancer is bawling. He does not even realise that Rosa has gathered him up in a hug, until he senses Andy there, breathless, hovering beside them. Dancer disengages awkwardly, embarrassed now.

'You ok?' Andy asks.

He nods. He doesn't know where to look.

'Rosa. Tim.' He can hear the tension in Andy's voice.

'Andy,' they answer together, not coldly, but there is a hesitancy.

No-one seems to know what to say next, until Andy plunges in. 'Tell me, Rosa, are we welcome here?'

'What?!'

'I thought you might be comin' to tell us to clear out. We've been here three days, an' no-one's come near us.'

'Fucken Two Bob! It'd be easier if he just explained things straight up sometimes. He asked for a few days on his own with you two. We couldn't wait any longer though, we wanted to meet this boy! Look at him, Tim, you can see he's a Rider!' She ruffles Dancer's hair, with tears in her eyes.

Two Bob comes down from his house and joins them, looking shamefaced. 'You right there, Dancer?' he asks.

'Yeah.'

There is another shuffling, uneasy silence. Rosa breaks the ice by changing the subject. 'So Andy, d'you reckon you and this uncle of mine can come up with a plan to save Highlands?'

As they wander up to Two Bob's verandah, Rosa drops back beside Dancer and says quietly, 'It's good to meet you, Dancer. It's good you've come here. We'll talk hey, but I've got to do some business now.' She strides ahead to join the others, calling cheerfully but firmly, 'Hey Riley, turn the bloody TV down will you. We can't hear ourselves think out here.' To Dancer's surprise, the volume is almost immediately muted.

30

Rosa and Tim decline Two Bob's offer of tucker. He sorts Riley out, then brings three plates of stew. Dancer forks down the meal as he listens to the talk bouncing around between Rosa and Andy and Two Bob, with an occasional contribution from Tim. He has a sense of unreality that almost touches on anger.

What about my mother? Last time you saw them, Dad, you drove away leaving her here, and you never saw her again! Maybe they know something. Who gives a fuck about cattle?

But there seems to be an unspoken consensus amongst them to ignore the elephant in the room as they talk station business.

It is a story of slow decline. Never enough money in the station account to do anything properly. Kenny who took over from Two Bob did his best, but things kept slipping further back. The feller after that didn't really give a bugger. They started resorting to contractors. Some were outright scumbags. Some were well intentioned, but as Two Bob points out, the good operators follow the money, and none of them reckoned they were going to make a killing out of Highlands. The last two years there hasn't even been a muster.

Rosa is scathing about the last council. They just gave up on the station, she says; reckoned they couldn't afford to keep throwing good money after bad. Not even repair work on the floodgates after the wet season. Tim said he'd go out and fix them, but they wouldn't put up the money for the wire and pickets. 'They could've used the CDEP account, the pricks,' she says angrily. 'It was just all these bloody family arguments getting in the way.' And since then two bores have fallen idle with no funds to repair them.

Now there is a crisis. She has discovered that the rents and rates on the pastoral lease are over a year in arrears. The Aboriginal Affairs mob aren't interested; they reckon their rules don't let them put money into a business that hasn't got – 'What was it?' Rosa tries to remember the government-speak. 'That's it, "a viable five-year enterprise development plan." What the fuck does that mean?'

'It means they reckon we're fucked,' Two Bob offers.

'They're saying they can send in a consultant to do a plan for us,' says Rosa.

'Prob'ly cost more than the rates bill,' says Two Bob.

'What are you saying we should do, unc?!' Rosa does not try to hide her exasperation. 'They're saying we might have to forfeit the lease!'

'What?' Dancer has spoken without meaning to. 'They can't take it off you.'

'They can. I'm not saying they will. But they can.'

'What? And kick you off?'

'Not kick us off. This square mile here where the community is, that's a different lease, with the Lands Trust mob. But they can take the cattle lease.'

'No way!'

'Hopefully not, Dancer. Not while I'm chair. The question is, what're we going to do now?' She turns to Andy and Two Bob. 'Have you two come up with any bright ideas yet?'

Two Bob pushes his plate aside and pulls out his tobacco tin. He coughs. But instead of speaking, he begins to roll a smoke. Andy gives him a sharp look. 'Listen, Rosa, I'm not sure exactly what this lambara of mine has told you. An' I don't know what you know about me after all these years, but I'm not the man who's goin' to save Highlands for you. I'm not a musterin' contractor. I've got no plant, just me truck. I only ever did two years ringin', you know.'

Two Bob rounds off an exhalation with a perfect smoke ring that expands as it rises above them. 'Nothin's gunna happen this year. It's too late in the season.'

He starts quizzing Rosa about whether she can find money from anywhere to pay the rent and rates, or even make a part payment to keep the buggers at bay for a while. She says she's working on it. He embarks on a long and intricate discourse about the various contractors who've been on the place over the years, and how not one of them knew the place or knew who to ask; how the back country on the far corners of the station is still full of cleanskins. Tim murmurs his agreement.

Two Bob tries to explain himself. 'I'm not sayin' Andy can save the station. That's not it. But if I'm gunna be any help to you, Rosa, I need someone I can trust to talk it all through with. Not some gov'ment idiot with a computer. Not some contractor hungry for money. I need someone who can read the country with me. We've gotta look those back country bullamon in the eye an' work out how to play 'em. They're clever buggers, livin' on their wits out there.'

He doesn't know the money side of it any more, what they might be worth. But he does know there are bullamon out there, if he can work out a way to bring them in next year that doesn't bust the bank; even if it's just enough to clear the debts and hold on for another year or two. He's not saying that Andy has to do the muster. He just needs someone to drive the country with him. Help him find a plan, or tell him no plan is going to work any more.

Half the time he seems to be talking to himself, trying not only to find the words, but the ideas behind the words, as if he is working it out in his mind as he speaks. But now he turns to Andy. 'I'm just an old pensioner these days. Rosa here's the one with the weight on her shoulders. But I've been here long time now. I don't want to lose this place, Andy. You might've only been a two-year ringer, but you were a bloody good one. You were born to be a manager.'

Tim chuckles into the silence that follows. 'He's right about one thing, sis. It's too late to do anythin' with the cattle this year. Let 'em have a go.'

❧

'Born to be a manager,' says Dancer. 'Wasn't just you and Mum had that dream by the sounds of it.'

'Life plays tricks on you,' Andy says.

'Was that your shooting star wish back then?'

'You're gettin' a bit close to the bone, son.'

They are back in their swags. Under the Kimberley stars, it is a mighty big room, but the elephant is still in it.

'Ol' Two Bob's still puffin' away. G'night Dancer.'

Dancer looks over to the verandah, and sees the glow of cigarette as Two Bob inhales. He pulls the swag cover over his face.

Be patient, he tells himself. *Suck it in and be patient.*

31

Two Bob flicks the butt.

I'm smokin' too much.

Nevertheless, he rolls another.

'*Fucken Two Bob! It'd be easier if he just explained things straight up sometimes.*'

He'd heard it.

Trouble is, Rosa girl, there's nothin' straight up about it.

A sudden random memory. Down at the waterhole. Marj nursing toddler Milly. Little Rosa throwing a tantrum. He doesn't like fishing much at the best of times, but wrestling with impenetrable knots in the tangled line of a screaming five-year-old who's just lost a fish in a snag is as bad as it gets.

Oh Bob, am I fuckin' this up?

He hears the low murmur of voices from up by the truck, and the rustle of movement in swags. He takes another drag. Tries to blow a smoke ring, but it disintegrates in the breeze.

I can't just spit it all out, Rosa, it's not that simple. It'd scare 'em off, I know it. An' what would you say? Straight up doesn't work after all this time. An' there's still another twist I've gotta work somehow.

All is silent up by the truck. He should've been asleep a couple of hours ago. But instead of going inside he makes his way back down to the boab tree. Another sign from his brother would be good. Maybe. But the breeze has gone. All is still. The old tree towers silently above him.

32

Driving and yarning. Yarning and driving.

Old man's bush track driving. Not once in the whole week over fifty kays. Caressing the road. Nursing the vehicle. Nursing the lads in the back as much as he can. The flat stretches are for examining the country, not for speeding up: for lip-pointing and gesturing to Andy; for explanation and speculation about those cattle pads wending their way up past that hill, wondering how many bullamon there are in Poddy's Pocket, the little valley that opens up behind it.

There's a good spring up there, plenty water. One year he pulled eighty-four head out of Poddy's. Choppers or horseback? That's the big question. No other way to check it out unless they pull up now and walk it. Motor car won't get in there.

It seems the flow of talk between the two never stops, on their own in the cab of the ute, or seated around the fire, pannikins in hand. The young fellers mostly listen, but sometimes drift away. Some nights they make it back to Highlands, some nights they camp out. There is always a leisurely dinner camp, and often another break to boil the billy.

The yarning interweaves Two Bob's tales of years past, and pondering this maybe muster. One informs the other. He has ridden every inch of this country many times over. For all that's changed in the last twenty years, he knows with an innate precision the habits of the cattle that eke their sustenance from the wiry grasses and scattered water points. For every beast they spy, he knows how many remain out of sight. Those two busted bores; he's figured how many will have perished, which watersheds the others will've crossed to stay alive. He's got that side of things figured. With a half-decent horse plant and six good men, he could bring in every last beast. But that's not the way of the world any more. Men or horses.

⚬

Dancer has never seen his father so animated as in this fireside conversation that bats back and forth. Testing and challenging Two Bob's thoughts, quizzing him about details, tossing up his own ideas. He comes to realise that in the aftermath of Milly's death, and in emerging from his lost years to become a father to him and Buddy, Andy has forsaken his true vocation as a man of the cattle country. That the years of driving road trains that bring cattle from the far-flung stations to Broome port are so much more than just a living; they are a way of keeping connected to this world.

There is a surreal quality to watching his father and his grandfather like this, one so familiar, one almost unknown. Day by day he can see Andy becoming more engaged with Two Bob's vision. The knowing looks the pair exchange, the twinkling in Two Bob's eye reflecting the gleam in Andy's as they leap to the same conclusion whilst turning over some intricate matter of mustering technique beyond his ken.

But Andy also brings a brutal realism to the discussions. They could yard every beast on the property, which would be a miracle, and still there would be no guarantee. The price for shorthorns is fickle at best, and that's if you can find somewhere that'll take them. The buyers only want brahman stock these days.

'I'm not arguin', Andy,' the old man sighs. 'This place is a bit like me. Ol' style, an' just about worn out. But there's got to be a way, somehow.'

'I've got me thinkin' cap on.'

33

Even at Two Bob speed a driver is not always in control on these backtracks. A tree shadow disguises the drop, and bang! The front end of the vehicle dips, then the whole machine judders as the front wheels hit the other side of the little washout. Dancer grips the top rail of the tray, but his feet fly out from under him.

'You right back there?' Andy calls.

'Yuw.' But he has banged the funny bone in his elbow in his fall, and curses as he rubs and shakes it, trying to ease the intense pain.

'You got big feet.' It is not until Riley speaks that Dancer realises he has landed with one leg sprawled across Riley's lap.

'S'pose so.'

He tries to straighten his leg, but his cousin is holding his foot. Smiling.

'I know this one foot.'

'What you talking about?'

'Long time. This the foot been kick my ear.'

'What?!'

'In your mummy's tummy.'

'Eh?' Dancer is feeling a bit weirded out.

'Before you been born. I was young feller then. Little kid. Auntie Milly been lookin' after me alla time. Your daddy come. Her tummy been grow big. She been take my head in her hand, turn me sideways, put my ear on her tummy. Boom! You were kickin'. Strong way! This big foot now!' Riley smiles. 'See. I been know you before you been born, Robbidy Dancer.'

Dancer waggles his foot. Riley releases his grip on it. Dancer does a mock kick, prodding Riley gently, before straightening himself out.

'Yeah! Like that!'

'Robbidy?'

'Robiddy. Your proper name, before that Broome mob been call you Dancer.'

'Oh ok. Robert.'

'Robbidy.' Riley starts to croon a nursery rhyme.

> *'Robbidy bub, Robbidy bub,*
> *Robbidy bub an' me*
> *Robert an' Andy an' mad mother Milly*
> *What's gunna happen to we?'*

Now Dancer is feeling totally weirded out.

'She been sing that to herself, when ...' Riley starts.

'When she came back here, and I ...?' He jerks his head in the general direction of faraway Broome. 'You were here then?'

Riley nods solemnly.

34

'What's the name of that hill again?'

Andy has swivelled away from the fire, and is pointing towards a distant flat-topped mesa. It is an outlier of the range that dominates the southern horizon, sitting a couple of miles west of the point where the range ends. Its red cliffs have a warm glow in the late afternoon light. Watching the hill, he does not see Two Bob glance in Riley's direction, before answering quietly, 'Unggulala. Flat Iron Hill.'

'That's it! Flat Iron Hill.'

The words carry to Riley, sitting on a swag carving a design on a boab nut. He drops the nut and the knife, and stares fiercely at Andy.

'We climbed up there once, me an' Milly,' Andy continues. 'We could see all the way to Bullfrog Hole.'

Riley springs up and strides away from the camp. Dancer can't read the look on Two Bob's face as he watches Riley disappear. But he can see the conscious effort his grandfather makes to compose himself before Andy turns back to face them.

The body language leaves no doubt; this is the first time Milly's name has been mentioned. From the look in his father's eye, Dancer is sure it was not accidental. But Two Bob changes the subject. 'You had a look at that ol' horse float back at the station, eh?' He reaches for his tobacco tin and busies himself rolling a smoke.

Andy decides not to force the issue. 'Yeah, but not real close. It's a big mother.'

'He'd hook up all right to your truck you reckon?'

'S'pose so. The turntable'd need a good greasin', if nothin' else.

How long since she's seen action?'

'Good while now. One of them contractors might've give it a run I think. Cartin' feed though, not horses. Not sure when the last time was before that.'

'How come there's a big ol' trailer float like that on a place like Highlands? More the sort of thing you'd see on Fossil Downs or somewhere.'

'It's been here since Smithton time. He was last owner bar one before we got the place back. He got it for takin' his horse plant into the races – always thought he was goin' to win the Derby Cup. He never came close.'

'Too big for a Toyota?'

'Needs a truck, Andy.'

'Prob'ly needs new tyres too. What you got in that head of yours, lambara?'

'Mmm ... How long since you've been on a horse?'

'What's goin' on, lambara? Spit it out.'

'What about you, Dancer? You much of a rider?'

'Nothing.'

'What? You never been on a horse?' Two Bob can hardly believe it.

'Couple of times, but just messing about.'

'He sit the horse all right, Andy?'

'Just all right. Come on, what's this all about?'

'Well ... there's some country south of Bullfrog Hole ...' He seems unsure what to say next. 'No road in there but.'

'I thought the river was your south boundary down that way.'

The old man taps a forefinger against the side of his nose. 'Yeah. But there's no station other side. An' plenty bullamon. It's good country.'

'More'n Poddy's Pocket?'

'Oh yeah.'

'Can you get 'em out of there? That sort of country they just disappear into the ranges.'

'I know how.'

Andy can't help a chuckle. 'I'm sure you do, ol' man, I'm sure you do. Listen, if we go ahead next year, we'll allow for a run through there, an' work out if we'll need chopper hours for it – all that stuff. But we're not geared up for workin' with horses this time round.'

⁂

Two Bob flicks his butt into the fire, takes off his akubra, gives the crown of his bare head a good scratching. The moment has come.

Yes, he has become engrossed with this mad plan that he and Andy are trying to devise. Yes, there is nothing that would please him more than saving Highlands Station. But when the idea first came to him at Jirroo Corner the morning after Buster's funeral, cattle and station business were but a means to an end.

He didn't know then, he doesn't know now, exactly what that end is. He cannot put it into words. But he can feel it as a knot of tensions sitting high in his guts; hopes and fears and memories and regrets writhing around a tight, mysterious kernel.

The kernel had taken root when he watched the grandson he had never known walking down the aisle of the church, bearing his Nyami Buster's coffin. The next morning, when Dancer was not at home, Two Bob, the steady one, had felt a flash of panic. Of losing all over again something he'd never had.

Somehow he'd got from that moment to this. His grandson is sitting at the fire with him here on Highlands. But it is not enough.

Two Bob levers himself to his feet. He turns his back to the fire, to Andy. All he can think to do is offer a piece of the truth.

'It's not just about the cattle, Andy. It's my country down there, my true country. I want to go back there one more time if I can. I want to show it to Dancer. Him an' Riley are the last ones in the line for it.'

35

When Two Bob dropped the bomb about his true country Dancer was watching his grandfather's hands, fingers twining fiercely at his back, revealing the turmoil his calm tone sought to disguise. Then he'd looked across at Andy. His father had a very slight smile, a look almost of admiration in his eyes as he shook his head slowly. He was a man checkmated, given an offer he could not refuse by a man who loved him.

Hardly a word was spoken after that until they got back to Highlands the next day.

⤙

'We've got to talk, Dancer. Want to go down the river, or sit in the truck?'

'Truck.'

'What's eating you, Dad?' he asks once they are settled.

'You want to do this trip don't you?'

'Of course I do.'

'Of course you do. And of course I'm up for it. I haven't really got a choice have I.'

'That's what's bugging you hey, no choice?'

'The ol' bugger's playin' me. All this cowboy dreamin's good fun at one level, don't get me wrong. I'd love to do this muster next year, an' there might even be half a chance we can. There's a chopper pilot I'm gunna have a yarn to if I get the chance in Broome. But I told him we had two weeks, maybe three at a pinch, an' he waits till now to spring this cockamamie idea of gettin' a horse plant together and ridin' off into the ranges. It doesn't make sense.'

'Maybe he's got his reasons.'

'I wish he'd fucken share 'em.' Andy thumps the steering wheel. 'We're gunna have to come back. You know how it sits, Dancer. Every week I'm not workin' I'm losin' money, with the payments on the truck. An' don't forget, I've got an extra debt to pay off now. We've got to be out of here in four days max or I'll lose that hay cartin' gig. An' we're not doin' any fucken horse trek into the ranges in the next four days are we.'

'Do I have to come back with you? I could stay here and help Grandpa.'

Andy is gobsmacked. This thought had not crossed his mind. 'The bikies?'

'Little bit, maybe. But I haven't thought about them for days till just now.'

'What about school?'

'Fuck school, Dad. I'll pull my finger out when I get back there, I promise. But that's not where my head's at.' He reads Andy's concern. 'Look, I'll even repeat next year if it comes to that. But not now.'

'Where is your head at, boyo?'

'Marnunbarrigu. Unggulala. Grandpa's country. Auntie Rosa and the Riders. My story, Dad.'

'Fair call ... Fair fucken call,' Andy says, nodding. 'You can put up with that evil eye from Riley for two weeks on your own?'

'You've got it wrong, Dad. You're the only one he gives the evil eye. I just get the eye. We've got a bromance happening in the back of the ute.'

Andy gives him a mock cuff around the ears.

⚓

Once Andy gives in to the inevitable, he and Two Bob turn to sorting out details of what will be required. Two Bob is adamant that there is no way in other than on foot or on horses. That means old style; packhorses, hobbles, all that. 'In the ol' days I'd do it in one day easy from Bullfrog to the place I'm thinkin' of,' he explains, 'but the pace we'll be goin' we've gotta allow two. Gettin' in's the tough part. After that it's pretty good goin.' Dancer can see Andy becoming intrigued despite himself, even enthused, as they draw up lists and talk logistics.

A slow drive around the horse paddock running an eye over the plant and they agree there's enough half-decent horses for the job. Two Bob confesses it's just as well he has a couple of weeks while Andy's away. He'll need the time to pull the horse team together and get them prepared. He reckons he'll have a word to Rosa to see if Tim and his boy Jimmy can give them a hand.

On the way back from the horse paddock they have a good look over the float. Andy confirms it will hook up to his truck, and they figure it should be up to the job with a bit of work. Two Bob reckons there's a fellow in the community who's handy with the tools, and will help them out. 'Stan'll patch any tyres that need it too. Any luck we won't need to buy any.'

'Ropin' everyone in,' Andy laughs. 'You've got Rosa lined up to cover the expenses, eh?' Two Bob's sideways look has him rolling his eyes. 'What? You haven't spoken to her yet? I can't cough up the money for all this, lambara. I was sort of hopin' Jimbala Wali'd cover my fuel.'

'I didn't want to say anythin' till I knew if you two were up for it.'

Andy shakes his head in bemusement. 'You don't like doin' things the easy way, do you.'

The old man tries to look sheepish, but the corners of his mouth are crinkling as he tips Dancer a wink.

36

When they get back to camp Two Bob suggests that Dancer go up to the office and ask Rosa if she can come and see them in the morning. 'If she's not there, she should be home. You know her place eh?'

'The one with the garden?'

'You gottim.'

He looks up at the row of houses as he cuts across toward the office, and there she is watering the lawn. He wheels towards her with a wave. 'I was just going up to look for you. Grandpa was hoping you could come down and see us in the morning.'

'Was he just? Wants me to come down to him. Want a cuppa tea?'

'Yeah, that'd be good.'

'Kettle's up there on the bench on the verandah.'

Her neighbours might have the dusty, unkempt yards so common in communities, but Rosa's is a much-loved oasis. None of the trees are fully grown yet, but the African mahogany is already tall enough to throw a thick circle of shade, and the mangoes and frangipanis are lush and healthy.

'It's so green,' he admires as he rejoins her. 'You're into gardening hey?'

'Sure am. It's good to stand here with a hose in the shade of a tree I've planted. Almost as good as being down the river, and easier to get to. What about you?'

'Maybe one day when I've got a place of my own.'

'Your granny had a green thumb. But she didn't have running water like this, she just had a few pot plants.'

'She was the chairman here too hey, like you?'

'That's right, Dancer. That was early days, when they did it tough. I've got it easy compared to her.'

She shuts off the hose and leads the way up to the verandah, signalling him to a chair whilst she makes the tea. She hands him a pannikin and plonks herself down in an armchair moulded to her shape.

'I've been wondering when you'd come to see me.'

'We've been camped out most nights, or back late.'

'I've noticed. Having fun?'

He takes a sip, thinking how to answer. 'Yeah, mostly.'

'You going all right in that bachelors' camp?'

He laughs, and the tea sloshes. 'Dunno about bachelors. Might be Riley, but ... I dunno, he's not exactly looking for love I don't think.' This gets a laugh from Rosa. 'I'm still a schoolkid, and Dad and Grandpa, well they're widowers aren't they, not bachelors.'

'I think I'm going to like getting to know you, Dancer,' she says, raising her pannikin in a silent toast. He grins and raises his back.

'So how's it going?'

'What?'

'The big drive. The big plan.'

'You better ask them for that.'

'Fair enough. Is that what they want to see me for?'

'I think Two Bob wants to ask you about the horse float.'

'The what?'

'You know, that old horse float behind the garage.'

'Whha? I don't get it. Listen, I've got clinic in the morning. After that I'll be here or the office. He can come and find me if there's something he wants.'

'I'll tell him. You work in the clinic?'

'Three days a week.'

'Nurse?'

'I wish. I nearly was. But my badge says Community Health Worker.'

There is a silence. Dancer is about to push himself out of his chair, when he finds himself asking, 'What do you know about Grandpa's country down from Bullfrog Hole?'

The look she throws at him is sharp, inquisitive. 'What's Uncle Wajarri up to? Horses, Bullfrog Hole?'

'Is that his bush name? Wajarri?'

'Yeah. It means boab nut, Bunuba way.'

'He wants to take me and Riley down there. His true country, he said. He reckons we're the last of the line for it.'

'What's he told you about it?'

'Bugger all really. He reckons more better to give us the story when we're down there.'

'Bugger all, hey. He likes his secrets does Two Bob. Debbil debbil country, that's what the old aunties called it.'

'Why?'

'I don't really know, Dancer. Olden days stuff.'

'Oi! Rosa!' The call comes from a woman up near the office.

'What now?' she yells back.

'Telephone.'

'Who now?'

'What his name. That 'countant feller, for money side.'

'Ok, tell him I'm coming.'

She is already up out of her chair. 'Sorry, I've got to take this. Hope he hangs on long enough for me to get up there. It's good to have a yarn, Robert Rider – that's how I think of you, you know. Let's do it again soon.' Then she is off at a jog towards the office.

37

Rosa makes cuppas and ushers them out the back of the office to sit under a shade cloth. She makes them squirm a bit, and earn her backing. Dancer has to work hard at times to suppress a smile, especially when Rosa catches his eye with a twinkle in hers.

Two Bob starts off with a spiel about getting the horse plant and gear sorted, and using an expedition to the Bullfrog Hole country as a test run for next year. She points out that they could do all that horse stuff around here; why Bullfrog Hole, and all the expense of the horse float and the hassles of trucking them down to the furthest corner of the station?

He talks up a storm about all the cattle he knows are down there south of the boundary, and how they can't get in there without horses. They'll still be there next year won't they, she asks. She knows he wants to look all those back country bullamon in the eye, she tells him, but we've got to be practical about this. Two Bob is struggling to hide his distress. Out of the corner of his eye Dancer catches Andy also hiding a smile.

'Hey Wajarri,' Rosa says. This time there is a softness in her tone. Two Bob looks up. 'It's all right. Dancer told me about your true country trip. I'm cool with it.'

She still drives a bargain though, once they get down to tintacks. If anyone asks, this is a CDEP back-to-country project, nothing to do with the station. CDEP's the only bucket that's got any money at all in it. Tim and Jimmy are his for the next fortnight as their top-up job, they'll like that better than the garden work, that's for sure. Yes, Stan can give them a hand as required. She thinks the CDEP account will be able to cover fuel, but she'll have to check.

She's going to be away for the next week on a training course, but they can spend up to seven hundred and fifty on the Elders account for essential gear. Just don't get silly about it, and anything over that has to wait until she gets back.

'Thank you, Rosa. Thank you. Seven hundred an' fifty. Not a penny more. Promise.'

Dancer can see the hope surging in the old man.

'It's a good thing, Uncle. I hope,' Rosa says. 'Just don't forget, when it's finished, you and Andy have to sit down with me and give me a plan. I'm not going to lose this station.'

38

Dancer tips his chair back to look up into the boab tree. A bowerbird hops from one branch to another, its beady eye fixed on him.

Dad'll be on the road again by now. He should make Broome by lunchtime.

There'd been an awkwardness to their parting yesterday. He'd helped his father pack the truck, then climbed up as Andy turned the key and let the engine warm up. They sat in silence until Andy gave the pedal a gentle nudge, and the revs signalled that the truck was ready to roll. They turned to look at each other.

'Take care of yourself while I'm gone, Dancer.' Andy cocked his fist, leaned across, and gave Dancer a shoulder punch so gentle it might have been a caress.

He had no matching gesture. He stared at the floor of the cab. 'You too, Dad. Say hi to Buddy.' Standing on the running board he looked back in at his father, and found a smile from somewhere. He walked in the truck's wake as Andy eased it down to the road, and headed west. Before it disappeared round a bend Andy gave a blast on the air horn. From the scrub beyond, a startled eagle rose above the trees. Dancer watched it take flight.

> *Gliding through the valley, the wedgetail is my friend*
> *Winding like a river ...*

He didn't sing the last phrase.

❧

The bowerbird alights briefly a few yards from him. He knows birds can't grin, but that's what it seems to do before flying away.

Why were we so uptight saying goodbye?

Dancer has no real answer for his question, except a sense that he and Andy are both feeling things move. In ways they don't understand.

He has woken today with a sense of anticipation. A nervous anticipation to be sure. But also a sense that all the fragments of information and new knowledge and unfamiliar emotions of the last couple of weeks might be starting to gel into something. He senses more than hears a tread.

'Hey, Grandpa! Billy's just about cold. You sleep in?'

'I never sleep in. Just gettin' some gear sorted.' He gently places a pile in Dancer's lap. A neatly folded checked shirt that Dancer recognises as the one Two Bob was wearing at the funeral; a silver buckled belt of woven leather, dubbinned to a gleam; his own boots, freshly polished, and resting on them a pair of spurs.

Two Bob busies himself with pouring tea as he says, 'You won't really be needin' the spurs, I'm guessin', but I figured you might as well look the part, seein' as you're gunna give me a hand gettin' these horses in.'

⚬

Dancer has never done the cowboy look favoured by Andy, but he can't help feeling a bit of a swagger as he climbs into the passenger seat of the Hilux. He is wearing the same old jeans, but the flash shirt and belt and shiny boots feel good. The spurs are a step too far though; he's not even sure how to strap them on. Two Bob gives him a wink. Tim is waiting for them down at the yards. He runs an approving eye over Dancer, and says Jimmy will join them tomorrow.

What is left of the Highlands horse herd is skittish, but they know Two Bob and his sugar cubes, and a mob is easily lured into the night paddock adjacent to the yards. Once the night paddock gate is closed and they realise they are confined, they begin to mill and stir. Two Bob and Tim spend an hour walking amongst them, with quietly soothing words and noises.

Two Bob reckons that is enough with the horses for day one. They head up to the garage, and with Stan work out exactly what patching up the horse float needs. Then there is a thorough inspection of the old saddle room to assess the gear. Two Bob is all business. It is as if he has shed twenty years as he steps back into this familiar world, and inhales the rich smells of horseflesh and leather.

They make it up to the office in time to call Elders. Rosa watches with amusement as Dancer performs the role of telephone intermediary for Two Bob and Stan, scribbling down prices, relaying questions back and forth about size and type of D rings, and other arcane matters of which he clearly has little understanding.

'Seven hundred and fifty,' she reminds Two Bob, when they are finished.

'Seven hundred an' fifty,' he repeats like a mantra.

'I'm off in the morning. I've lined up meetings with the Shire and the funding mob while I'm in Derby,' she tells them. 'I'll try and get some breathing room on these bills.'

It feels like maths class that evening as Two Bob works out the best way to spend his allowance, with Dancer doing the calculations. In the end Two Bob decides to put off a new tyre for the float, and hope that Stan can make do with the existing ones. 'We could get by without the horse nuts,' he muses, 'but they'll make life a whole lot easier. If we finish up needin' a new tyre you'll just have to sweet-talk Rosa.'

'Me?!'

Two Bob chuckles. 'You're her new favourite nephew.'

ॐ

After the dawn cuppa under the boab Dancer and Two Bob jump into the Hilux and head down to the night paddock, leaving Riley still in bed.

'The float'll take a dozen,' Two Bob says as they pull up at the gate and cast their eyes over the quietly milling mob. 'But we'll only take eight I reckon. Two each, and two packhorses.'

'Doesn't that make ten?' Dancer asks.

'Riley won't get on a horse. He'll walk.'

'What!'

'Don't worry, he can walk all day that young feller. An' fast. We'll only be pokin' along on the horses. See any you fancy in this mob?'

Dancer is the fourth cog in the wheel as they work the horses in the days that follow. The others have the job very much in hand. They narrow the candidates down to a dozen, all reshod and becoming reaccustomed to the feel of a rider on their backs. He picks his pair – the quietest two – and survives his few hours on horseback better than he thought he might. He is more use as an offsider to Stan, as they get the horse float in shape.

One of the pair chosen as packhorses is skittish at first, but responds to the gentle persuasions of Two Bob and Tim. The intricate business of getting the saddles and straps in place goes smoothly enough, as does securing the load of carefully balanced saddlebags, swags and gear. A slow loop around the horse paddock and nearby country is completed with no dramas. And so the first of the three benchmarks Two Bob has set for them to complete before Andy's return is ticked off.

The initial attempt at getting the horses used to the float does not go so well. They have to take them to where the float sits behind the garage shed. The unfamiliar surroundings put the horses on edge, and the crowd of kids watching noisily doesn't help. Every one of them shies away from the ramp at least once. The big bay gelding Two Bob has earmarked for Andy causes a flurry of excitement when he rears high, and has Jimmy at the end of the lead struggling to hold his feet, bringing whoops from the kids.

The next day it is still not smooth, but they do get the full dozen loaded. Two recalcitrants are nothing but trouble on board, rearing in their stalls, and unsettling the others. The pair are unloaded. Their dozen has been trimmed to ten. These are left in their stalls for a couple of hours, with horse nuts and much petting and praise, before they are led off and returned to the night paddock.

'Not bad, not too bad,' is Two Bob's assessment. With benchmark number two achieved, he declares tomorrow a holiday, before they gear up for the third test.

39

With Two Bob busy, cooking duties back at the house have fallen to Riley. This means two or three random tins with a spoon of blachan sauce heated up in a single saucepan, and grilled toast with bread straight from the freezer. One evening when Riley is distracted by some excitement in the gameshow on TV, the toast and the orange spaghetti and Irish stew mix are all burnt. Two Bob and Riley eat theirs without comment. Dancer grits his teeth and tries, but can't force it down, and has to open another tin and make his own supper.

The evenings have a different feel. There is no escaping the obvious: Riley has calmed down now that Andy is not there. And a calmer Riley makes for an easier atmosphere. Dancer comes to realise that the more tense Riley is the louder the TV volume gets, as if it might drown out whatever is agitating his soul. As the days pass the volume seems to go down a notch each night.

Two Bob spends the evenings at the kitchen table with a saddler's needle and twine and dubbin, repairing bridles and hobbles. Or out on the verandah preparing the larger items – the saddles and packs. Once Dancer has done the washing up he gives Two Bob a hand, or wanders out to contemplate the boab tree in the moonlight and listen to the night birds, or plonks down on the sofa for a while to see what Riley is watching. One night all of a sudden the man boy of few words asks him, 'You like Phantom?'

'What?'

'Phantom. Ghost who walks. He narrugu for me an' Two Bob. Kit Walker.'

'You mean the comic?'

'Yuw.'

'Dunno. Never read one.'

'What! You don't know Phantom!'

'Nuh.'

'Here.' Riley is thrusting a comic book at him. 'Read him.'

'Ok, when I go to bed.'

'No, no. Read him now.'

Dancer starts to flick through the comic in a cursory fashion. 'No. Out loud.'

It is not until that moment that Dancer realises Riley can't read. He leans in, hanging on every word. Then Two Bob pulls his chair up behind the sofa to watch and listen as well. It evokes dim memories of Mimi Bella reading him bedtime stories, but he does not recall being as entranced as these two. When he is finished Riley has an enormous smile. He springs and turns to kneel on the sofa, facing backwards, and gives Two Bob a high five.

'Us Walkers have got a thing about the Phantom,' a shamefaced Two Bob explains. 'Goes back to when I was a kid.'

'You had Phantom comics here then?'

'Just one. I used to humbug my father to read it to me.'

It is not until later that Dancer thinks of the obvious question. Two Bob's father could read, but he can't?

❧

The next night he wanders back in from the boab, his head full of the strange resonances of the coucal's call, the sinking, echoing cadences that feel like they are trying to draw a song from him. Riley thrusts a sketchpad at him, exclaiming, 'Phantom Meets His Narrugu!' Song thoughts vanish. If last night was odd, this is surreal. Riley has drawn a Phantom cartoon, complete with speech balloons that are all blank. As Dancer works his way through it, Riley points to each balloon, speaking the words he has imagined.

Dancer loves the intricacy and energy of the drawings. The Phantom stepping off a plane; standing resolute and tall in the back of a Hilux, hands on the rail, with Riley beside him, hair blowing in the wind; sharing a cup of tea with Two Bob under the boab tree. Riley hauling in a barramundi under the Phantom's approving gaze. A gang of baddies descends, and there is a mad fight sequence of bam-kapow panels. The final scenes of Riley triumphant, standing with a foot on the back of his prone, black-clad adversary, before a manly handshake with the Phantom, and the two of them striding off towards the horizon.

40

'You can drive?' Two Bob asks, the morning of their day off.

'I've got no licence. Too young.'

'Not much traffic policeman out here, Dancer. You can drive?'

'Not real good, but yeah.'

Two Bob tosses him the car keys. 'Me an' Riley go bush every weekend. But I'm a bit buggered today, too much work this week. Why don't you take him fishin'.'

～

Up here in the high country the rivers seem to slim down. Dancer could almost cast his handline to the far bank with a slightly bigger sinker and a good release. But the waterhole is long; to the north he can just make out the sandbar where it starts, to the south it disappears around a distant bend. The water is a deep dark green. On the other side the bank is mostly thickets of pandanus palms. But here where he is sitting the sand shelves gently down to the water, shaded thickly by river figs that tower above and reach out over it. Just down to his right a magnificent paperbark leans towards the centre of the hole. Its lower branches, pocked with dried streamers of flood debris, almost kiss the water's surface.

He soon realises that his cousin is no fisherman. Too eager, Riley is prone to give the line a mighty jerk at the first touch, before the bream can actually take the bait. He does manage to get a couple to Dancer's five. There's more than enough for lunch.

Dancer guts the fish, builds the fire, and puts them on to cook. He can sense a pent-up excitement in Riley, who is singing quietly to himself, and hopping from foot to foot; but he's started to work out that it's better to just ride with Riley's moods and whims and see where they lead than to ask questions or seek understanding.

'Ever caught a barra?' he asks idly.

'You been see. In Phantom Meets His Narrugu. Big one!' Riley extends his hands to show just how big. He keeps a straight face, but there is something about his manner that suggests a joke.

'Come on. I mean proper way.'

'Proper way! Ol' man barramundi too clever for Riley!' Riley cackles and all of a sudden bursts into a sprint that finishes with a cartwheel in the sand and an improbably athletic standing somersault that has him land at Dancer's feet. He collapses in the sand, seizes Dancer's foot, and pulls it into his stomach. 'Boom!' he pretends to have been kicked, rolls and springs to his feet. 'Robbidy Bob, Robbidy Bob!' he sings, as he runs down to the bank and leaps into the water.

Dancer wakes, sits up, shaking the sand out of his hair. The fire is still smoking in a half-hearted sort of way, a couple of charred bream skeletons showing amongst the ashes. A small breeze ripples the surface of the waterhole. The dried leaves floating on its surface dance. Riley is nowhere to be seen.

Dancer goes for a little wander to clear his head, savouring the beauty of this place, then sits back down in his fishing spot and lazes the midafternoon away catching another half-dozen. Then he hears Riley's call. And again, closer. Riley bursts into the clearing. 'I been walkin'. Sorry, I been walkin'. I forgot. Sorry. Come on. We'll be late. Come on.'

'Late for what?'

'You'll see. You'll see.'

Riley can hardly contain himself as Dancer gathers up their gear and they make their way back up to the Hilux.

41

Rosa does the talking, but not with her chairman's hat on. This is a family gathering of the Rider clan. She has seated Dancer between herself and Tim. Riley is tying a bandanna of white cotton around his forehead to match the other men. 'Your grandfather Wajarri, Two Bob, he came here long time. Before I was born. But his country is south from here. And on Highlands, us mob say a Rider is a boss for a Walker.'

Two Bob has heard the joke many times, and laughs along. 'That's what my Marj always used to say.'

Then Rosa's tone takes on a formality, a gravitas, that marks this night as different to a meeting or a verandah chat. 'My Auntie Marj, your grandma, she was a proper Rider, a proper boss for this Jimbala Wali country here. She was a big woman for the Kimberley your granny Marj. All the Land Council mob, all the Kimberley bosses came here to Jimbala Wali for her funeral.

'Your grandpa Walker, he's brought you back here. But you've gotta know your granny Rider's story too. And your mother, poor thing. She was one of us. That means you're one of us, Robert Rider.

'You've just started to get that story little bit. But underneath that story is a song. And underneath that song is country, and law. You've gotta listen now to the junba for this Jimbala Wali country.'

And so the night begins. Tim and Riley lead the singing, backed by Rosa and a chorus of women. Two Bob is amongst the dancers, as is Jimmy. Dancer has no idea of the story being sung, but that knowledge can come later. Right now there is fierce contentment to be here in this circle, absorbing the song. Riley is transformed. The boyish innocence that seems so much a part of his character has dropped away. There is an intensity to his whole manner and bearing.

Dancer studies the dancers closely, watching the patterns and movements, noting the subtle differences to the Broome-side style he is familiar with. Sitting there cross-legged between Tim and Rosa he is starting to move from the hips up, feeling the dance.

Before he knows it Two Bob and Jimmy have stepped out, grabbed him by an arm each, and led him up to join them. He is dancing the Jimbala Wali junba. His new family can soon see why his Nyami Buster dubbed him Dancer. After a couple of verses his hesitancy is gone. Once he has the feel, there is a rhythm to his movement that belies the heavy set of his body, a firmness to his stamping with a quick strong lift into the next step, a sharp grace about the way he moves into each new position. There are calls of encouragement from the women and knowing smiles exchanged amongst the men. He looks up to see Riley's eyes fixed on him. They both break into broad grins, without Riley missing a beat of the song.

He feels momentarily deflated when the junba comes to an end. Jimmy escorts him back to the spot between the Rider siblings. Tim ties a white strip around his forehead, and slaps him on the back. Rosa's gravitas has gone. The twinkle is back in her eye as she asks, 'Anybody let on?'

'I had no idea.'

She sees the tears glinting in the corners of his eyes, and gathers him into a hug. 'Welcome to your other country,' she whispers, before releasing him, and saying in her normal voice, 'Get ready for the fun now.'

Tim gives him an elbow nudge, 'Looks like you're bringin' ol' Two Bob back to life. Can't remember the last time I saw him dancin'.' And then a sly wink. 'You're a more better dancer than horse rider, boy.' Blowing raspberries to loosen up his cheeks, he reaches back for his dijeridoo. 'Watch this kind dancin' now.'

❧

Dancer dreamed that night that he was dancing a wangga.

He was entranced, from the moment of the slow, almost mournful start of Tim on dij, joined by Riley as singer. The prowling of the young men, then the surge as the clapsticks beat faster. The outburst of free-spirited exuberance, the flashiness of the dancers who each gave their all in whirls and leaps as the short crescendo peaked. Jimmy tried to drag him up to have a go after he had watched a few. But he resisted. He was tempted, but needed to wrap his head around this dance, so unlike anything he had seen before.

As the night wound down and everybody drifted back to their camps, he was still hearing Riley's song, and choreographing moves in his head. After the last goodnights, as the three of them walked back to Two Bob's camp, he suggested to Riley, only half jokingly, that next time they were down the river he should sing a few wanggas for him so he could practise some moves.

'Yuw, yuw! We can do that. You'll be best wangga dancer, Dancer! Dancer dancer!' Riley did a jig, delighted with his pun.

When they reached Two Bob's yard, Dancer tried an opening step; the crouching prowl, hands held low with fingers pointing.

'Woorroooh!' Riley purred his approval and followed suit.

Dancer pivoted, stretched another step.

Riley straightened and began to sing.

'Down the river,' said Dancer, holding his hand out for a low five.

Riley tapped his hand. 'Yuw.'

42

The next morning Dancer makes a prearranged call to Andy from the phone box by the office. Andy is in good spirits. The hay carting gig is going smoothly. Not long to go now, then he'll head back up after a day getting gear sorted and doing a bit of shopping. Dancer asks if he can put in a couple of requests for the shops. His first one draws a guffaw from Andy at the other end of the line. 'Ol' Two Bob still into the Phantom is he?'

'Yep, and Riley.'

'He used to make me read the bloody things to him. Milly thought we were nuts. I'll see if I can get a few. Only you can do the bloody readin', mate. What else?'

'See if the newsagent's got any of those sketchpads. You know, the big ones, double the size of a notepad. A couple of them, and a few of those drawing pens for Riley.'

'See what I can do. Sounds like you're gettin' on ok up there then?'

'Yep. I was dancing last night. The Jimbala Wali junba for all the Rider mob.'

There is real pleasure in Andy's laugh down the line. 'Two Bob need anythin' else?'

'Nah, he reckons it's all good this end. He said to tell you he's got a couple of good horses for you.'

'Not sure I can trust the ol' bugger on that. He can be a bit of a trickster you know.'

'We've been walking them on and off the float, and they're just about right with that. We're doing another run-through today.'

'He was always a stickler for detail. You're in good hands with your grandpa.'

'Yep. We're gunna take the plant out on a night camp tomorrow. Day's ride to Ruby's Bore, then hobble them out, and come back the next day. He reckons if they handle that all right, we'll be set to go.'

'Proper old style! Gotta say I'm lookin' forward to a bit of ridin' after all these years. See you in a few days time.'

'See you, Dad.'

He feels good this morning! He gives a stomp, and shimmies a move from last night's dance as he leaves the phone box.

'Whoo Dancer!' It is a couple of teenage girls who were there last night, heading towards the store. One of them copies his shimmy, and they burst into giggles. He does not even feel embarrassed; just laughs back, and heads down towards the yards. He reports to Two Bob on the conversation with Andy, adding that Andy is a bit dubious about what sort of horses they've lined up for him. The other three can't quite hide their conspiratorial smiles.

'You're not setting him up are you?'

'No, promise. You an' me are gunna poke along at a walk, but I reckon your ol' man'll want to go for a bit of a gallop, just to remember what it used to be like. Andy's a good man on a horse. Falcon here'll give him a good run if he wants it.'

No-one talks about the dancing, but Tim and Jimmy are more chatty than they have been. Dancer floats through the day. He's not sure why, but he decides on a name for the little gelding he's chosen as his main horse – Buddy. He'll find the jokes before he gets back to Broome. They leave Buddy in the night paddock. Dancer's job in the morning will be to bring in the rest of the plant whilst the real horsemen get everything ready for the third test.

The result is bizarre, but the intention is clear. Riley has put in an effort. He's made a rare trip down to the store. Every tin plate and plastic bowl from Two Bob's meagre kitchen cupboard has been commandeered. There is ice-cream – already starting to melt – and tinned apricots. The spaghetti and the Irish stew have been heated in separate saucepans. There is margarine on the toast.

And there's a sparkle in Two Bob's eyes as they enjoy the feast. He tries to not smoke in the evenings, but tonight he pulls out his tin and rolls up. He lets out a burp, gives his stomach a pat, and excuses himself to head out to the verandah. Dancer can feel Riley watching as he does the dishes. He wipes down the bench, squeezes out the rag, and turns to see Riley standing in the doorway of his bedroom, waving Dancer towards him. He ushers Dancer into the room, peers back out suspiciously, then pushes the door shut.

Dancer hasn't been in here before. He's surprised at how orderly it is. With Riley, he'd expected a chaotic mess. Riley motions him to sit on the bed, puts a finger to his lips, then goes to a cupboard. He pulls out a spiral-bound sketchpad and clasps it tight to his chest. Dancer assumes it is the same one he saw the other night. 'Have you done another Phantom comic?'

Riley shakes his head firmly. 'Two Bob.' A downward handflick – the 'nothing' sign. Then thumb and forefinger drawn slowly across his lips – 'mouth zipped'.

'Don't say anything to Two Bob?' Dancer interprets.

Riley nods. Then, 'Andy.' He repeats the pantomime.

'Don't say anything to Dad.'

Riley double-nods, then licks his middle finger, dashes it in a cross across his chest. 'Cross my heart an' hope to die,' he blurts. Dancer is hesitant. Riley repeats the lick, the gesture, the words, more urgently. With an uneasy feeling Dancer repeats the ritual and the words. He can sense how tightly wound his cousin is, as Riley lowers the pad down onto his lap, then slides it across.

Dancer flips the stiff cardboard cover open. He's only paying cursory attention to the details, until his eye is caught by a panel at the foot of the second page. It is the young woman and the child who have featured in most of the other panels. In this one the child has his head close to the woman's rounded stomach, eyes wide with delight, and a huge smile. Tremor lines around the stomach suggest movement. The woman too is smiling happily. Her face is the same as the one in the picture in the hallway at home. His mother's.

Riley sees that Dancer has twigged, and is almost bursting with pride.

Dancer goes back to the start. It is obvious now. Idyllic scenes of Milly and Riley fishing. The bad guy in black clothes and hat, scowl-faced as he towers over Milly, is clearly Andy. In one panel the child Riley cries forlornly in the foreground as black-hat Andy and Milly drive away. He's not sure he wants to turn the page. He runs his eye over the panels of the first two pages again, astounded at the intricacy and accuracy of the drawing.

The next two pages tell a story he knows, though there are details which are new to him. A white nurse examining Milly with a worried look on her face, and a series of panels showing Milly and Andy and the nurse in tense then angry exchanges, all drawn from the low perspective of a child. The final panel shows young Riley on Two Bob's hip, head buried, refusing to watch as Milly and Andy drive off, with Milly looking back, crying and waving.

He turns another page. The cartoon is interrupted. Across the two opened pages is one large line drawing. The boab tree from a distance. The station track disappearing into scrub as it winds towards the distant Gibb River Road. Under the boab tree two figures sitting on flour drums; Two Bob in profile, and a little boy with his back turned. Something about the pair, small in the landscape, speaks of loneliness and sadness.

The next double-page is blank.

'Is that all?'

Riley gives a short shake of the head, twisting away as Dancer licks a finger, and turns a sheet to reveal the next spread. Dancer can't help the gasp that escapes him. The first page is taken up by a portrait of his mother's face that is too painful to look at. He briefly takes in the wild hair and the haunted, vacant eyes, then with a shudder folds the spine of the sketchbook, to hide her away.

He thinks he should stop, but cannot.

The other page has six panels, all framing exactly the same view. A woman with wild hair seen from behind, sitting cross-legged on a sandy bank with a waterhole in front of her. Pandanus thickets on the far bank. A big paperbark on the right, branches kissing the water. His mother is sitting in exactly the same spot where he sat most of yesterday.

In the first five panels Riley is cavorting around her. Catching a fish. Offering it to Milly. He cartwheels in front of her. The water explodes in a splash as he does a bombie. In each panel she sits, unmoved. In the last panel on the page, the boy is walking out of frame, head bowed, and still she sits, exactly the same. Dancer wipes a tear from his cheek with the back of his hand, then briefly places the hand on Riley's knee.

The next two spreads are a series of half-page sketches, four to a spread. In each the landscape is similar; a range on the horizon. In the first the wild-haired woman looms large in the left foreground, half a head and right shoulder, seen from behind. The landscape stays the same, but with each drawing she grows smaller and more distant, moving across the frame of the pictures from left to right, but always walking straight into the distance. Dancer does not know how Riley has achieved the effect, but as his mother disappears further into the distance she becomes fainter, with the landscape starting to be seen through her form. In the last she is barely a distant glimmer.

Riley has edged away from him. There is now a metre between

them, as his cousin sits frozen on the corner of the bed. Dancer stares for a long, long time at the last frame.

There is a single smallish panel on the next spread. A boy lies curled in sleep, in the spot on the sandbank where Milly sat. There is a caption bubble. But there are no words: the bubble shows the boy's dream, a miniature of almost the same landscape that Milly disappeared into. But the view has shifted slightly. The horizon range is further to the left, and in the centre of the landscape is a flat-topped mesa which Dancer immediately recognises as Flat Iron Hill.

'Unggulala,' he murmurs as he turns the page.

The left sheet is blank. The right is drawn in a completely different style to what has come before. The boy is a small, crude stick figure in shorts. Unggulala is drawn in thick outline, with the rest of the landscape only faintly sketched. He turns another page. The same small stick figure. This time Unggulala is larger and darker, the rest of the landscape has disappeared altogether.

And again. Unggulala almost fills the page, hatched in darkly, overwhelming the small figure which now has shiver lines, and this time a small speaking caption, filled with the asterisks and exclamation marks used to indicate swearing.

The final page of the sketchbook is inked black. Completely. With hard, fierce strokes that have torn at the paper.

⁓

Dancer sits staring at the black page. Eventually he leafs backwards until he finds one of the landscapes with his mother disappearing. Yep, there is Unggulala, cut in half by the right edge of the panel. He keeps leafing backwards until he knows the next page will be his mother's face. He closes the sketchpad and places it on the bed between them.

'Tell me,' he says.

Silence.

'Tell me,' he says, more forcefully.

More silence.

He gets up. He kneels in front of Riley, who is twisting his neck almost off his shoulders to avoid looking at him. He struggles to keep his voice even. 'Fucken tell me.'

The words are almost unintelligible as Riley contorts rigidly, straining away from him. 'Not yet. Later. Not ready yet.'

'Then why the fuck did you show me this?!'

He grabs the sketchpad and throws it at Riley, who lets out a scream as he catches and cradles the pad. He slips around Dancer and stashes the pad away and slams the cupboard door shut. He throws himself on the bed, and lies there rocking himself whilst frantically crossing his chest with his middle finger and muttering over and over, 'Cross your heart an' hope to die. Cross your heart an' hope to die. Cross your heart an' hope to die ...'

Dancer is still kneeling by the bed, stunned, when Two Bob throws the door open and takes in the scene. He takes Riley in his arms and begins to rock him, giving Dancer an angry glare and waving him out of the room with a dismissive gesture.

43

'Hey Buddy, am I stressing you out?'

To his surprise the horse gives a toss of its head, which he takes as a no. He realises that the name is not about playing a joke on his little brother. They have never been apart for this long. In some odd way talking to horse Buddy helps bridge the gap.

Tim has already gone, driving to Ruby's Bore. Jimmy is somewhere up ahead, riding Falcon. And Two Bob is not far behind, leading the packhorses. Before they set off, Two Bob had instructed him, 'If you start feelin' cranky, you just pull up an' climb out of the saddle an' have a spell. Your horse can always tell, Dancer. You get cranky, Buddy'll get nervous. If he gets nervous, anythin' can happen. You always gotta be careful travellin' with packhorses. Can't have 'em shyin' with that load on their back.'

Dancer leans forward and gives Buddy a rub between the ears. 'This is life in slow-motion, bro. Bit hard to stay wound-up at this pace.'

⁕

Last night he'd been wound tight, pacing a groove in the dirt around the boab tree.

Riley knows something!

I've got to tell Dad. This is bullshit. We should pull out.

After Two Bob had glared at him and waved him out of the house, his first instinct had been to ring Andy. But his father was probably about halfway between Halls Creek and Fitzroy

Crossing hauling two trailer-loads of hay.

He's a fucken retard. It could all be bullshit.

No way I'm going to fucken camp at Ruby's fucken Bore with him tomorrow and pretend everything is fucken sweet.

The image of his mother's haunted face will not leave him. Maybe ever.

It could all be bullshit. I've had enough of fucken riddles.

Maybe Rosa knows something. Too late to go up to hers now.

Fuck. We're supposed to be taking off at daybreak.

Fuck you Riley!

Eventually he slowed down enough to head back up to the house and throw himself onto his swag on the verandah. There was movement inside. Two Bob coming and going. Riley's bedroom door opening and closing. He heard the pop of the tobacco tin opening. Half a minute later the flywire door creaked. Two Bob lowered himself onto the front step of the verandah and lit up. He took a few drags before speaking.

'You still right for tomorrer?'

No answer.

'You can't growl him, Dancer. Even when you want to, you can't growl him. It just makes things worse.'

Two Bob finished the smoke in silence. He flicked the butt, hard. They both watched it soar and land, and glow there in the dirt.

'Riley's gunna stop back. I've sorted his tucker for him for the next coupla days.'

❧

Dancer loses track of the hours. Shifting occasionally in the saddle. Rolling his shoulders to loosen a back muscle that is starting to make itself felt. Watching the country slide past at the pace of a walking horse.

The campsite is perfect, under a spreading bauhinia tree with a pair of willy wagtails skittering and chirping. Tim has the billy boiling when they arrive, and he's raking the coals over the camp oven to finish off the damper. Tim and Jimmy take charge of the horses, unloading the packs, watering them at the trough, then hobbling them out, with Two Bob happy to just keep an eye on things. Dancer doesn't even watch. He cradles his tea and stares at the hills.

Fuck you Riley.

He can't put it aside. He has no idea what Two Bob has or hasn't said to the other two, but he can feel them giving him space, and their disappointment. He was not the only one who'd expected camaraderie tonight. 'Good damper, uncle,' is the best he can offer before they all turn in to their swags just after dark.

∾

The knot in his guts is not quite so tight in the morning, and he joins the others in getting the day moving. He gives Buddy an ear rub and some nuts, tells him he's got the day off, then saddles up his second horse, which he has not found a name for yet.

'They're goin' well, Dancer,' Two Bob says as he runs his eye over the horses standing quietly by the trough. 'If we get back to Highlands today with no balls-ups, I reckon we're gunna be good to go.'

A quick breakfast of damper spread thick with jam, and they are ready to ride.

∾

Two Bob pulls up the packhorses and string of spares and dismounts for a piss. He times his remount for Dancer's approach so the two fall in together. 'Feelin' any better today, jaminyi?'

'Little bit.'

'Want to talk?'

'About what?'

'Anythin' ... Riley ...'

'Cross my heart and hope to die! We're not fucken kids.'

'He's got this thing about secrets.'

'Rosa reckons you like 'em too.'

'Does she just. Whatever secret he gave you, Dancer, it means he trusts you. That's a big thing for Riley.'

'I get that. But he only gave me half the secret, see. Which means he doesn't really, really trust me. Or maybe it's just some dream, or some mad thing in his head. That's what I'm starting to think, but that'd be worse.' He sniffs, and shifts awkwardly; suddenly the horse is skipping sideways, and he has to concentrate for a few moments on settling her. 'I'm pretty cranky with him, Grandpa. I've been wondering if I should ask Rosa if I can put my swag on her verandah.'

Two Bob winces. They ride on in silence for a while.

'They wanted to take him away, one time.'

'Riley?'

'Yeah. They reckoned he needed some kinda treatment. Can't remember what they called it. He can sing. He can walk. He can draw. There's not much else Riley's good for, I know that. But they're three good things. Just think about Riley in some fucken hospital or whatever it was they wanted.'

The old man lip-points at a bush turkey. The bird watches them warily, but does not take flight. Two Bob looks back to check on the packhorses. Lets some more time pass.

'We used to go bush every time Rosa told us the special doctor was comin' out an' wanted to see him. She didn't give me a hard time about it, so I figured she must've been on my side. He's got no-one else. An' I've got him. What's that thing they say when you get married?'

'Uh ... oh, you mean "for better or worse"?'

'That's the one. There's a bit of both in it, Dancer.'

Dancer looks across at him, and there is an enigma in the slightest of smiles that he gets back.

'I know you've got this big argument goin' on inside your

head, boy. We can all see it an' feel it, even if we don't know what it's about. I'm not you, but if I was, I'd keep his secret. It's a heavy thing to break ...'

He leaves a silence for Dancer, but when he gets nothing, he continues. 'If you really need to say somethin', talk to your dad when he gets back. Don't tell me. If Riley stops trustin' me, I don't know what'll happen.' Suddenly he is coughing loudly, thumping his chest as he reins his horse in. He gives his horse a rub. 'Sorry Nellie. You right there?'

Dancer suspects he's manufactured it, but halts his horse and turns in the saddle. 'You ok?'

'Now I've stopped, I might check those packs. You keep goin'. Jimmy'll be at dinner camp by now I reckon. I'll join you there.'

There is a half stumble as he dismounts. He grabs at his calf.

'You sure you're all right there, Grandpa?'

'I'm right. Go on.' Dancer is unsure. Two Bob gives him a backhand wave as if to say get going.

Dancer flicks the reins, and the mare breaks into her slow walk.

'Move camp to Rosa's if you have to ...' Dancer turns in his saddle again. 'But I'd like you to stay.' They watch each other for a couple of moments, until Two Bob repeats his get going wave.

⚬

'Hey Sally, there's a good girl. We've made it!' He dismounts, feeling foolishly pleased. He found her name on this last leg between dinner camp and the station yards. She ain't no mustang, but it feels right. He opens the gate for Two Bob to lead his string through, then closes it behind, leading Sally.

Jimmy has been back a while already, and has Falcon's saddle on a rail, and the horse rubbed down. The horse prances round the yard, clearly pleased with himself for leading the expedition. Rosa has joined Tim and Jimmy, all sitting on a rail beside the saddle, watching them come in.

Two Bob makes no allowance for his aches and pains as they go through the business of unsaddling, rub-downs and kind words and nuts for the horses, and loading gear back into vehicles. All the talk is upbeat. They're good to go is the consensus. Jimmy is only half joking when he points out that they still have ten good horses, they could take an extra rider on this trip. Dancer is caught up in the mood. When Rosa asks him in a quiet moment, with a meaningful look, how he's going, he tells her he is fine.

'Want to come round for dinner tomorrow night?' she asks.

'That'd be great.'

44

'We'll unload the ute in the mornin' eh?' Two Bob suggests as he eases himself stiffly out of the ute.

'I reckon,' Dancer agrees.

They notice the ground in front of the verandah has been raked. The grooves from the spokes are still showing; not a cigarette butt or a stray leaf in sight. The verandah has been swept, Dancer's stuff is neatly stacked beside the bed frame, just waiting for his swag. They look at each other as they step inside.

The living room is spotless. The TV is off. A spaghetti tin on the table holds a slightly limp arrangement of yellow flowers from a cotton tree. Riley is humming edgily to himself as he scoops ice-cream fresh from the freezer into bowls of tinned apricots.

Two Bob and Dancer look at each other again, and sit at the table. Riley says nothing and refuses their urgings to join them as he serves a three-course meal of ice-cream and apricots, baked beans, and braised beef. When they are finished Two Bob disappears to his room yawning. Riley vanishes too. Dancer is left to do the dishes, get his swag from the back of the ute, and wonder what the hell.

∾

He almost stands on the sheet of paper when he gets up. The drawing is held down by a pebble on each corner. A coucal whoops its throaty 'frog in a drainpipe' call. It is still too dark to see properly. Dancer picks up the sheet and heads down to the boab tree, catching a glimpse of the bird with its improbably long tail as it flies off.

He makes a fire and fills the billy, waiting for the light to strengthen. He doesn't want to look. When he has warmed himself with a first gulp of tea he gives it a glance.

What the ...?!

Andy's truck. Right down to the dent in the bullbar where they hit that bullamon coming into Willare on the way up. Through the windscreen he can see Andy at the wheel and himself in the passenger seat. The truck is swooping down out of the sky, top right to bottom left, with a pair of angel wings extending on either side.

There is a small panel in the top left corner. A black hat on the ground. Andy taking off his black shirt. In the bottom right there are two more. Dancer and Andy – in white hat and shirt – emerging from the truck. Then four figures walking towards the horizon.

45

'How are you this morning?' Dancer asks as Two Bob settles on his flour drum.

'Little bit sore, jaminyi, but I'll be good. You?'

'Yeah, ok. Back's a bit stiff. Anything planned for today?'

'Day off I reckon. I'll check the horses later on.'

'Your washing machine work?'

'Little bit.'

'What you mean little bit?'

'He can do that back and forwards, back and forwards part for washin'. That spin around part, he don't like that much. I just take 'em out after the washin' part an' hang 'em on the fence.'

'Sounds good. Rosa's asked me round for dinner tonight. Thought I should clean myself up a bit.'

Two Bob is trying to look at the drawing without being too intrusive. Dancer passes it across. Watches the old man deep in thought as he traces the drawing with a finger. He is hoping for a comment, an explanation, perhaps even some sort of enlightenment, but when Two Bob finally turns to him there is just a question in his eye.

Dancer can only shake his head. 'He's saying sorry, maybe? I don't know. I'm hoping it means he'll stop giving Dad such a hard time at least.'

'I like that last little picture.'

❧

He hears the Hilux start up while he's busy tending the washing machine, wringing out clothes, and hanging them carefully over the dilapidated fence to avoid them dragging in the dirt. When he goes in he realises that Riley has disappeared along with Two Bob. He idles through the day, deciding to wash the grotty sheets in his swag as well, and beat the dust out of the blanket, and polish his boots. He even doodles for a while with the guitar he has not touched since arriving at Highlands.

Maybe he's taken Riley for his dose of walking down the river.

He reads through the Phantom comics again. The thought occurs that perhaps Two Bob is managing the situation, keeping him and Riley from having too much time together. Eventually the sun starts to dip. His clothes are dried stiff, he has to shake his jeans and shirt out to loosen them up. He feels strange dressing up for a date with his auntie.

๛

'I'm not too early am I?'

'You're fine.' Rosa runs an eye over him. 'Looking good there, Dancer. All spruced up.' She looks again. 'You've even had a shave?'

He blushes. She flicks the hose, spraying his feet lightly. 'I like it, nephew. Making an effort. Dinner'll be a little bit. You know where the kettle is.'

She joins him up on the verandah as he's making the tea, and they settle into the comfy chairs. 'D'you like goulash?'

'Don't think I've ever had it.'

'Hungarian stew. Lots of paprika. I learned to make it when I was down in Perth. Good winter tucker – a potful would last me a week. I still make it now, even though there's not much of a winter here.'

'When were you down there?'

'Round the time you were born. When I came through Broome on my way back up for summer holidays at the end of my first year, Milly's stomach was out here, fit to burst,' Rosa holds her rounded palms in front of her stomach. 'It was only three or four days after that you popped out.'

She leaves a silence for him, but he can't think what to say.

'I never saw her again. Flew out of Derby going back. I think about her a lot though. And you wouldn't know how many times I've wondered about you over the years.'

This time she lets the silence hang, waiting for him. But he can't meet her eye.

'So you knew Mum – I mean of course you knew her, but ...'

'We grew up together. Cousin sisters. And you are making me remember her. That slow, gentle voice of yours.'

This time he meets her eye. 'I've got no memories of her.'

Rosa wipes a tear. Squeezes his knee briefly. Wipes the other eye. 'She used to camp with us, back when we were little, when Two Bob was out on the stock camp and Marj had to go away for meetings. It changed a bit after I went to the hostel in Derby – I was a couple of years older than her. But we were close.'

'Didn't she go down to the hostel?' asks Dancer.

Rosa laughs. 'Yeah, but not by choice. I was the opposite, I loved it. Don't get me wrong, your mum was sharp as a pin, she just didn't give a bugger about school, and she couldn't hack the hostel at all. She missed this place and her family so, so much every day she was there. She was out of there the day she turned fifteen. Auntie Marj didn't approve, but she knew there was no use arguing about it.'

Rosa pushes out of her chair. 'The goulash should be just about ready. Can you light the mossie coils under the table there. Plenty of cold water in the fridge if you want some.'

The table sits under a boughshed with a roof and one wall of spinifex held by chicken wire. A jasmine creeper is making progress towards enveloping it all in green. She has sprayed the spinifex, and the breeze blowing through creates wafts of cool, scented air. There are two glasses chilling in the fridge with the cold water. He pours them one each and sits at the table, thinking. Rosa has opened a door for him. He is going to walk on through, but that doesn't stop him being apprehensive. What are the right questions to ask?

She makes a couple of trips in and out rather than asking him to help. He senses that indoors is a private domain, and is glad he didn't ask to camp here. When she eventually seats herself there are not only the bowls of goulash, but a salad, pita bread, and dips. He can't help a big smile.

'What?'

'This is the first meal since Broome that I won't be eating off a tin plate.'

'I don't think your grandpa's ever got past the stock camp school of cooking.'

'Riley does a line in ice-cream and tinned apricots.'

'Yum. Mind you, I prefer black cherries to apricots. That's dessert.'

'He does it for first course. Then tinned spaghetti.'

'Don't criticise the cook unless you're willing to have a go yourself.'

'Ooh Auntie, this is good.'

As he eats he can feel her watching him, waiting. He decides to go straight to the point. 'Tell me what happened. I mean I know the basics, Dad's version. But you mob. Her family. What happened, Auntie?'

⁓

She seems to evade the question. Is she trying to spare his feelings? He feels kind of angry; she has opened the subject up, after all. But he begins to realise that this is hard for her too, that she has to work her way into the story.

'When I got into the nursing course, I can't tell you how happy I was. Mum and Dad were pretty pleased too. Everybody here. First kid from Jimbala Wali to get past high school. I was fine with the studies. Good at them. For a while there I even fancied the idea of doing a bridging course, trying to get into medicine.

That would've been something hey! Doctor Rider. But all that time down there I was sitting on a secret. I had my eyes on the big wide world. I was going to leave this place behind.'

She pushes her empty bowl aside, tears at her pita bread, almost angrily. 'There was a white boy I thought I was in love with. Medical student. Then he dropped me. Cold. Not a word. I think he figured a blackfeller wife and Kimberley munjons for his in-laws was going to be too complicated for the smart young doctor he was planning to be. But he never had the balls to say so. Bastard. All of a sudden the Perth dream didn't make so much sense.

'Then your granny died. That last spell she did in Perth on the dialysis, I don't know how many hours I sat with her. In the hostel. At the hospital. Didn't do much for my study routine, I can tell you. I organised for Two Bob and Riley to come down when the end was near. Don't think the poor old feller even realised I was there. I came back up for the funeral. The Greyhound all the way from Perth to Derby. I couldn't not come.' Rosa blinks hard.

'Sitting here with Mum and the aunties crying for Auntie Marj ... Oh, I dunno. We don't honour people like her enough. The ones who led the way. But I wasn't only crying for her. I was crying for myself. And angry at myself. Proper wild. For thinking I was too good for this place. For thinking I could leave my family and my country behind.

'I went back down and finished the course, but my heart wasn't in it any more. I never did my last prac. Never became a nurse. I came home, and here I am. And I don't regret it ... much.'

She gets up, takes their water glasses to the fridge to top them up. 'The reason for telling you my sorry story, nephew, is to try to explain why I can't answer your question very well. Between high school and nursing school, and having my head in the clouds all those years, I missed so much. All those struggle times when this place was born. I sort of turned my back on it all, and I'm ashamed of that.

STEVE HAWKE

'And I more or less missed the last couple of years of Milly's life. I saw her in Broome that time when I was passing through, and then ...' Rosa trails off. After a moment she says, 'All the stuff with your mum, Dancer – when it went wrong for her ... I just heard about it in my phone calls to Mum. It didn't seem real.

'What eats away at me, still, is thinking that I might have been able to make a difference. If there was one person in the world, it would have been me. Maybe it wouldn't have changed anything. But her cousin sister wasn't even paying attention.'

Each is lost in thoughts and memories. In the end, he ignores her story and asks, 'What about your mum, and the others here? What did they think?'

'Riders and Walkers,' she answers ruefully. 'I like Two Bob. I always have. But he's a strange old bird. I can only just remember his brother Bob, but by all accounts he was even stranger. And scary with it. The white witchdoctor, some people used to call him.

'There was one old granny who never liked either of them. The one that was always carrying on about the debbil debbil country. She used to stick it into Two Bob for ever taking Milly there, and blame him and Andy for cursing her. A couple of the aunties used to talk the same sort of way ...'

'So people were blaming Dad?'

She holds up a placating hand. 'I don't think many people really believed all that debbil debbil stuff. But same time, none of it made any sense. Specially the way she just disappeared. Everyone was freaked out.' She sees Dancer's furrowed brow. 'I shouldn't be talking like this, should I.'

'Yes, you should!' They are both shocked by his vehemence. 'I need to know.'

There is a wave of jasmine scent as a gust of wind sets Rosa's trees to swirling.

46

The waxing moon is directly above, throwing enough light for the boab's branches to speckle Dancer with a tracery of moonshadow. It's later than he has been up in many weeks. Rosa switched gear and started quizzing him about his Broome family. It'd taken a few moments to get back into remembering that world; three weeks seem a lifetime ago. But he was more than happy to reconnect in his mind, and rabbit on about the uncles and aunties, brother Buddy and the cousins, tales of Broome. Even Nyami Buster, so recently lost.

Rosa was so easy to talk to. Like no-one else he could think of. Maybe it was because she had offered something of herself first. By the time she got to her feet and started to gather up the remains of the meal, he felt like he had told his life story, such as it was to date. And that it had been welcomed, valued.

She refused his offers to clear the table or do the dishes, and re-emerged with a wicked grin and two big bowls of ice-cream, topped with half a tin each of black cherries. The rustling of the jasmine creeper, the slurp of soft tucker sucked off the spoon, small sounds of pleasure. They finished together. No words were necessary, his smile said it all.

'Tim tells me you're not much of a horse rider.'

'Thanks Tim.'

'He reckons it's not a problem though. Two Bob's got it all worked out. You and him are just going to mosey along at a walk.'

'That's the plan.'

'And two horses still to be culled out?'

'Mmm.' He was feeling his full stomach, not really paying attention. Until.

'Your mum told me a story one time.'

He sat up in his chair.

'D'you ever do that "cross your heart and hope to die" thing when you were a kid?'

He was struck dumb, but if she noticed, she ignored it.

'I don't know where she got that from. Bush kids we were, no TV or any of that stuff. Must have been some story Marj read to her I s'pose. But that's what she made me do, cross my heart and hope to die. I'd forgot it till the other day, when you told me about Two Bob's true country trip. I didn't twig straight away, it was later that night it came back to me. I mean, we were only – I was nine and she was seven or something like that, maybe younger even. Do you remember all the things you did when you were nine?'

'Nup.'

'That was only a few years ago for you. Bloody lifetime for me.'

'What d'you remember?'

'Cross my heart and hope to die. I s'pose it doesn't count now. She's gone. I honestly can't remember the details. But she told me about this secret place she'd been. About grannies and little boys and a secret pool full of birds. I thought she was just telling stories, Dancer. Little girl stories like we do.' The smile is more for herself and the memory than for Dancer.

'Put the kettle on will you.'

He made the tea, and they settled back into the soft chairs.

'I want to come, Dancer. You're going to that secret pool full of birds, far as I can reckon. I know it doesn't change anything. I know it doesn't make any sense. But it's like ... my way of saying sorry. That I believe you, Milly. I'd like to come.'

'Fuck.'

'Yeah. I get that.'

'Can you ride?'

'Good as you, from all reports.'

'This trip isn't about Mum.'

'I get that too. But it is for me.'

'You're freaking me out, Auntie.'

'Sorry.'

They sipped at their teas for a bit.

'Listen, Dancer. I'm not putting all my eggs in this flimsy old basket your grandpa is weaving. Jimbala Wali is not going to lose Highlands Station. Full stop. I love the idea of Two Bob and Andy pulling this mad scheme off, of pulling this place out of the shit. But I'm working on Plan B and Plan C. I have to.

'And I've got this feeling in my guts that this plan, whatever it is, is worth giving a go. Every cattleman I've talked to reckons your grandpa is as good as they come. I've juggled everything I can without breaking the silly fucken government rules to give it a chance.

'The thing is, though, all of that's got nothing to do with what I'm asking you. I'm not talking with my chairman's hat on here. This adventure you're about to go on is his plan, his game, his rules. If he says it's a boys-only trip for him and you and Riley and Andy, that's ok. I wouldn't hold that against him.

'I can't ask him myself. But I'd love to come, Dancer. I'm asking you a favour. Tim reckons those last two horses'd be all right for an old girl like me.'

'You're the same age as Dad, aren't you?'

'Same same.'

⁓❧

Dancer stretches, waggles his fingers, watches the moonshadows flicker across them, looks up to the yellow orb, laughs to himself.

Gunna be an interesting yarn with Grandpa in the morning.

47

'It's a bloody convoy,' Andy remarks drily, as they pull away from the station, waved off by a gaggle of kids.

'Are you pissed off about Auntie Rosa?'

'No skin off my nose. Not sure what the point is though.'

Rosa's ahead, with Tim and Jimmy aboard her Landcruiser. Two Bob and Riley are bringing up the rear in the Hilux. It's the first time Andy and Dancer have been alone. 'You're gunna have some explainin' to do to your brother when you finally get back to Broome. You wouldn't believe how cranky he is to be missin' this. I had to make sure he hadn't stowed away.'

Andy splutters when Dancer explains about his number one horse. After being brought up to date on family news from Broome, Dancer asks, 'Any word on the bikies?'

'I've given 'em a down payment.' Andy drums the wheel fiercely. 'I'm not takin' it lyin' down though. I'm sort of hopeful they might finish up decidin' Broome's not a good town for 'em to do business.'

'Meaning?'

'Don't ask.'

'Dad?!'

'Don't worry. I haven't done anythin' silly. An' I'm not takin' any chances. They'll get their fucken money from me, the scum.'

'How?'

'Dunno yet.'

'There's something I should tell you,' Dancer says sheepishly.

'Yeah?'

'I, um … let slip about the bikies.'

'You what!'

'It was just Grandpa – and Riley was there. It just sort of came out one night.' He is starting to babble because he is embarrassed. 'It won't matter, no-one back in Broome'll find out. There's no way —'

Andy holds up a hand to cut him off. 'What's done's done. I'll have a word to Two Bob about keepin' shtoom.' He changes the topic. 'So how's it been?'

Dancer breathes a sigh of relief. 'Mostly good. I've been getting to know Auntie Rosa a bit. I really like her.'

'She was away down south when I was hangin' round up here.'

'Yeah, she said. Her and Mum more or less grew up together.'

'Mmm. Any stories for me?'

'Don't think I'll be looking for a job as a ringer anytime soon.' This gets a laugh. 'Lots of stories, Dad. Maybe too many. I'm sort of thinking let's just do this ride, and then do all the talking when we're driving back home ... Is that all right?'

Andy takes his eyes off the track long enough to look at his son for a couple of moments. 'Yeah, that's all right. Prob'ly a good call in fact.'

⚬

'Bullfrog Hole. Remember it?'

'Of course,' Dancer murmurs.

'There's been a bit of water under the bridge since last time we were here,' Andy says as he eases the truck to a halt where Tim is indicating. 'Come on then, we better get these horses offloaded.'

The Rider mob have pressed on ahead and got on with the preparations. They have half the horses unloaded and clipped to a tether rope rigged between a couple of sturdy trees by the time they hear Two Bob's Hilux approaching. He cuts his engine at a good distance. Dancer glances up and sees Riley almost burst out of the car, bouncing with energy and excitement. Two Bob waves him down, they talk briefly, and Riley heads down to the waterhole. The old man doesn't want all that buzz around the horses.

Two Bob stays in his car, watching. Once all the horses are settled Dancer wanders over and climbs in beside his grandfather. 'Thought you'd be checking the horses out.'

'You lot got it covered. I'm just havin' a bit of a think, jaminyi. Got a big story to tell tonight.'

'Everybody's waiting.'

'Yuw.' He taps his nose with a long forefinger, and tries a grin, but the unease shows. He changes the subject. 'Look at your dad an' Jimmy.' The two are deep in conversation as Andy inspects Falcon. Jimmy looks up at the sun, nods, and leaves Andy with the horse. In a few moments he is on his way back with a saddle and all the accoutrements.

'Told you,' Two Bob says, and this time the smile is real. They wait until Andy has trotted off on Falcon before they join the others.

◆

There is half an hour of daylight left when the unpacking and camp chores are completed. Andy is not back yet. Dancer slips away and heads down to the waterhole, hoping for some solitude, but Riley is there, sitting on the sand, singing. Dancer sits beside him. Riley finishes the song before he turns to Dancer. 'This your Unggurr place eh?'

'This is my Unggurr place.'

Riley bounces to his feet. 'Mine down thataway. Where we're goin'.' He lip-points to the south, then prances off. Dancer eases himself into a more comfortable position as he gazes over the waterhole. It is as beautiful as the memory he has held these last three years. It is a bigger river than the one back near Highlands; wider, deeper, still in the evening light. Even the birds are quiet for the moment.

'*Your mother dreamed you here, before you were born. Bunuba way, that means you were runnin' round this place when you were a spirit child.*'

Without looking down, he sifts through the sand until he finds a stone of the right weight. He rubs it under his armpits, then tosses it into the water. He feels a flash of resentment, wishing that everyone else would disappear so he could just sit and absorb this place, and feel his connection to it. But he knows now is not the time.

Yesterday, waiting for Andy to arrive, he'd finally decided to stay silent about Riley's drawings, and their strange encounter. It wasn't just because of the promise he'd given so uneasily. He feels overloaded with stories, confidences and unresolved tensions. With so many different agendas and memories swirling around this journey, he finished up figuring it was better for him, and probably for Andy, if he kept his own counsel and waited for things to unfold. There is no way he could tell Andy the story without freaking him out.

But that did not stop him feeling like a traitor as they drove past Unggulala today on the way here, fighting off memories of that terrible portrait, and saying nothing to his father.

The light is all but gone when he gets to his feet.

48

'I dunno how long this story gunna take, we're supposed to be makin' early start in the mornin'.'

They are all gathered in a circle except for Riley, who prowls the outskirts of the firelight behind them. Two Bob eases himself into his tale. 'Where we sittin' now, Bullfrog Hole, I call him no-man's-land. Bunuba word is different. Malayi. That means shared country. He's little bit Ngarinyin, little bit Andinyin, little bit Bunuba. Proper Ngarinyin that way, back Highlands side. Proper Bunuba down that way. Proper Andinyin over there. But here, he's mixed up. Malayi. Where we goin' tomorrer, that's gettin' more on proper Bunuba side.

'An' that's my true country. Me an' Riley. Not that native title way. My mummy was proper Bunuba, but her really country, that's down Fish Creek side, more longa Fitzroy way. I mean our born country. Where we born. Where we been grow. Me. My brother Bob. Riley. Nobody knows that country now, 'cept me an' Riley. Nobody belongs that country now, 'cept me an' Riley. An' my jaminyi, Dancer.

'This story starts long time. Olden days. Jandamarra time. Where we goin', that was his secret hideout place, where no whitefeller, no policeman, no black tracker ever been find him. His secret place. An' still today, no road, no track, nothin' goin' in there.

'Those early days now, ol' Jandamarra, one of his main men was a feller called Marralam. They been put him in jail for long time. When he got out, Jandamarra was finish. No Bunuba people still livin' old way. All slavin' away on the stations.

'That Marralam, he made a promise never to live under the white man. When he got out from jail, he remembered this valley. He been grab his wife back from Fish Creek, and he been come to this place. He been live there rest of his life, away from the white man, away from the stations. Ol' Marralam was uncle for my mummy.'

He pauses to roll a smoke. His audience waits.

'My daddy was a white man. His name was Charlie Walker.'

He catches the look, the little nod from Tim to Rosa.

'That's right, Tim. Bob an' Two Bob. Janga an' Wajarri. Born together from a black mummy an' a white daddy. Proper mixed up buggers us two. Born down there in the valley.'

He tells them the story of the killing of Twelve Inch. Of his parents' flight. Of the sanctuary they found with Marralam. Of the terrible fear they had of the killing being discovered, of punishment for Billy's crime, of being separated. Of their love. Of Sarah. Of the fear compounded and multiplied when he and Bob were born. Of the awful certainty that they would be torn asunder if ever they were discovered.

They have all sat through Two Bob's yarns at other fires, some of them more times than they could count. But tonight there is none of his stock-in-trade of wry humour, and nod-and-a-wink exaggeration. These tellings are dredged, wrestled from a place deep within. Each memory, each detail, has to break free of the chains with which he has bound it for decades. The anguish of revelation is writ in his voice and his body.

He tells them the story of the deal done between his father and Stumpy Maclean, with an aside to Rosa, reminding her that he wasn't humbugging when he told her about all the bullamon down there.

He omits the story of the chaining of Janga, talking only of an almighty argument between Janga and their father that led to Janga's flight to Highlands.

'You gotta understand,' he says. 'Us mob, our whole life been secret. Hidin'. Janga, he was wild when he been take off. But that didn't mean he could give away that secret. That's why he been give you Highlands mob different story.

'I couldn't stop behind without my brother. He been call me with a dream. An' I been foller him. To Highlands. But me too, I couldn't give away that secret. Liar ones, that's us two.'

He waves his empty pannikin, and Riley comes running to take it for a top-up. Rosa is the first to break the silence. 'How much of this did Auntie Marj know?'

Two Bob rolls up another smoke. Waits for his top-up. Takes a slow sip. Lights up. 'Nothin', for long time.'

'Bullshit! Can't be.'

'No, nothin' bullshit, Rosa. Me an' her, we had our own way. We worked things out between us. Bob the one been tell her first, when they been drivin' round the country doin' that Land Council politics ... She had most of that story by the end.'

He relights his rollie, waiting.

Dancer can't hold back. 'What about Riley?'

After delivering the tea and putting another log on the fire, Riley has sat down in the fireshadow cast by Two Bob, half hidden, knees clasped to his chest, feet touching Two Bob. He does not move, does not react.

'Jinda?' Tim asks.

'You gottim again, Tim. Jenny Jinda. Sarah's girl.'

'An' you brought her back here?' Tim says. 'I'll be buggered.'

'I brought her back.'

'The coppers thought that whitefeller must've killed her and dumped the body.'

'He near enough did kill her. I wish they'd charged him. But I brought her back. An' then Riley was born.'

He tells them of the years he spent keeping his family alive, carting in stores bought with Billy's gold, salting the killers. Of the deaths; Jenny Jinda, Parli, Bessie. Of the stubborn refusal of Billy and Sarah to contemplate coming out. Of the love they showered on Riley. Of the desperate impossibility of knowing what to do. Of the smoke signal. Of mourning for Sarah. Of walking out with Riley on his shoulders, leaving his father behind.

It is only when he finally runs out of words that they realise Riley is humming a song, barely audible, as he rocks back and forth.

Eventually a dingo howls.

'You used to take Milly in there hey?' Rosa asks.

'Coupla times,' he affirms.

'And what —'

Two Bob holds up a hand to cut her off. 'I got no more words left in me tonight.' Riley is by his side, helping him to rise, ushering him to his swag. 'Early start tomorrer,' he reminds them as he subsides into it.

Looks are exchanged across the flicker of fire. But no-one speaks.

49

Hardly a word is spoken as they get themselves and the horses organised. There is no sign of Riley. Two Bob tells Dancer he's started walking. 'He'll be waitin' for us.'

Tim and Jimmy watch them head off, and settle in for a few days of fishing. Two Bob leads the way, with the string of packhorses and the spares following. Rosa and Dancer fan out on either side a few lengths behind him, each content to pursue their own thoughts for now. Falcon is champing at the bit, trying to convince Andy to let him run.

It is not long before Two Bob picks a path from the open plain down towards the river, finds a gentle gradient, and leads his team into a dry section of the riverbed. Soon they are across and up the other side, heading upstream along the south bank, past a round hillock covered in spinifex.

They are on undulating ground swelling up towards a range that parallels the river. The range is tall, and steep. Rugged, somehow forbidding. Two Bob angles across the undulations towards a rocky point where river and range both turn to the south. It is slow going as the ground underfoot becomes rockier and less even. They have to let the horses pick a path, step by step. Dancer imagines Riley skipping across this ground at twice the pace they are managing.

Once they have rounded the point, the country ahead smooths out, sloping evenly down towards the river on their left. The range begins to resolve itself into a sharper shape; a scree slope rising steeply to the base of a cliff that stretches into the distance. Just before the cliff starts there is a notch in the skyline of the range.

The four riders have drawn together. Only when they are almost upon it does it become apparent that the notch in the skyline is at the top of a narrow defile that cuts through the range. Riley is sitting on a boulder at the foot of the ravine. Two Bob signals a halt. Eases himself off Nellie, and hands the reins to Dancer. He walks to where he can face up into the ravine, standing on the bank of the creek emerging from it. He cups his hands to his mouth.

'Waliyooooo ...'

His call trails away, then begins to echo off the rocks. A mob of startled shorthorns bursts out of the trees, galloping towards the river.

Riley stokes a fire while billy, pannikins and the makings are extracted from packs. Once the horses are tethered Dancer and Andy walk to the ravine. The late morning sun is high enough to throw good light into the slash in the range. It opens up slightly, a hundred yards in, to a small bowl with a grove of bauhinia trees and spindly white gums reaching for the light. It seems to be a dead-end, but shifting to another angle, Dancer thinks he can see the gorge continue, angling up behind a house-sized boulder.

'We're supposed to ride up there?' he asks disbelievingly.

'We'll be leadin' the horses, not ridin' 'em,' Andy answers. 'Look.' He points to the grey groove of a cattle pad winding through the spinifex. 'Bullamon can get up an' down. We'll make it.'

Two Bob has come up to join them. 'No cattle pad like that olden days. We had bush gate up there to block 'em in. All driftwood an' that kind.'

'An' you used to bring a mob down through here every year?' Andy asks.

'Every year. Nice cattle too. We worked 'em every year up there in the valley. Make 'em quiet. Ol' Stumpy reckoned they made the best coachers in the Kimberley.'

Andy lets out a low whistle. 'Bugger me, lambara. What a fucken story!'

⌀

Two Bob tells them to have something to eat with their tea. 'We'll be halfway up that climb proper dinnertime. Nice little waterhole not far when we get up the top. We'll make early camp there.' Rosa digs out a packet of dried fruit and nuts to top off the damper and jam. Whilst they eat, Two Bob gives his orders.

The ascent is a hard, hard slog, but remarkably trouble-free. One little jump-up causes Buddy to scramble. Dancer helps Two Bob cajole Nellie and the string past this hurdle, but the horses are all willing; they want to be out of this gorge as much as the humans do. The loads all hold on the packhorses. He is starting to appreciate just how well Tim and Two Bob have prepared the animals and the gear for this trek.

His attention is focused on the trail ahead; choosing his footsteps, making sure he does not stumble and jerk Buddy's lead rope. The gorge has opened up a little, and the creek is now well below the track. He doesn't really notice the lessening in the gradient. The downward steps are just another dip in the trail.

'Oi.'

He looks up at the soft call from Riley. Blinks. Looks again. The majesty of the country almost undoes him. He is at the high point of a plateau that unfolds into the distance. The creek – it seems too insignificant to have cut a path through the mighty range at his back – is down below to his left. A glimpse of water, glinting with reflected sunlight, indicates a pool. Diverging treelines show that it sits at a junction. In a line of sight beyond the pool is a magnificent bluff that commands the landscape.

The smaller tributary winds down from the east. But his eye is drawn to the south. The plateau slopes gently down, gradually narrowing to become the floor of a valley that spears in a straight line into the distance, hemmed on either side. The right wall is

219

a fierce looking tumble of jagged rock. The left wall, from its beginning at the bluff, is a sheer red cliff, just starting to pick up the rich light of the westering sun.

Jiir, jiir.

Dancer looks up to see the pair of white-bellied eagles spiralling on a downdraft.

⚬

By the time they reach camp at the pool on the creek bend, Two Bob has almost seized up. He has to call Riley over to help take his weight as he eases himself gingerly out of the saddle, clutching at that calf again. Despite his protestations Rosa takes charge, settling him in the shade, checking pulse and temperature, whilst Riley hovers.

Dancer and Andy are left to deal with the business of unpacking and unsaddling the horses, leading them down in pairs to drink, and finally hobbling them out. Rosa has grabbed her medical kit as soon as it was unloaded and given Two Bob some Panadol and salt tablets, and they can see that he is starting to pick up. She comes over to join them as they watch the horses slowly disperse, nickering to each other as they forage. She turns a full circle, drinking in the country with her eyes. 'What a place! I like the look of this country of yours, Dancer.'

With her words he gets a surge of feeling rising from his guts into his chest that has him standing taller, straighter, as a slow smile spreads across his face.

⚬

Two Bob insists he is fine, tomorrow will be easy, nice steady going. Riley has smuggled some sheets from the sketchpad into the packs, and sits off to one side a bit doodling patterns. Once he has some tea to sip on, Two Bob talks them through the geography of the valley and the plan for tomorrow while the others prepare and cook supper.

From that bluff, to the south and the east it is all proper rocky ranges country going on forever, he explains. 'No good for horse, no good for bullamon. Only goanna an' hill kangaroo, an' olden days footwalkin' blackfeller. Ol' Jandamarra used to come up through there to get away from police mob. Nobody couldn't track him.'

He points to the east, 'That creek comin' down, he don't go far. Might be three miles.' They used to block the pass in the range there, keep their bullamon here in the valley. There's an old foot track through the bottom side of Highlands, up into the old outlaw country, through to Halls Creek, Wyndham, anywhere. 'I been walk that road one time.'

He swivels to point to the jagged range forming the west wall, 'Other side them rocks, that big river cuts through, where he swings round down from Bullfrog Hole. Biggest gorge. Then he opens up into station country.'

A half-turn this time. He lifts his shoulders and sits straighter as he points to the south. 'That big valley, that's our really home. He runs riiight down, straight down, till he finish up in them ranges.' They won't be going right to the end of the valley. Somewhere past there was his father's gold place. His old camp is about two thirds of the way down, 'But you won't see him, even if you lookin'.' If they get away early and everything goes smoothly, they can be there by midafternoon.

He tells Andy to be sure to keep a count on the cattle that he sees. 'But if you an' Falcon are out ahead, when you come up to where there's two big boab trees together on west side, you gotta pull up there an' wait.' He looks over at Riley, who is listening without watching. 'Riley been ask me for somethin'. He wants to go in first. Just him, an' Dancer. The rest of us gotta come behind way little bit. He didn't say why. He just been ask me for that.'

It is a quiet supper. They are finished and washed up before it is dark. Dancer and Andy pack away everything except the thin swags and the makings for tea and a cold breakfast. Riley has drawn until it is too dark to see, but now they can sense him watching them in the torchlight as they move about stowing gear in saddlebags, tightening straps. The boyish bounce has gone; there is a stillness about Riley this evening.

'Big day tomorrer,' Andy murmurs.

They all find a spot for their swags, as flat and as sandy as they can.

'I feel like I've earned my sleep tonight,' Rosa says softly, to no-one in particular.

'You've done good, girl,' Two Bob answers.

It is not long before Andy is snoring, and Dancer can sense from their even breathing that Two Bob and Rosa have drifted off. But sleep is slow to come to him tonight. And he can hear Riley prowling.

50

Most of the cattle they see are on the move, disturbed by Andy up ahead, but there seem to be plenty. Each time Andy circles back he updates Two Bob and Rosa. Rosa is impressed. 'Too much,' reckons Two Bob. 'Ol' days we managed 'em proper. Kep' the country better – more grass.'

'We'll just have to clean 'em out next year eh,' Andy grins, with a wink for Rosa. 'Come on boy,' he flicks the reins and wheels Falcon off again at a brisk canter.

Rosa laughs. 'He's enjoying himself, your old man.'

'Isn't he,' Dancer acknowledges. But he is only half paying attention. He is watching the country. Watching, listening, absorbing. And thinking about what is to come.

A bit earlier in the day Two Bob had signalled him closer. They rode beside each other for a few minutes. Eventually the old man spoke. 'That Riley, he never asks for nothin' ... That's not his style.'

'You talking about him wanting me to go in front with him?'

'Yuw.' They rode on a bit more. 'I gotta make sure you're clear on somethin' ...'

'What's that?'

'When Daddy sent up that smoke signal, an' I came in here to get Riley ... I had no horse that time. Just footwalk, with him on my shoulders most of the way, all the way back to Bullfrog Hole. Daddy, he was sick, proper sick. An' proper old. He wouldn't come. Dancer, there was no-one left behind to bury him.'

'You never came back?'

Two Bob doesn't answer, instead he asks, 'You right to go in front with Riley?'

'If that's what he wants.'

~&~

The sun is still high when Dancer spots the twin boabs. They've made good progress on the open, even ground. Riley, with his rhythmic, ground-swallowing gait, has stayed well ahead of them though.

Andy looks relaxed, back resting against the smaller of the boabs. Falcon is the first to spot them approaching. He turns and lifts his head inquisitively. They see Andy get to his feet, alerted by the horse's movement. He waves, and goes over to soothe the horse.

The second boab is a monster, nearly the size of the giant back at Highlands. It has multiple trunks, one of which lies parallel to the ground. It is not until they are almost there that they spot Riley as he springs down from his perch on the trunk.

51

The faint path veers right, but three steps to the left on the trackless granite, a different, hidden path beckons. Riley does not hesitate, despite the years. Coming from the south the opening would've been easy to spot, but until Riley ducks around the boulder, Dancer has no idea there is a break in the rockface.

The afternoon sun is warm as they make their way beneath the looming overhang, but the morning cold lingers in the shadowy depths. Dancer glimpses desiccated animal bones, but Riley's quick tread allows no close examination, and before he knows it the vista opens on a small glistening valley enclosed on all sides.

The cousins halt as one, hands touching featherishly. Riley, slight and dark. Dancer, heavy-set and gangling all at once, yellow more than brown, like an adder asleep in the sun. The skeleton of the hut is weathered grey beneath the reds and browns of the cliff. The rusted sheets of iron lie amongst the green vegetation like twisted flakes from the rockface. As their eyes sweep across the stark remains, they both see the bones. They hesitate only a moment.

The bones lie with arms folded, at peace. The flesh had withered before the hut's walls had crumbled, before dingoes or other predators could disturb the remains. Riley shows no fear, even when the skull falls apart at his touch. He merely steps back.

This is my great-grandfather.

At the foot of the bed is an ancient tin trunk. With the lightest of nudges, Riley elbows Dancer forward. 'That his treasure box.'

Riley's whisper is insistent. 'Go on.'

Dancer carefully removes the two smooth stones weighing down the lid. As he reaches out to touch it, the disintegrating skull fills his mind's eye. He eases the lid open, amazed at how readily it comes free.

A parcel wrapped in oilcloth sits at the top. Dancer gently unwraps it. He senses Riley step closer, feels his cousin's breath on his shoulder.

There are two pouches of worn leather. He can't help a small smile as he realises that each is made from the balls sac of an old-man kangaroo. Carefully he lifts them, and holds them up. Riley reaches over to take them.

Bending close, Dancer can just make out the pencilled scrawl on the top page of the fragile, yellowed papers: *The Last Will & Testament of William Noakes.*

52

Dancer kneels before the trunk, staring at the will, unable to think.

Eventually he places the papers gently back in the oilcloth and carefully rewraps them. He lays the parcel on the ground beside him.

He peers into the trunk again. There is another cloth-wrapped bundle. He feels it gingerly, tests its weight. More papers, he guesses. An ancient looking locket, the silver case and chain tarnished dark. These are resting on a cotton dress of faded red; it looks fragile enough to crumble at a touch. A handful of books. The one on top is just a bundle of pages tied together with two ribbons. On the worn cover, indents with just a trace of the original embossing seem to indicate it is *Robinson Crusoe*.

He closes the lid of the trunk. He picks up the parcel with the will, joins Riley outside the remains of the hut.

'You lived here?' Dancer looks at Riley.

'Yuw. Little one.'

'D'you remember?'

'I remember. I know that treasure box for Poppy Pop eh.'

'True. Poppy Pop?'

'That his name belongin' to me. He been say I can't call him Poppy, like Grandpa, you know, because he more older'n that. He father for Nanna Sarah. So I been call him Poppy Pop. Make him laugh.'

'What else do you remember?'

Riley points. 'Camp for me and Nanna Sarah.' Dancer can just make out the traces; little more than the ant-eaten stumps of corner posts. 'Not flash like Poppy Pop, only bark roof. We been go inside his camp big rain time.'

Riley starts walking. Dancer can see the bulges of the leather pouches in his pockets. He stops near the foot of the cliff, in the shade of a fig tree, looks about in the undergrowth until he locates a mound. 'Nanna Sarah. Poppy Pop been bury her here, then Two Bob been come for me.' He pulls vines away from another mound. 'Look. That one Nanna Nan, from before me. See, I remember. Come on.'

Riley seems almost jaunty as he takes Dancer on a tour. Back past the skeleton hut to the creek. 'Ol' veggie garden,' he says kicking at some rusted fragments of chicken wire. As they cross the creek Dancer can see the remnants of a stone wall that must have once created a small dam. Up over the other side to where some old pickets and other detritus suggest former usage. 'Ol' Camp. Nanna Sarah used to be, before she come back to Poppy Pop side.'

He points upstream, 'That way Jaliwala. I remember Jaliwala. He got a song. Come on.'

'Hang on, Riley, here come the other lot.'

53

On the other side of the small valley, beyond the Old Camp, there is an overhang like the one at the valley's entrance, but deeper, and taller. It is too open, too full of light to be a cave, but it's an almost perfect natural shelter.

Rosa has supper cooking, and has just distributed teas, calling up Riley, who's been engrossed with something down by the creek. Two Bob blows on his pannikin, takes a sip, then lights up a rollie. 'This is where Jandamarra been camp, long time. An' ol' Marralam when he first been come back here, before he make that Ol' Camp. My old man the one been make that new camp, other side creek.'

No-one had wanted to make camp over that side.

Two Bob has said very little until now. He'd been at the lead walking the horses in. He'd dropped the reins, walked to the skeleton hut and removed his hat, then stood there for a long, long minute. Since then he seems to have been lost in his thoughts.

Riley repeated his tour for Andy and Rosa. Two Bob did pipe up when he wanted to take them to Jaliwala. 'Tomorrer, Riley. Tomorrer.' As they'd gone about the business of unloading and sorting the horses Dancer, Rosa and Andy said little, but each time one caught another's eye, they would share a sense of disbelief. Disbelief that this place is. That it could've been. That barely twenty years ago Riley lived here with a Nanna and a Poppy Pop. That Two Bob has carried such a secret.

Now Two Bob's words cause the three of them to take another look around the shelter. To think that Jandamarra had ... that they are sharing this space with him.

'Woorroooh.' Rosa's voice resonates from the walls.

Andy shivers.

Dancer places a hand on the dry, dusty ground, cups the hand over his mouth and nose, and breathes in the smell.

For a few minutes there is nothing but Two Bob smoking his cigarette, watching his exhalations drift upwards. Until he stubs out the butt on the tin, and puts it in his top pocket. Just as Dancer is about to speak, Rosa breaks the silence. 'I've been thinking, Uncle. In the morning we should bury your father with the others.'

'Yuw.' The answer is emphatic. He gets up and moves the few paces to the fire to deposit the cigarette butt, and on his way back to his spot bends to place a hand on Rosa's shoulder in a gesture of thanks. Once Two Bob is seated again Dancer speaks.

'Grandpa, Riley got me to open the treasure box.'

'Whha?'

'That tin trunk, next to his bed.'

Two Bob is flummoxed. 'What for?'

'I don't know why. He just asked me.'

He reaches behind, feels for the oilskin package he has put in his swag, tries to pass it to Two Bob. But the old man is reluctant to take it.

'What now?'

'It's a will, Grandpa. Poppy Pop's – William Noakes' will.'

'Oh fuck me.' Two Bob is panting. This wasn't part of his plan. 'What he say?'

'I don't know. I haven't read it.'

'Read him.' His voice is almost panicky. 'Read him. Read him.'

Dancer looks around. Riley is listening, but not watching. If Rosa and Andy had seats, they would be on the edges. Both are leaning forward, hands clasping ankles, intent. They each give him a small nod.

Once again he unwraps the oilskin. His hands are trembling. 'This paper's so dry. It feels like it's going to fall to bits. Hang on.'

He puts down the sheets on the open oilskin, opens his swag and stretches out, propped on his elbows, so that he can read without holding the paper.

'*The Last Will & Testament of William Noakes,*' he reads. 'It's in pencil. It's so faint.' He glances up at the sky beyond the shelter. The light is starting to fade. 'Rosa, you've got the best torch.'

She springs up and grabs it from beside the fire. 'Hang on,' she calls. 'This tucker's going to burn.' She pulls the pair of billies off the coals. Dinner can wait. Careful not to tread on the oilskin, she flicks the torch on and passes it to Dancer. He turns the cover page over. He has to pause a number of times to decipher the faded writing. But the others wait, perfectly still and silent, until he finishes.

'*My name, my true name, is William Noakes.*

'*I have also used at times the name Charlie Walker.*

'*I was born in the Nullagine goldfield in the year of 1900. Mother Mary Noakes, boarding house proprietress. Father Rudolph Noakes, mining engineer and prospector.*

'*I assert that I am the rightful owner of pastoral lease number 1836/98 in the District of Omalinde, known to me as Maryvale. The lease papers and my agreement, in the name of Charlie Walker, with the late Stumpy Maclean are herewith enclosed. I am led to understand that Mr Maclean died at war, in the service of his country.*

'*I know not what may have become of this lease in the offices of the Lands Department in far-off Perth, as I have not been in a position to pay the annual rental since the disappearance of Mr Maclean so many years ago.*

'*But let me say that no other person has shown themselves on this place to make a claim upon it. And I do hereby assert by right of the original lease, and by right of my continuing occupation, my ownership of this land.*'

There is a collective intake and release of breath as Dancer turns to the next page.

'I cannot follow all that my son Othello tells me of the world beyond, but gather many things have changed, and that the natives may now hold their own lands. I pray it be so.

'And if this prayer be answered, I do hereby bequeath this property to my son, Othello Noakes, whom I am led to believe is known in the wider world as Two Bob Walker, he being one of a pair of twin boys born here on Maryvale, before it had that name, in the year, I think, of 1929.

'As of the date of writing, I know him to be alive and well, residing upon Highlands Station, formerly owned by the above named Stumpy Maclean.

'I beg of Othello, if ever this be read to him, to care for his grand-nephew, Riley Noakes, and hope that he may see fit to one day let Riley take the title.

'I have no Executor. I know not when, or if, this document may be found, nor by whom. Yet I also ask and pray, that if perchance Othello has passed, and young Riley has attained his majority, my bequest pass to him.

'I bequeath also, to Riley, the contents of the pouches enclosed with this document. The small collection of yellow nuggets and flakes will no doubt be easily recognised. The clearish stones may be of no value, but when I chanced upon them I was reminded of mother's diamond engagement ring.

'If neither Othello nor Riley are positioned to accept this bequest
...

'Then I do not care.

'I know not the date, and am uncertain even of the year.

'Alas, I have no witness, but I append my signature.

'William Noakes.'

54

There are more papers. The others wait, still silent, as Dancer holds the torch close to examine the next page. 'I can't read it. Too faded. Fuck ... *in trust*, I think ... that might be *Maryvale* ... and signatures, might be.'

He gives up and lays the sheet with the will. The last document is on a heavier, parchment type paper, the ink faded but clear, in a fancy old font. Dancer grins. 'It's the lease paper for Maryvale.'

He rolls out of his lying position, sits up and looks at Two Bob. His grandfather takes off his hat, scratches his head.

'Bugger me,' is all Two Bob can say as he reaches for his tobacco tin.

Rosa gets to her feet, speechless, as she stirs up the coals and puts the billies back on the fire. Riley disappears for a moment, then is back with two sheets from the sketchpad. He smooths them out as well as he can on the ground next to the oilskin.

He pulls one of the pouches from a pocket. Loosens the leather thong. Gently pours the contents onto the first sheet of paper. A tobacco tin's worth of flecks and flakes and small nuggets gleam yellow in the light of the torch. He pulls the other pouch from the other pocket. Repeats the process. A dozen small clear stones tumble out.

Andy reaches out, takes the largest of them, sits it in the palm of his hand. Dancer shines the torch on it. 'Quartz?' Andy wonders. 'It's all over these hills.'

'Ol' man liked lookin' at rocks,' says Two Bob. 'Specially that quartz. I remember him always pickin' it up, holdin' it up to the sun, lookin' close. Must be some reason he hung on to this lot.

Somethin' different.'

'Hey lambara, you're a station owner. Boss of Maryvale! Rosa'll have to pay you for all these bullamon now.'

'Can't be. That lease must be finished up long time now.'

Andy's jest has broken the spell, unleashing a torrent of questions and speculations.

How much would that gold be worth?

Where would they get the maybe diamonds tested?

Is there any chance Two Bob would have a case for the Maryvale lease?

There must be some kind of place in Perth for looking at old papers that can make out what that agreement with Stumpy says, mustn't there?

Riley ignores it all. He carefully folds each sheet of paper into a vee, and empties the contents back into the respective pouches, gets his torch, then disappears.

The flurry of questions is left hanging in the still night air.

55

Dancer wakes with fragments of yesterday's events tumbling through his mind in an overwhelming jumble. He rolls onto his back and opens his eyes. He can just make out the arching rock of the overhang above him, and he finds his mind settling on thoughts of Jandamarra. Of sleeping and eating and being with family here, in the same space the great warrior once inhabited. Nothing seems quite real.

He hears Two Bob stirring, and climbs out of his swag to wait in the mouth of the shelter. 'Eh jaminyi, good morning,' Dancer says, turning to greet him.

The smile on his grandfather's face makes his heart dance. It is not lost on either of them that this is the first time he has used the reciprocal term. Two Bob embraces him in a fierce hug. 'Wulyu gumanda, jaminyi,' he whispers. They sit watching the outlines of the small valley beginning to emerge from the pre-dawn gloom.

'Is it good to come home?' Dancer asks.

'Not yet,' is the cryptic answer. Two Bob gets up. 'I'm gunna find a shovel over there. I know where he always put 'em. Might be white ants got the handle by now but better than nothin.'' He holds up a hand when Dancer starts to get up. 'I might just poke round little bit meself eh.'

'No worries.' He watches the old man walk stiffly down the slope, pausing for a few moments to inspect the Old Camp. Then Dancer starts looking around for kindling.

◦

They've finished breakfast and are on their second cup of tea by the time they see Two Bob making his way up the slope. Riley seems to be still asleep, but as soon as Two Bob joins the others, he sits up in his swag. The others pay no attention to his rustlings and bustlings until he calls, 'Oi.'

He indicates to each of them where to sit: Rosa, Dancer and Andy in a row opposite him, with his swag in between them, Two Bob beside him. He is trying to be solemn, but can't quite control the twitching at the corners of his mouth. With great ceremony, he pulls the flap of the swag back. There are three folded sheets of paper. He looks at Dancer. 'That milli milli for Poppy Pop, he says that gold and them stones belongin' to me, right?'

'Yeah.'

He looks across at Two Bob for confirmation. 'Yuwai.'

From between the folds of the first sheet he slides out one of the ball sac pouches, empty. He opens the fold of the paper, revealing a small mound of gold and four stones. Like last night, he uses the vee to pour them into the pouch, then places the pouch on the centre of the sheet, obscuring a drawing.

He repeats the procedure for the second sheet, four stones and a small mound of gold the same size as the first. For the third sheet there is no pouch. Instead he uses the bandanna that is normally tied around his neck.

'Rider.' He slides the first pouch towards Rosa, revealing the drawing. One side of the fold is Rosa and Tim on horseback. On the other side Rosa is handing a cartoon style bag of money with a dollar sign to a man with glasses wearing shorts and long socks.

'Dancer.' He slides the second pouch towards Andy. On one side Dancer is dancing the junba. On the other Andy is watching two motorbikes disappear, one rider holding a dollars bag.

'Walker.' He passes his bandanna to Two Bob. The first picture shows him and Two Bob walking in the bush. The second is another shorts-and-long-socks man with a bag of money. Riley and Two Bob are standing in front of a big dual-cab four-wheel drive.

With a single movement he bounces to his feet. 'That torch got no more battery!' And then he is gone. He stops short of the Old Camp, cups his hands to his mouth and calls, 'Thank you, Poppy Pop. Thank you.' He turns upstream, heading for Jaliwala.

'Bugger me,' says Two Bob.

Rosa reaches out and picks up her drawing. 'Is that what I think it is?'

'It's your rents and rates Rosa,' Andy confirms. 'You should get some change.'

'And that?' Rosa asks, pointing at Dancer's picture.

'Tell you later,' says Andy. There are tears rolling down his cheeks.

56

Using a shovel blade like a trowel, Andy and Dancer take turns to hack out a small grave. Rosa goes back and forth to the creek with a canteen bringing water to soften the ground, and helps Two Bob with clearing fig litter and vines from around Bessie's and Sarah's graves. When the work is done they share a drink from the canteen before walking together up to the remains of the hut.

'Should I go look for Riley?' Dancer asks.

'Not yet,' Two Bob answers.

He picks up his swag cover, takes a deep breath, steps across the threshold. He kneels, smooths the canvas out. Bone by bone, he places the skeleton on the swag. Some break as he picks them up. He doesn't react, just gathers the fragments and puts them with the bones. Finally only the crumbled skull remains. Piece by piece it is placed in the canvas.

He puts his hands in the small of his back and straightens for a few moments. He does a final inspection of the bed, finds two more small pieces of bone, which join the rest. He folds the canvas over, then gently, carefully, rolls it up. The others can see his shoulders trembling as he stands with his back to them.

Two Bob leads the procession back to the fig tree, and tenderly lays the swag roll into the hole. Kneeling by the grave he asks, 'Anybody want to say somethin'?'

They all shake their heads. He stands up and steps back. Rosa keens softly as Dancer and Riley backfill the hole and pat the small mound smooth.

Riley goes to the base of the fig tree and retrieves the flowers he has collected – yellow and red, cotton tree and kurrajong – and arranges them on the mound.

Two Bob is the first to turn. He leads them silently back to their camp in the shelter.

57

'There's somethin' else we've still gotta do.'

There is a weight in the words. As one, Dancer, Rosa and Andy put down their pannikins and turn. Two Bob squeezes Riley's shoulders in a hug, then gets up and steps out of the shelter's shade. He pushes back his weather-beaten akubra, and looks up at a sun just past its zenith and beginning its westerly descent, reckoning.

'Might be enough time if we take off now. These ol' legs of mine are slowin' down, you know. Or we can do it in the mornin'.'

'Enough time for what?' Dancer asks.

'You'll see, young feller.'

They know there is no point in pressing for more. Andy is first to his feet. 'Let's go, lambara. Do we need anythin'?'

'Water bottle might come in handy.'

❧

Two Bob leads them across the creek to the cliff face behind his father's camp. He follows an old footpath along the base of the cliff. It has become tangled with undergrowth from below, and fallen branches from above. Andy steps up to join him. They exchange nods, and Andy takes the lead, and the hard work of clearing the path.

Dancer assumes they are heading to the spring. Andy pulls up at a low call from Two Bob. The five of them gather. He points with his lips. Through the tangled growth they can glimpse the darkness of a small cave, and hear the trickle and splash of water. 'Jaliwala,' says Two Bob. 'Might have to come back tomorrer, eh.

Clean him up little bit.'

To the right of the spring a gully has been carved into the cliff face, the steep slope littered with scree. He puts a hand on Dancer's shoulder, breathing deeply a couple of times, before gesturing again with his lips. 'See that path?'

'Sort of,' Dancer lies.

'I gotta go first, clear the ground for us. Riley, you come last one, behind Rosa. When we level out, you gotta sing. You know what song eh?'

'Yuwai.'

Two Bob gathers himself, pushes aside a low branch, and sets off up the gully. As soon as he comes out into a clear patch of ground, he stands tall, and calls. For a minute or more he talks in Bunuba, loud and strong, to someone or something up there.

He starts to climb again. There is little vegetation on the stony, boulder-strewn slope but the pace is slow. Andy has to pull one big fallen tree branch aside, but otherwise Two Bob leads them, pausing frequently to continue his chanted dialogue with the country.

He stops, leaning against a vertical rockface, his breath fast and shallow as he struggles to regain his poise. One by one the others join him, all gasping at the climb. Dancer is the first to turn and look out. Beneath them lies the small valley, sparkling in the afternoon sun; a timeless speckle of eucalypts and spinifex in greens and yellows, shot through with rocks and patches of pindan.

Two Bob lets them absorb it for a minute as the canteen is passed around, then he gently nudges Riley. In a high treble voice, Riley begins to sing. The sweet lament floating out over the valley both thrills Dancer and sets him on edge.

Two Bob picks his way along a narrow, dusty path clinging to the rockface. Tracks and droppings reveal it as a pad of the rock wallabies. Andy follows a step behind, then Dancer, Rosa and Riley, still singing. Dancer's left hand trails against the cliff face, helping him to keep his bearings on the vertiginous track. He senses a change in the texture of the rock beneath his fingers, glances, gasps. He is stroking a red ochre dingo.

They round a protuberance in the cliff, and Two Bob comes to a halt. The others gather behind him. Riley's song tails away.

⚬

They are at the front of a cave. The height of three men at the mouth, it curves back deep into the rock, narrowing into the darkness in a graceful wavelike shape. The rockface is a profusion of paintings: dingoes, wandjinas, crocodiles, human figures, echidnas, mysteries. But there is no time to examine and absorb. Two Bob leads them into the cave.

He intones. 'Jawandi. Marralam. Grandpa for my sister's man. Uncle for my Mummy.' Dancer's eyes begin to adjust to the gloom, and he sees the bones, stained red with ochre. Beside them, an ancient rifle. 'Fighter for Jandamarra. Countryman.'

The bones lie on a ledge at waist height that sweeps in a curve along the back of the cave. Two steps on, Two Bob comes to another arrangement of bones. 'Nyawurru. Wiyala, wife for Marralam. My big sister Sarah been tell me stories for you. Always makin' her laugh when she was little one.'

They follow him as he steps along. 'An' Nawangari. Parli. Born here too like me. For those two there, your daddy Marralam and mummy Wiyala. Aaiee, poor thing.'

Dancer is gripping Andy's arm. Riley has begun a soft keening that Dancer feels like a scalpel tracing a line on the skin protecting his heart. Two Bob moves to Riley's side, places an arm tight around his shoulders, then inches them forward to the next skeleton.

'Nyambiyindi, Jinda, Jenny girl. Look at your boy ... He's a good one, Jenny. He can sing. He can talk our lingo. Your Mummy Sarah been start him off, then I been grow him up for you. He's a good boy, Jenny.' He whispers in Riley's ear.

The curve of the cave leans back towards the light as Two Bob moves them on again. There is one more set of bones. A beam from the lowering sun picks them out. Andy cries out and steps back, shrugging Dancer off. Two Bob is lost in the ritual as he steps towards them, strokes them. There is a paperbark shroud almost intact around this skeleton. But peeping through, incongruous in this cave of earth colours, is the faded purple of a terry towelling material, with the barely discernible outline of a baby elephant in pale blue.

A fearful intuition sweeps through Dancer, turning his guts to water.

'Nyawajarri. Daughter mine.' Two Bob falls to his knees, oblivious to the others despite his words. 'Milly ... Milly my girl. I been bring 'em. Like I promised ... Your man, your boy! They're good ones, I tell you. Good ones, good ones, good ones.' His voice trails away into quiet sobs.

58

Andy left the cave before Two Bob had finished his crying for Milly. Dancer hovered in the mouth, torn, until Two Bob looked up, and signalled that he should go with Andy. He couldn't catch up until they reached the flatter ground at the foot of the gully. Andy turned, but could find no words. Fighting back tears, he headed on down the path. Dancer dropped back, giving him space but not letting him out of sight. Fear for his father left no room to absorb what he had just seen and heard in the cave.

By the time they reached camp the sun had dropped behind the ranges. Andy set about gathering his gear, stuffing it willy-nilly into his sausage bag. He started to roll his swag, but stopped and knelt there, staring into the distance. He spoke with his back to Dancer. 'If we had a Toyota I'd leave. It's a bit fucken late in the day to catch the horses and pack saddlebags though, isn't it. A bit fucken late in the day.'

Andy turned to face Dancer. 'I don't trust meself, Dancer. I don't know what I'm goin' to do when he shows up.'

'There's got to be a reason, Dad.'

'A reason? For what?'

'For not telling you. For bringing us now.'

'I might do him harm.'

'No, you won't. You wouldn't.'

With a wrenching sob Andy let himself down onto the swag. Dancer could do nothing but come and sit on the ground beside him. Eventually the sobbing eased, Andy's heaving chest subsided to a quiver, and he was able to speak between sniffs. 'I'm sorry, Dancer, sorry ... can't make space for you yet ... your mother, I know. You're her great gift to me ... but you didn't know her.'

He rolled over onto his back, finally meeting Dancer's eye. 'I loved her, man. Those bones up there. I loved her like you wouldn't believe. Like I hope you get to love a girl one day.' With the back of a hand, Andy wiped tears and snot from his face. 'How could he do this to me?'

He reached out to Dancer, placing a hand on his knee. 'We'll talk, eh. But just let me lie here for a bit.'

Dancer got the fire going and set about slicing salt beef and yesterday's damper for dinner. It was full dark, and he'd just taken a pannikin to Andy when he heard the others approaching. He sat by the fire and watched Two Bob limp in, leaning on Riley, with Rosa on his other side. He lip-pointed at Andy, back in the darkness on his swag, raising a hand to indicate they should leave him be.

In silence he handed out pannikins and plates of damper and beef, to Andy on his swag, to Two Bob and Riley by the fire, and to Rosa. She put her plate down and grabbed his arm. Used his weight to pull herself to her feet, and wrapped him in her arms.

When there were no more sounds of eating Two Bob cleared his throat. The four of them by the fire heard the small cough from Andy, and the sound of him sitting up. Two Bob gestured at the fire, and Riley placed a large piece of wood on the coals. They all watched the flames start to grow, licking at the fresh fuel, while Two Bob rolled himself a smoke. After taking a couple of drags, he began to speak, never taking his eyes from the dancing fire.

❧

'Us Walkers've got secrets an' lies in our blood. I'm not sayin' that's a good thing or a bad thing, it's just how we are. We keep things close ... Even Milly. She kep' Riley's secret.

'You're the last one, Dancer. The last one, an' the first one not caught up in the secrets an' lies ... At least not till now.'

'I kep' the secret,' said Riley, head low.

'Riley's the one been find her.' Two Bob glanced nervously in

Andy's direction. They could all hear him shift his position on the swag. Riley began to hum the lament he had sung earlier that day. Two Bob flicked his cigarette into the fire, and shifted in his seat.

'He was only a kid, but Riley kep' lookin', after everyone else been give up. She was high up on Flat Iron Hill. On a ledge lookin' out Bullfrog Hole way ...'

'I been get a dream,' Riley murmured, with a look at Dancer.

A long pause.

'I've gotta talk this story through now, don't I,' says Two Bob.

A gathering of breath.

'Riley went missin' one day. It was nearly dark before I found his track. Me an' Marj set out first light next mornin', follerin' him. He was little kid, an' he been walk right through from Highlands to Unggulala, climb that hill, find her, come back down.

'We been find him walkin' back, poor little bugger. We tried to take him home, but he just been cryin', "Milly, Milly, Milly," till we been turn around.

'Marj couldn't climb up.'

He had to prepare himself before he could continue, but still he choked on the words. 'I had to cut her down from where she was hangin'. Those baby clothes you been see. It was tucked into her bra, close to her heart. She was keepin' you close, Dancer.

'I had to carry her back down the hill to where Marj been waitin'.'

Riley didn't respond to his nudge. Rosa got up and took his pannikin. He rolled another smoke while she topped it up and stirred in the powdered milk.

～❖～

'I didn't know what to do. Marj was the one been say.

'We were thinkin' about that boy Johnny that hanged himself at Snake Springs the year before. Police been take his body away. They been slice up his body, makin' tests and everythin'. Detectives been come. His family couldn't bury him for longest time ... We didn't want 'em slicin' up our Milly, Andy. We didn't want 'em to take her away.

'Riley been fall asleep. We been sittin' there in the motor car bottom of Unggulala. She been look at me an' say, "You reckon she was facin' Bullfrog Hole way?" "Yuw." "Well that's where she can go," Marj been say. "With your mob. Ol' style. We won't tell nobody."

'So ... I found right kind tree, right place, quiet one, there near Unggulala. I made little platform with dead branches, an' we been put her there. Ol' style. We went home to Highlands, never told nobody ... We didn't want 'em slicin' up our Milly.'

He relit and took a few more drags.

'I never told Marj, but I been ring up to Buster, askin' after you, Andy. I didn't tell him 'bout Milly, he didn't know, I swear. But he been tell me you were drinkin' heavy, that you weren't in a good way. I kep' quiet.

'Couple months later Marj had to go Perth for that dialysis. Second one. I reckon she knew she wasn't ever gunna come back. Before she went she said to me, "Take her."

'Only time I ever left Riley till he growed up. I been trick Tim, told him I was goin' with Marj for one week, an' he took Riley. After I been drop Marj in Broome I cut in the back way an' up to Unggulala. Wrap her up. No horse that time. I been walk, carry her to the cave. Put her there.

'I been cryin' too much that time to worry for my daddy. That hut been still standin' then, an' I been walk straight past. I been cryin' too much ... I haven't been back here since then.'

He hurled his butt into the fire.

'Another fucken secret.

'Always. Always I was goin' to tell you, Andy. But I couldn't find right time. Right way. I had to trick you into comin' here before I could tell you.

'Just think if I been tell you this story before ...

'Fucken secrets an' lies. They get a hold of you.'

Sparks soared into the darkness as the fire took hold of a new log.

Andy got up from his swag. He turned and walked into the night.

59

Dancer shakes himself into the new day. He wants to hug his father's sleeping form in the swag a few feet away. He'd fallen asleep in the early hours, still listening for Andy's return. He looks to the fire, and realises that Two Bob is sitting there watching, exactly where he was last night when Dancer crawled into his swag.

'I'm goin' up to Jaliwala. You want to come with me?'

Dancer nods, climbing out of his swag. He grabs a hunk of damper and follows Two Bob.

'You wild at me?'

'Not really. I can see why Dad is, though.'

'Yuwai.'

They walk in silence, listening to the dawn chorus.

'When I hooked up with Andy at Boxwood, he was about same age you are now.'

'He's told me about it. You knew my other grandpa too, hey? Old Joe Black?'

'Only little bit. We put up a mill together one time. Good feller.'

Two Bob starts to sing. He looks at Dancer with a question in his eyes. Dancer nods. Two Bob sings again. Third time round Dancer joins in hesitantly, stumbling over the unfamiliar words. Twice more Two Bob leads him through it, before he breaks off with a smile. 'You'll get him. Riley can teach you.'

They force their way through the dense growth towards the spring. The temperature drops. The birdsong and the sound of water grow stronger together. The pool is less than the size of a house; half in speckled sunlight, half in the deep shadow of the cave. Creepers and low-hanging branches drape into the water. The surface is dappled with leaf litter, some backed up, and some swirling in slow currents. Wrens and bee-eaters swoop and call.

A secret pool full of birds.

Two Bob stoops, and comes up with two pebbles, hands one to Dancer. Talking in language, he rubs his under one armpit, then the other, then tosses it deep towards the rear of the pool. Dancer follows suit.

'I'm a bit buggered up from all that climbin' yesterday. You right to give me a hand on this job, jaminyi?'

'No worries, jaminyi.'

Two Bob pulls a knife from his belt and hands it to Dancer, then sits himself on a water-smoothed rock. He has Dancer wade through the pool, sweeping the thickest of the surface litter to the sides, then scooping it out onto the banks. He tells him to pull the water-rotted deadwood out. At the mouth of the cave Two Bob gets him to work with the knife, cutting back creepers and overhanging branches that are choking the entrance.

As Dancer starts on this task Two Bob asks quietly, 'He right if I talk to you little bit?'

'Yuw,' Dancer grunts, as he slashes another vine.

'Ol' man Buster, your Nyami, him an' me talked sometimes. When he been give you your name, I was happy. Your mum, she was a good dancer, I tell you.'

Dancer works away at the growth in the cave mouth.

'But I couldn't come close because ... because of what I been tell you last night. The secrets an' lies were like a barbwire fence holdin' me back. That, an' I s'pose I got tangled up with lookin' after Riley all the time ... An' the longer it went the more shame I been feel for not tellin' Andy.

'You've got the story now. All the story I can give you on the family side.

'Might be you're too young for me puttin' all this word on

you, but I don't reckon. You've got strong blood in you, Dancer. Both sides. An' you're a finder. You keep findin' stories. I reckon you know how to find the true way.

'Me, I'm an' ol' bushman. Proper bushman. Even the Highlands mob reckon I'm like an' old-time munjon. And look at you, my grandson, a city boy down there in Broome. You prob'ly even know how to work one of them computer things eh.'

'Little bit,' Dancer admits.

'This ol' munjon's been wantin' to unload all his secrets for a long time now. I knew, soon as I seen you in that church in Broome carryin' your Nyami's coffin.'

Dancer places a last armful of cut brush on the bank, and looks at his grandfather. 'That good enough now?'

'Yuwai. Foller me.'

Two Bob unfolds from his spot on the rock, and wades into the depths of the cave, as far as a branch wedged into a crevice of rock. Together the pair of them work at it until it pulls free. Two more steps, and they are at the source; the springwater bubbles directly from the rockface, feeding the stream. Standing waist deep, Two Bob cups his hands, then spreads the sweet, cool water across his face. His smile lights up the dimness of the cave.

He cups his hands again.

'Jaliwala,' he murmurs, as he runs his wet hands through Dancer's hair.

As they make their way out of the cave back into the dappled light a water goanna scrambles off the rock where Two Bob had been sitting a few minutes earlier, and disappears into the pool. The two of them climb up and take its place.

'No need for secrets any more, boy. You carry this story any way you want to. Inside yourself if you want. Or tell everybody if you need to. God knows if my daddy's will means anythin' to that government mob. Crazy ol' bastard. One thing I got to ask you though. For Riley. Look out for him if you can.'

'I live in Broome.'

'I know. But you belong this country too. You're a Kimberley man, Dancer Jirroo. You've got the saltwater dreamin', that law for Jiir and Marnburr from Nyami Buster. He told me you dance it better'n anyone he's seen. But you're a river man too, a freshwater man from your mother's side. These hills, all this high country is in your blood too. Your line goes back to Marralam, to those red bones and that ol' rifle up there.

'You've got everythin' 'cept the desert in you. An' might be you've even got that somewhere on your Jirroo side.

'It's time for you to go back home to Broome. But you can come back here anytime an' learn the way for this country. If you want to.'

A silence falls, except for the twitter of the birds, and the running of the water.

'This was our playground when we were little, me an' Janga. We were always swimmin' here.'

Dancer pulls off his shirt, and slides into the water. He breaststrokes underwater across the pool, toes trailing in the sand, then back again. He rolls over to float on his back, and drifts. When he rights himself, and shakes the water out of his ears, Two Bob is singing the song of the spring. Dancer sits in the pool, water up to his chest, and sings with his grandfather.

They don't stop when they hear the rustle of Riley and Rosa and Andy approaching. Riley sits beside Two Bob on the goanna rock, and joins the song. Rosa stands behind them. Andy sits on the bank near Dancer.

Dancer slides across to him. 'You ok, Dad?'

'I'm goin' up to the cave. Gimme ten, then come up if you want.'

60

Andy is sitting cross-legged on the dusty floor of the cave. The bones lie still in their paperbark shroud. Dancer hovers uncertainly.

Treading as gently as he can, he moves closer. He lowers himself to sit behind Andy, places his hands on his father's shoulders.

After a time, Andy reaches up to grip Dancer's hand. Tight.

A moment, an aeon? Dancer has no sense of how long that intense, almost ecstatic, yet serene connection is held. When Andy loosens his grip, Dancer gets slowly to his feet and makes his way into the daylight. He finds a spot at the mouth of the cave where he can sit, looking down over the valley with his feet dangling.

He can't think. He doesn't want to think. He just wants to feel the sun on his face.

Andy settles beside him on the ledge.

The staccato, truncated chortle of a blue-winged kookaburra somewhere down below intrudes on their silence.

Dancer smiles.

'There's going to be a bit left over from that gold after you've paid off the bikies isn't there?'

'Fair bit I'd say.'

'I don't care what we do with the rest of it, but you know what the first thing we're doing is?'

'Tell me.'

'Buying you a saxophone.'

Andy's body starts to shudder. Dancer thinks he is about to burst into tears, but it is the beginning of a laugh, a great convulsion that contains more than a hint of tears. He puts his arm around his son's shoulders.

'That was another time, son.'

'This is another time, Dad. Starting now. That's what it feels like to me. And I don't give a bugger if you never play a note on it. I'm getting you a sax!'

Andy ruffles Dancer's hair fiercely, pulls him close so their heads touch for a moment, then lets his arm drop.

'Feel that?' Dancer asks.

A swirl in the air; an eddy that sweeps through the cave, and blows warm against their backs for a few seconds.

'Mmm,' Andy murmurs.

Riley and Rosa come into view, picking their way across the valley floor towards the campsite on the other side. After a bit, Two Bob also emerges. The old man pauses, stretches, feeling at his back. He turns and looks up towards the cave.

Andy extends an arm.

Two Bob sees the movement, straightens.

Andy puts two fingers to his forehead in salute, then lifts his hand, and waves in a big arc.

The valley floor is a long way down, but Dancer is sure that he can see Two Bob repeat Andy's gesture.

They sit with their feet dangling over the ledge, watching the play of light and shadow in the valley as clouds scud across the sun.

Glossary

Blachan	Malay	A very hot sauce of Malay origin commonly homemade in Broome and the Kimberley.
Bogey	Colloquial	A wash, be it in the river or under the shower.
Bullamon	Kimberley Kriol	Bullock.
Bush (v)	Colloquial	Dismiss / send away / fire.
CDEP	Acronym	Community Development Employment Program; a work for the dole program providing top-up payments for work undertaken within the community. Used in many Aboriginal communities up until about 2010.
Coachers	Colloquial	Quiet cattle, used to handling, that can be used at mustering time to lure and lead wilder feral cattle.
Countryman	Colloquial	Used amongst the Kimberley mob to describe Indigenous people.
Cudja cudja	Broome colloquial	Gambling game played in old Broome, similar to mahjong; also called 'sticks'.
Floodgate		A fence at a creek or river crossing that usually needs to be replaced or repaired after each wet season.
Gudia	Kimberley Kriol	White person. (Numerous spellings: gardia, kartiya, etc.)
Jalgangurru	Ngarinyin/ Bunuba	Healer, medicine man.
Jaminyi	Bunuba	Reciprocal term. A boy or young man calls his mother's father jaminyi. An older man calls his daughter's son the same.
Janga	Bunuba	The pith of the boab nut.
Jiir	Yawuru	Sea eagle.
Junba	Ngarinyin/ Bunuba	Story song.

Lambara	Bunuba	Father-in-law.
Malayi	Bunuba	An area of country that is acknowledged as being shared with another group.
Manburr	Yawuru	Ghost crab.
Milli milli	Kimberley Kriol	Generic term for papers, documents.
Mimi	Yawuru	Grandmother, or equivalent, e.g. great-aunt.
Munjon	Colloquial	Term used in the 1800s and first half of the 1900s to describe Aboriginal people still living in the bush, i.e. not under the control of the stations.
Narrugu	Bunuba	Someone with the same name.
Nicki nicki	Kimberley Kriol	Chewing tobacco.
Nyami	Yawuru	Grandfather, or equivalent, e.g. great-uncle. (In the case of Dancer and Buster, grandmother's brother.)
Poddy dodger	Colloquial	A small-time station operator who thieves unbranded calves ('poddies') from neighbouring stations.
Ringer	Colloquial	Stockman.
Sugarbag	Colloquial	Honey from native bees.
Unggurr	Bunuba	The place where a person's spirit lived before s/he was born.
Wadu	Bunuba	Brother-in-law.
Wajarri	Bunuba	Boab nut.
Wandjina	Bunuba and others	Spirit beings often depicted in Kimberley rock art.
Wangga	Ngarinyin/ Bunuba	Dancing song.
Wida	Bunuba	Native bee.
Yuwai	Kimberley Kriol	Yes. Often shortened to 'Yuw'.

Acknowledgements

Alan and Stephen Pigram. It could be said that this is all your fault, and I thank you for it.

Grants from the Western Australian Department of Culture and the Arts and the Australia Council supported me during the research and initial writing phase of work on this book.

Sharon and Tony Gavranich for their generosity and hospitality in the early days of this journey.

The Bunuba mob. As the author's note explains, this is on my head, not yours. But I would like to thank you for the privilege of getting to know you and your beautiful country. For those who read it, I hope it does not disappoint.

For help along the way. Lesley Corbett, my editor of first resort, amongst other things. Sam and Kel Corbett for their intelligent readings and feedback. My agent Clive Newman, always dependable. Ray Coffey for important input at the time it was most needed. And my official editor Naama Grey-Smith, a wonderful collaborator; it's always good to work with someone who's on the same page.

The lyrics from 'Roadtrain' on the Pigram Brothers' *Saltwater Country* album are reproduced with permission, courtesy of Pigram Music.